LISA STROMME

The Strawberry Girl

VINTAGE

1 3 5 7 9 10 8 6 4 2

Vintage
20 Vauxhall Bridge Road,
London SW1V 2SA

Vintage is part of the Penguin Random House
group of companies whose addresses can be found at
global.penguinrandomhouse.com

Copyright © Lisa Stromme 2016

First published in Vintage in 2017
First published in hardback by Chatto & Windus in 2016

penguin.co.uk/vintage

A CIP catalogue record for this book
is available from the British Library

ISBN 9781784702175

Printed and bound by Clays Ltd, St Ives plc

Penguin Random House is committed to a sustainable future
for our business, our readers and our planet. This book is made
from Forest Stewardship Council® certified paper.

For Dagfinn
the palette in which I mix my colours

ÅSGÅRDSTRAND
1893

I

Blank canvas

The greatest brightness, short of dazzling,
acts near the greatest darkness

Theory of Colours, Johann Wolfgang von Goethe

I hid inside the Painting hoping she wouldn't see what I had become. Sometimes it still worked. If I closed my eyes and thought of strawberries I could feel the threads of the ripped dress tickling my bare shoulder while Herr Heyerdahl's brush swept the palette and daubed the canvas. When I concentrated hard I could make my face sullen, yet obedient, as it was when he captured it. I could even feel the fine stems of the jasmine laced through my fingers like cobwebs. My other hand, trembling with fatigue, gripping the bowl. That itch on my shoulder that I couldn't scratch; must not move, must not talk, must keep still.

During the winter when there were no guests she saw me as I had been then: ten years old, simple and useful. But at sixteen it was getting harder to be the Strawberry Girl. The label had replaced me, hidden me firmly behind it. From the moment the Painting was finished and displayed at the Grand Hotel for all the Kristiania guests to admire, my title was set like lacquer. As a child, I wore the label with enforced pride. Now it wore me, but the veneer was cracking and peeling like old paint.

Mother was on her knees at the stove; she swished her rag in the pail as if bathing a small child. When she saw me coming she wrung it out with a forceful twist as though the thing had tried to talk back to her.

'Move, Johanne,' she spat. 'Why are you dragging your feet when there's so much work to be done? It's the start of the season, for heaven's sake! The Heyerdahls are arriving this afternoon. You know how he likes the cottage to be light and airy, free from . . . ?' Her voice rose and she paused, awaiting my answer. 'Free from?'

'Clutter,' I said, through clenched teeth.

'You can lose that attitude, my girl.' Her sleeves were already rolled to the elbow but she pushed them higher as if to make a point. 'He's bringing canvases and paints, all his supplies. He can't be working if it's not *free from clutter* in here.'

Hans Heyerdahl couldn't care less about that sort of thing. He was a painter. He *made* more clutter than the four of us ever did.

I drew a shape on the wall with my finger.

'Well, don't just stand there,' she said. 'I read you the letter, didn't I? Out loud?'

'Yes, Mother. First the boat, then the wagon. We've to send Father and Andreas to fetch them.'

'So we need to get a move on.'

4

She brushed past me and stretched to the high shelf, then slammed a wooden bowl down onto the stove.

'Find some fruit, will you?' she said. 'Fill the bowl. Quickly. I need you back here to sweep the floors and air the sheets.'

'It's still early,' I said. 'I won't be able to pick that many strawberries for a few weeks yet.'

'I said lose that attitude. Go on, lose it, out there in the woods.' She clapped her hands in front of my face. 'And if that Thomas comes running after you, you tell him you're not interested in that kind of attention. Do you hear me?'

'Yes, Mother.'

'And don't dawdle near the other painter's house. The Sinful Man. Fru Jørgensen said he arrived last night. He's brought his evil back again. That man's not right,' she prodded at her own temple. 'Not like our Herr Heyerdahl. Not right in the head. You keep walking past the hut. Don't even look in the garden. You know he leaves those dreadful pictures outside to dry. Sinful. That's what they are. He hangs his depravity in full view, like he's proud of it. You keep your head down, Johanne Lien. Think of this family's name, think of your reputation. Now go and find some fruit for the Heyerdahls.'

She planted the bowl in my hand and shooed me from the house, muttering about my bare feet and straggly hair as I dashed out into the bright morning sun. I left her grumbling amid the mess of her own words.

The strawberries would still be buds, hard and reluctant like small white fists. Nature had mixed her colours but not yet brought them to her canvas. Fruits and flowers needed light and warmth before they could blossom, but Mother seemed to think I could force them to ripen, as if by magic, because I was the Strawberry Girl. For her, the title had little to do with my occupation and more to do with the Painting. It was currency, the bridge that linked us to the upper classes, the rich holidaymakers from Kristiania, Herr Heyerdahl's patrons who flocked to Åsgårdstrand every summer.

It was an accurate portrait of me as I was then. The blues and yellows merged to form a tatty little girl in a scruffy dress whose folds and crevices were darkened by shadow. The flash of skin at the torn sleeve made my shoulder look clean, although I was always covered in grazes from my wild ramblings in the forest. I didn't see how the Painting could possibly have united us with the ladies who paraded around town in their fine white dresses and hats and ribbons. But Herr Heyerdahl stayed in *our* cottage. That meant something, didn't it? The Painting set us apart. This collection of shapes, contours, tone and light seemed to transform me into a princess in the eyes of the Kristiania guests. To my mother, it was all the proof she needed that we were practically one of them.

There was only one strawberry bush that could be ready. Perfectly located on a hill by a wall, it was easily accessible and bathed in sunlight even this early in the season. The only complication was that it happened to be in *his* garden.

If Hans Heyerdahl was Mother's god, the Sinful Man was her devil. It was forbidden for Andreas and me to say his name. Even thinking about him was considered a betrayal.

Mother didn't know about what he had given me, or the conversations I'd had with him. The times I'd met him in the forest.

Neither distinguished nor successful, he was something of an oddity in the town. He was the summer neighbour the locals liked but could not hope to understand. He was as poor as the rest of us, barely able to pay the rent for his hut, so poor that we didn't even bother to set the word 'Herr' before his name, as though he wasn't a gentleman at all.

His strange paintings did nothing to strengthen his reputation, and rumour liked to make him a madman and a drunk. Our upper-class guests from Kristiania, with whom Mother was so keen to make her allegiance, shunned him completely. The ladies were advised to avert their eyes from the paintings and use their parasols to shield themselves from the vulgarity on open display.

Out in the fresh air I dared myself to say his name, treading heavily to dampen the sound of my voice. Quietly at first, I whispered the two words that dripped with wickedness. I said his name, out loud.

'Edvard Munch.'

Something snapped behind me as the name escaped my lips. Had I been cursed as I'd said it? So instantly condemned? I spun round to find Thomas sauntering out from behind a cluster of silver birches by the road. His open face beamed and his dark-brown eyes twinkled so brightly that, even against the glare of the sun, I could see exactly what was on his mind.

'Johanne! Wait!' he said. 'Where are you going?'

'I've to pick fruit for the Heyerdahls.'

'Can I help?'

I gestured for Thomas to join me, without seeming too eager. My hand leapt to my shoulder, touched the fabric, smoothed out the seams of my blouse.

7

'How long have you got?' he said, snatching the bowl from my hand.

'Give me that!' I reached out, but he lifted it high above his head, stepping back towards the trees and inviting me closer. 'Thomas! I don't have time for this, not today. Give it back.'

'All right then,' he said, lowering the bowl. 'But at least come with me to the beach. A quick paddle won't do any harm, will it?'

He darted off, leaving me staring out to sea with a familiar longing swelling in my body. The vast expanse of water dominated my life. It always entranced me. The sheer scale of it was so infinite that I barely believed the fishermen's stories of what was out there where the fjord met the open sea. Punctuated only by the island of Bastøy and the ships and sailboats that passed our bay, the endless blue could be seen from every part of Åsgårdstrand, a town that seemed to have been carved into the steep hill as an act of defiance by the people who belonged to the fjord.

Thomas was already running ahead of me. I was drawn to the water and needed no further invitation. Our hill was steep and the gradient unforgiving, so it was difficult to walk down it slowly. I reeled after him, down Nygårdsgaten until it levelled out at the bottom. We passed the fishermen's huts that would house us for the summer while the Heyerdahls stayed at our cottage. I averted my eyes through force of habit when we came to the little mustard-coloured hut at the end, the one Munch was renting from Fru Jørgensen. Breaking into a sprint, we tore down Havnagata where the cobbles spread out beneath us, leading to the pier and the bathing house on the rocky side of the coast where the water coursed in from the fjord. My chest opened with relief and I inhaled the freedom of the fresh sea air.

Rolling his trousers to his knees, Thomas waded out into the water. I hitched up my skirt and petticoat. Soon the silt was filling the spaces between my toes. Out on the sea the sailboats drifted by, moving quietly with the tides as if in a daydream. The beach was still. A few young girls were playing with stones at the water's edge under the watchful eye of their mother, perched on a rock beneath a parasol. Further along, an old fisherman was scrubbing at the base of his upturned boat while a bearded man with a rope stood behind him tying knots. They paid us no attention and I was glad of it.

'Come on! Up to your knees,' Thomas said, striding out ahead of me. 'I dare you!'

I set my bowl down on a stone and followed him, splashing in the cool water as it rose above my ankles. He was heading for a group of rocks that jutted out from the surface, the place where I used to sit as a girl and pretend I was a mermaid.

'I can't get that far out today,' I shouted, thinking about the book in my front pocket, 'not without my bathing clothes.'

'Spoilsport,' he said.

He cupped his hands and scooped up water, then blew it through his fingers, spraying fountains all around me.

'Thomas!' I shrieked.

If it hadn't been for the book I would have drenched him. Instead, I sploshed away, searching for treasures. But soon he was behind me, slipping his arms around my waist and pressing his chest against my back.

'Look,' he said, pointing to a spot on the horizon, 'one day I'll take you out there, Johanne.' I felt his breath against my ear and my stomach fluttered, then tightened as his lips dusted my skin and he began telling the story he liked to recite. 'I'll take you away from here, on an adventure,' he said, lowering his mouth to my neck. 'I'll be the skipper on a big ship.'

'And where will you take me?' I said, as if I didn't know.

'We'll head out to sea, to Denmark, then down to France and to Egypt. We'll find riches and return decked in jewels and they'll call us the King and Queen of Åsgårdstrand.'

'You sound like Peer Gynt,' I said, 'and look where his seafaring got him.'

'At least he was rich,' Thomas said, 'in the end.'

I wriggled out of his arms and turned to face him.

'No, he was selfish and lost his riches.'

He shrugged.

'You will come with me, though, one day, won't you, Johanne?' he said, his confidence leaking like water from a broken bucket.

'Will I?'

'Don't you want to see what's out there?' he said, taking my hands in his. 'To *explore*?'

A low horn sounded out on the fjord and I turned round to see the *Jarlsberg* sailing in towards the pier, its flags flapping in the wind to announce its arrival.

I picked up my skirt and shook out the soaked hem as I ran back to the beach in search of my bowl.

'Wait!' Thomas shouted. 'Johanne, come back!'

'I don't have time,' I said.

'But wait! Johanne, stop!'

I was already hurrying away.

'There's a dance tonight, at the Grand Hotel,' he shouted, 'you will come, won't you?'

'Maybe,' I called. *Maybe, if my mother hasn't killed me by then*.

I ran across the beach, over rocks and clumps of seaweed. My feet knew the way and easily found the smooth tracks that years of bathers had padded away. I grabbed my bowl and hurried along the shoreline past the Grand Hotel and onto the path that led to Fjugstad forest. Munch's house was adjacent to the path and spanned a steep hill with the house at the top and the path at the bottom. The fruit trees and bushes on the other side of the fence beckoned me with outstretched arms.

The fence had never stopped me before. I balanced my bowl on the post and lifted my skirt to my knees, scanning the neighbouring windows for witnesses to my crime. I saw and heard nothing but the screeching gulls circling above me. My feet sank into the wire and I wobbled as it bent to carry my weight. My skirt tore, snagging on a stray splinter as I jumped over.

Avoiding the nettles, I landed in the long grass and set to work searching the bushes for fruit. I kicked away twigs and brushed aside the dainty white flowers and serrated leaves of the strawberry bush, but found nothing. Dropping to my knees, I crawled along the ground, checking the undergrowth. I plunged my arms into the tangle of the hedge, scratching my fingers and forearms until welts appeared on my skin.

'Oh, curse it!' I said. 'Damned Heyerdahls!'

My face was buried in the bushes.

'You're wasting your time.'

The voice flung open a door in my memory.

I released the leaves in my hand and froze as a shiver travelled the length of my spine.

My arms stung as I turned to find Munch looking down at me. He was wearing a dark jacket that hung from him as though he might have inherited it from an older brother. A grey waistcoat held him in place. He had a shapely, sensuous mouth, which I felt guilty for noticing. The top lip, curving and full, was framed by a light moustache, the bottom lip was plump, almost petted like a child's. He had a strong jawline and pale-blue, doleful eyes that sang with sadness. It struck me that the sadness was not a fleeting emotion but something that inhabited him permanently, like an anchor.

'Johanne?' he said, half smiling.

'Yes, it's me.' I straightened my torn skirt. 'Mother wanted me to find fruit for the Heyerdahls.'

'My sister and I collected the ripe ones this morning,' he said. 'Come up to the house.'

I wanted to refuse him. Mother would skin me alive if she knew I had been caught trying to steal strawberries, let alone from him. But I could not return empty-handed and although Munch's face was serious, his eyes were kind.

'We can't let Hans go without now, can we?' he said, fetching my bowl from the fence.

He was carrying a beige sketchbook. The edges of it were frayed and the cover was marked with scribbles and coffee stains. He tucked it under his arm and turned to go up the hill. I walked in his footsteps, my dirty feet stepping where his boots flattened the grass. When I raised my head at the brow of the hill I immediately noticed the paintings.

Two large canvases, almost as tall as me, loomed in the near-distance. Like bathers reclining in the sun, they were leaning against the wall of the burgundy outbuilding, his temporary studio. The pictures were so compelling I couldn't help but look. One was of a lady, a dark figure, staring mournfully at what looked like her own shadow. She was so utterly desolate that my chest tightened and a wave of sadness invaded my throat.

The other painting was of a lush scene where a man and woman were resting by a tree. The woman was wearing a light-blue apron and holding a bowl of red berries that ignited my curiosity and somehow intensified my sadness. I wanted to reach out and touch the couple. They seemed wounded.

When we reached the hut, Munch called out to his sister.

'Inger! Johanne's looking for strawberries.'

I hovered outside while he climbed the steps to the back door.

Returning to the couple in the painting, I saw that the woman holding the berries was with child, her swelling belly visible above the bowl. They were cherries and the tree was ripe, like her, abundant and in its prime. But the man was tired and his bones were heavy. He was slumped on a tree stump with a walking cane resting by his side. At the centre of the painting, the circle from a freshly cut bough blemished the tree trunk and robbed them both of their happiness.

'Hello,' Inger said, appearing in the open doorway.

I tugged my gaze from the pictures and looked at her with a fixed smile. She was dressed in black from head to toe, with the exception of a white collar that frilled around her neck. Her dark-brown hair was scraped into a severe bun at the back of her head.

'We collected them this morning,' she said, presenting me with the bowl as though she owed me the fruit. 'There's plenty.'

I looked at the small collection of strawberries, knowing they were everything they had.

Inger's features were similar to Munch's although her expression was more open than his and her eyes were darker and wider. In a way she resembled the woman on the canvas, tormented by her own shadow.

'It's for the Heyerdahls,' I said, guiltily.

'Yes, I saw the boat come in from up here – we have a splendid view,' said Inger, smiling as she handed me the bowl. 'You're the Strawberry Girl, aren't you? You've grown since last summer.'

Munch emerged again from the house.

'Subjects in paintings grow and change, Inger, like life. They *are* life. They change with our moods and the time of day. Different each time we look at them.'

I watched him as he talked, waving his hands, carving pictures into the air.

'How are your own paintings coming along, Johanne?' he said.

'Oh, they're just sketches,' I said. 'I don't have paints, Mother would consider them dirty. Although I do read the book you gave me, every day.'

'Why don't you come back again tomorrow?' he said. 'You can have some of my paints. I'm going to start mixing them from . . .' His soft voice drifted away and his hands moved in circles, as if completing his sentence.

'Mother won't allow it,' I said.

'She doesn't have to know, does she?' he said, looking pointedly at the strawberries in my hands.

'I suppose not.'

'Then tomorrow it is,' he said. 'I'll set aside a canvas for you.'

The sun branded my back as I ran up Nygårdsgaten and reminded me how late I was. With my ripped skirt and grimy arms, I was like a sketch that had been crumpled and cast away, an idea that had been scribbled out. But all I could think about was tomorrow. Tomorrow, I would see him again. Tomorrow, I would paint.

Mother's friend, Fru Berg, was at our gate when I rounded the top of the hill. Plump and puffy-cheeked, she looked as tired from coming a few paces down the hill as I was from having run up the whole of it. Her substantial bosom was hanging over the fence, which strained to prop her up for her daily gossip with my mother. I slowed to a walk.

'Goodness, Johanne, look at you,' Fru Berg said, staring at my dress and my mucky feet, 'have you been in a war?' She was a washerwoman and, like my mother, was obsessed with starched collars and pristine skirts. Smears and stains on clothes were the marks that tainted a person's character. To Fru Berg, I must have been a lost cause.

Mother came flying from the kitchen. She had changed into her best pinstriped skirt and the white blouse she saved for

15

church. Her slight body, already tense, tightened further when she saw me.

'Where've you *been*, Johanne? It's past twelve. They'll be here any minute. I've had to do the floors and sheets myself.' She glanced at the tear in my skirt. 'How did you . . .? Look at the *state* of you,' she said, her voice high-pitched and resentful.

'You wanted a full bowl,' I said.

Her lips pressed together and her cheeks ballooned as though filling with steam. If we had been alone she would have slapped me, hard, but Fru Berg's beady eyes deflated her rage.

'You see, Benedikte,' she said, 'this is why she needs a job. She runs around looking like an urchin all summer. She sells fruit, yes, but we'll get more out of her as a housemaid.'

'What do you mean?' I said.

'Fru Berg and I have found you a job. You are to be a house-maid for Admiral Ihlen and his family in Borre.'

'But I pick strawberries,' I said, incredulously.

'And you'll continue to pick your fruit. You can do that in your spare time, but from Monday to Saturday you will be a housemaid. You start tomorrow.'

2

Primer

In the process of colouring, the preparation merely washed
as it were underneath, was always effective

Theory of Colours, Johann Wolfgang von Goethe

I was washing my feet at the water pump when they arrived. A clop of hooves echoed meekly on the dusty road and I looked up to see a dappled pony straining against the weight of a heavily loaded cart. The horse nodded its head, as though trying to draw strength from its neck muscles, where perspiration beaded and coated its skin.

My father looked out of place on the wagon. He was a sail-maker and never used a cart or a horse; he didn't like the way they jiggled his bones and preferred the gentle rock of the sea. The wagon was borrowed from Father's friend, Svein Karlsen, but it was my brother, Andreas, who was adept with the reins. He was sitting in the middle, bolstered by Father and Herr Heyerdahl. Easing in the fatigued pony, he brought them to a standstill. Mother had forced Andreas into his Sunday best

17

and he looked stiff in his black waistcoat and white shirt. Even his cap had been cleaned.

'Well done, boy,' Herr Heyerdahl's voice boomed as he patted Andreas on the knee.

Thirteen, and shy to the point of silence, Andreas barely spoke at all. He hopped down from the wagon with his chin pressed into his neck and tied the horse's reins to our fence.

Herr Heyerdahl had become rounder in the last year. The buttons on his waistcoat were challenged by his protruding belly, which he clasped as he huffed to the ground. His beard and moustache were also longer and tapered to a neat point below his chin. Father was already at the back of the wagon assisting Fru Heyerdahl, a prim lady in a flowery bonnet. She was squashed between trunks and large canvases that looked as though they could topple and crush her at any moment. Their two children, Sigrid and Hans, jumped from the wagon and flew around the garden like birds freed from a cage.

Mother trotted across to greet her guests.

'Welcome back to Åsgårdstrand,' she said, in a sugary voice.

I pushed the handle of the water pump with renewed force to drown out her platitudes.

'Sara, what a pleasure,' Herr Heyerdahl was saying. 'Halvor tells me you've been working hard for us again. You shouldn't go to such trouble.'

'Oh, it's no trouble at all,' Mother gushed. 'I hope you'll find everything to your liking.'

While she continued to fuss, I noticed Herr Heyerdahl's attention begin to slip and it was only his manners that glued

18

the smile to his face. He glanced over Mother's shoulder and looked at me like a man overboard, reaching for a hand.

'Johanne!' he said.

'She's been out picking fruit, hasn't had time to get cleaned up,' Mother babbled, 'don't pay any attention to—'

'Goodness, you've grown,' he said. 'You still have the cornfield hair and those lovely blue eyes, though.'

I shook the water from my feet and dipped my head.

'Hello, Herr Heyerdahl,' I said. I may have been the opposite of my mother, but I wasn't impolite.

'You've been collecting fruit? So early in the season? What did you find?' he said, studying me with his painter's eyes.

My cheeks reddened. 'Strawberries,' I said, desperately aware of my mother's stare.

'It's still early,' she interrupted, 'but you can be sure she'll bring you plenty more when they ripen.' She was trying hard to find words that would turn him, anything to divert his attention from me. She seemed afraid that by simply looking at me, Herr Heyerdahl would change his mind about the summer rental and immediately order everyone back onto the wagon. But he was unflinching.

'They don't call you the Strawberry Girl for nothing! Where did you find them?' he said.

'Oh, down by the forest,' I said, casually.

'Really, Johanne, you must get your boots on now,' Mother continued, 'we need to leave the Heyerdahls to settle in. Halvor!' she yelled. 'What about *our* trunk? Is it on yet?'

'We're ready, Sara,' Father whispered, his voice reduced by the silence that governed him.

I climbed into the back of the wagon and sat on a trunk containing the clothes and the bed linen. Mother settled down beside me and threw my boots and a pair of stockings at me.

'Get these on,' she said, gripping the edge of the wagon as she sat down. 'Honestly, Johanne, the sooner we get you into a proper uniform, the better.'

Andreas snapped the reins and pulled at the pony's bit to steer her around. We rattled away from our home and down the hill towards the pier. The road faded away in front of me and at this oblique angle everything appeared to be in reverse. Not just the familiar white timber cottages and the lilac draping over the fences, but me. My life was in reverse. For many months I had tried to disassociate myself from the Painting, for the innocence and expectation of it were heavy burdens to bear, but now I sorely needed it. I needed its freedom. As the Strawberry Girl, I was free to dance with nature, to ramble and run, untethered by the bindings that fixed others to their post. I could roam the forests and hedgerows, explore the beach and the rocks. I was a wanderer, like *him*. That was how we kept finding each other. And tomorrow I would have painted. I would have finally been able to put what I'd read in the book into practice, to mix colours and experiment with them on a real canvas. But instead I would be a maid in a uniform with no freedom at all.

I saw my summer in the distance at the top of the hill, shrinking and dimming, as though I was leaving it at home for the Heyerdahls alone to enjoy. This season was mine. Could she be so cruel as to take it from me?

Mother flinched as we passed Munch's hut.

'Look away, Johanne,' she said, as the wagon rolled past the paintings, still leaning against the outbuilding in the sun.

'They're only paintings,' I said. 'What harm can they do?'

'Johanne Lien!'

I might as well have taken the Lord's name in vain.

'I don't want you seeing it,' she said, twisting in her seat. 'The medical doctors in Kristiania say those paintings can cause illnesses. I don't want you looking at that kind of filth. At least you won't have to be exposed to all of that this summer,' she said, dropping her hand from her face. 'The Ihlens are a very respectable family and you'll be surrounded by ladies. They have three daughters and they wear the finest clothes in all of Kristiania. Fru Berg does their laundry.'

'So what do they need me for?' I said.

'Oh, Johanne, you have a lot to learn,' she said.

I pulled at the tear in my skirt and made curling shapes from the frayed threads.

The air was downy and warm when we reached the back of the fishermen's huts. Usually the water offered a breeze, something to grasp onto, but our lungs were tight as we inhaled. There was complete pandemonium as half the local townsfolk were relocating to the huts, and the tranquillity of the morning was shattered by the invasion.

The place was packed with families, carts and trunks. Men were carrying boxes high above their heads. Sweat trickled from their brows as they navigated the carts and stepped over the piles of fresh horse-dung that steamed in the road. Children ran amuck, scattering out along the pier, running with hoops to the bathing house; some of the little ones were crying from the heat and confusion. Dogs chased after seagulls, barking excitedly, tongues hanging. Horses whinnied, swatting flies with their tails. Women beat the air with their hats whilst trying to keep track of their children, their husbands, their belongings. Tempers were beginning to fray in the heat and a wave of arguments had erupted: disagreements concerning keys and rooms.

The wagon drew to a halt under the full force of the sun. My legs and feet were suffocating in my stockings and boots and I had the urge to rip them off and run down to the water. I was perspiring from every pore. My blouse was tight and the bones of my corset threatened to puncture my rib cage.

'Can't you get into the shade?' Mother moaned.

'The road is blocked,' Father said, his gaze drifting to the sailboats in the bay. 'We'll just have to wait our turn.'

'But that could take hours,' she said. Attracted to chaos as if it were dust on a ledge, she became agitated. 'Look! There's Fru Hansen. Let me get down and ask her what's going on. Halvor! Help me.'

Father hopped down obediently. Mother stepped over the chests and mats and candlesticks that were piled around us, inching her way to the back, where my father lifted her down in an ungainly fashion, revealing her lower legs. She checked all around her to see if anyone had noticed and muttered a criticism to my father, waving a hand at him as she merged into the crowd, determined to tidy it all away.

'What's she doing?' I said.

'Oh, something about Fru Hansen having our keys,' Father said, shaking his head and returning to his spot on the driver's seat.

'How's that going to clear the road?' said Andreas, lifting his cap and wiping his brow.

As I watched my mother disappear into the throng behind us, my eyes were drawn to a mop of curly hair. Thomas. He was carrying a pallet of cod. The freshly caught silver skins shimmered in the sunlight. He had not noticed me and for a moment I watched him as he paced purposefully down the street. Everything about Thomas had a sense of purpose and I envied him for it. His muscular arms flexed with confidence, caring nothing for the burden of the pallet. The sea of people eddied around him and he lifted his chin. Something warm brushed my chest and flushed my neck and cheeks. With no time to examine this quiver of nerves, I consigned it to the room in my head that I kept clear for thinking.

With my mother gone and Thomas advancing, I seized the moment. Twisting round in the wagon, I patted my father's arm.

'Hmm?'

'You've heard that Mother's sending me off to Borre for the summer?'

'She's not sending you away, dear,' he said. The light drained from his face and his senses clouded at the thought of my absence. 'You'll be back on Sundays, and maybe some evenings too, if you're not needed.' From his reply, I knew he had already had the *Johanne will be a housemaid* discussion and, like thousands of others, it was an argument he had pitifully lost.

'It's just . . . there's a dance tonight at the Grand Hotel,' I said, 'and I thought, since I'll be leaving tomorrow, that you might allow me to go?'

The question hung in the heat. Thomas thundered towards us.

'It's the last chance I'll get,' I pressed.

My father stretched his hand back and stroked my sticky hair.

'All right, dear,' he said, 'if you tell me when you're leaving and promise you won't be too late.'

With his arms full of fish, Thomas could not wave, but he grinned at me anyway.

'Hello!' he called. 'I have your dinner here.' He tipped the pallet my way as though every single cod was just for me. The salty smell filled my nostrils and I found it oddly fresh and alluring.

'Where are you going?' I said.

'I'm delivering these to the ladies. We caught them this morning. They'll be delicious with boiled potatoes and a glass of beer. You will be at the beach, won't you?'

'If we ever get out of the road.'

'And the dance? Later? Will you come?'

I nodded and he grinned again; the twinkle had returned to his eyes. As he walked away I could see the edge of his broad smile.

Movement was painstakingly slow, but when the sun finally released us from her molten grip the wagons began to roll and the ties that bound everyone's good humour loosened and gave way to a lighter mood. We offloaded our belongings and heaved everything into the hut. Our own cottage on the hill was not roomy but it always seemed larger due to Mother's obsessive tidiness, although there would be nothing even she could do to make this seem bigger. Cramped and dark, the huts were built for men who needed no more than a primitive shelter to sleep in. They were divided horizontally. Some families would live upstairs, with doors that faced Nygårdsgaten, and others, like our family, would be downstairs, facing the beach.

There were three rooms inside. The front door opened onto a kitchen at the centre. It contained nothing more than an iron stove and a side table. To the right was a small bedroom where Andreas and I shared bunks, and to the left was a parlour. Mother and Father stored mattresses under the sofa and pulled them out at night to make beds on the floor. In the corner of the parlour was an old table with flecks of paint on the surface and four odd chairs that sat at different heights around it.

We dodged around each other as we brought in our things, banging our elbows on the edge of the furniture and stepping over the homeless chests. I wondered how the Andersens living upstairs would manage. They had the same amount of space as us and were a family of seven, with five children ranging in age from six months to six years.

With the Heyerdahls gone, there was no longer any reason for show, so my mother changed back into her ordinary clothes and set about the hut with a rag. Andreas and I unpacked. My first thought was to find a hiding place for the book and I slipped it under my mattress as a temporary measure. Mother would be washing the bed linen often and turning the mattresses to beat them. It would not be safe there for long.

25

I rummaged in my trunk to find a dress for the dance, but all I had was a blouse with a sailor collar and sleeves that puffed to my elbow, a cotton skirt and a belt to cinch my waist.

'Oh!' Mother said, when she saw me. 'Well, that wasn't such a chore, was it, Johanne? If you run a brush through your hair you might look half decent.'

I hadn't told her about the dance. I would wait until we were on the beach in front of the whole town, where she wouldn't want a scene. For now, I would let her believe I wanted to look like the Ihlens, the darlings of Kristiania whose housemaid I was about to become.

'Would you do my hair for me?' I said.

Her eyes lit up and she rushed to her trunk.

'The tortoiseshell combs are in here somewhere. We can fix it into place with those,' she said, hauling me through to the highest of the odd chairs at the dining table. 'Andreas, fetch water for the pitcher,' she said. 'We all have to get cleaned up for dinner.'

I allowed my mother to groom and primp, fastening combs here and there like a child with a doll. My thumbnail found a clump of dried paint on the table and I began to sketch out a curving shape in it, scratching backwards and forwards like I did with my pencil.

'Oh, stop fidgeting, Johanne,' Mother said, pulling my head aside with my hair. 'Look at the mess you're making. Keep still, I'm trying to make you look nice. You can be such a pretty girl when you want to be. Didn't you hear Herr Heyerdahl say so himself?'

I had heard no such remark, only that my eyes were blue and my hair was like a cornfield.

'He might paint you again this summer,' she said, gripping a comb between her teeth as she braided my hair into painful ropes that clamped my head. 'Be sure to visit them, won't you? Take them strawberries, and cherries too, when they ripen.' She took the comb from her mouth and scraped my scalp with it as she fixed my hair tightly into place. 'Nobody said you only have to pick strawberries. Cherries can look just as good in a painting, can't they?'

The bowl in the other painting sprang back to mind: the ripe fruit, the pregnant woman and the cut bough that had stolen her happiness.

We gathered at the sandy beach on the other side of the pier. The temperature had fallen and a warm breeze whispered around the small packs of townsfolk. Women were washing plates and cutlery in a pot over the fire. The older ladies sang folk songs as they worked, while the younger ones hummed sweet harmonies with subdued respect. Tired after the chaotic frenzy of the day and mellowed by beer, men were slumped into deckchairs and sitting on the edge of fishing boats, talking about netting and timber prices and telling lewd jokes. Their voices rumbled and boomed on the air amidst the cracks of the fire and the women's song. With the tireless energy that only summer evenings can bring, the children paddled in the water and played running games, squealing with delight as they chased each other along the shore. Andreas and his friends were skimming stones, bouncing them skilfully across the rippling sea.

The liquid sun melted in orange streaks on the water's surface and pulled me to it, mesmerised. Resisting the temptation to remove my boots and wade in, I paced along the beach, running sideways like a crab when the waves rushed in. I had almost reached the curve of the bay when Thomas found me.

'Johanne!' he called. 'Wait.'

I turned to see him running towards me, his wild curls bouncing as his pace quickened. He was going so fast I thought he would knock me over, but when he reached me he stopped dead in his tracks as though he had mistaken me for someone else.

'What is it?' I said.

'No, nothing – you just look . . .' He swept his hand through his hair, panting. 'Are you ready? For the dance?'

'Yes,' I said, lifting my chin.

'You look *different*,' he said, retrieving his lost sentence.

'Mother braided my hair.'

'She's allowing you to go?'

'She doesn't know yet. Father gave me permission,' I said, 'with it being my last night and everything.'

'Last night? What do you mean?'

'Mother's found a job for me in Borre for the summer, as a housemaid.'

'Oh.' His face paled the way my father's had.

'I'll be back on Sundays, though, and on evenings when I'm not needed.'

'A *housemaid*,' he said, baffled by the word. 'But you pick strawberries.'

I couldn't tell whether he was confused about my qualification for such a job, or if he was already mourning the secret kisses he stole from me while I foraged for fruit in the woods.

'I'll still pick them,' I said, 'when I have time.'

He snatched my hand and jerked me towards him.

'Come on then, Johanne,' he said, 'let's go.'

We hurried back along the beach, my eyes scanning the crowds for my father. It was almost impossible to find him. Halvor Lien was a thin, quiet figure who blended with his surroundings and could be difficult to locate, even in an empty room. As we stood there at the water's edge trawling the beach for him, I heard my mother screech my name like a crazed gull.

'Johanne! I've been looking for you everywhere,' she said, flicking a glance at Thomas. 'What are you doing? We're going home now.'

'I'm going to the Grand Hotel – there's a dance,' I said.

'You're doing no such thing,' she said, her face firing. 'You start your new job in the morning and you'll need to be up early.'

'I asked Father for permission and he granted it,' I said, beginning to walk away.

She dug her hands into her hips as she pieced together my treachery, seeing the part she had played in my preparation for the dance, fixing my hair and fussing around me, making me pretty. I thought she would start screaming, but my father appeared at her side and hovered over the eruption he must have predicted.

'Halvor!' she blurted. 'Tell her she's not going anywhere. Especially not with *that*—'

Before she had time to say '*that* Thomas', my father had slipped his arm round her waist and begun to twirl her around.

It was clear that he had drunk his fair share of beer, perhaps to quell my mother's inevitable fury.

'Oh, come on, Sara,' he said. 'You were young once, don't you remember?'

'But she's starting that job. I never went dancing at her age, not when there was work to be done – why should she? Halvor!' she squirmed. 'What if she's late? What will they think of her? What will they say?'

'I don't believe you will let her be late, dear,' he said. 'Come now, let your hair down, woman, I rather fancy a dance myself.' He whirled her under his arm and pulled her towards him, tottering into a jig. For a second my mother held him and allowed herself to be spun on his arm, but then a cheer burst out from a group of men sitting on a fishing boat and one of them raised a bottle.

'Halvor!' Mother wailed. 'Halvor! Really!'

The Grand Hotel sat between the two beaches at the foot of the steam pier. A handsome white building, it cornered Havnegata and the shore, opposite the Kiøsterud house that Herr Heyerdahl and Munch liked to paint. The hotel was glowing when we arrived. Light poured from its windows and the plink of fiddles drew us in with a sense of rhythmic urgency. Thomas took my hand again and we ran up the steps.

'Come on,' he said. 'My cousin Christian's playing.'

The doors were open and the sound of chatter and laughter swelled as we entered.

People were drifting from the dining room where a dinner had been held for the summer guests. Waitresses were clearing away plates and I could hear the clinking of china and cutlery. Cigar smoke snaked and hung in wisps in the air and at once I felt grown-up and recklessly free.

Thomas steered me into the lounge where the dance was beginning. The fiddlers sat on stools at the back of the room, dipping their elbows and tapping their feet, immersed in their own music. Armchairs had been pushed to the side to make way for the dancing. Guests were grouped in small cliques. Some had pulled chairs from the wall to form circles.

Several couples were already whirling round the floor in the centre of the room. Thomas and I skirted around them as he waved to his cousin at the back. We lingered by the wall for a moment to watch the city guests as they poured in. The women wore evening dresses with frills and bows and bustles at the back. Intricate detail had been worked into them as though they were entries in a competition. One of the dancers had a dress embroidered with pearls and appliquéd swallows and butterflies. Another wore a gown adorned with golden leaves and trimmed with lace. Some women had piled their hair up in a stack of braids hung with pearls; others had worked flowers into their hair and teased out tendrils to curl about their faces.

A willowy woman in her early twenties stood alone, detached from the others. She was wearing a delicate white dress with short sleeves that sat just off the shoulder. A single red rose was fitted into her low neckline. Her corset was drawn in so impossibly tightly that her waist was barely even visible. She was holding her skirt and sweeping it back and forth slowly, not in time to the music, but gently and purposefully as though she was listening to a different tune entirely. She had blue eyes that would have been piercing had they not looked so glazed, and wavy red hair that simply hung loose around her bare shoulders.

When the band struck up a new tune, Thomas clutched my arm and leapt forward.

'Let's dance!'

He pulled me into his arms and wheeled me around so quickly my stomach lurched. My feet barely touched the ground as we spun to the quickening tempo of the jig. I laughed with exhilaration as the rest of the room whizzed past me in a blur of gold and white and a unified shriek of laughter and drunken cries. I clung to Thomas's upper arm and felt wonderfully secure, despite the rhythm and pace of the dance. I gazed into his gleaming eyes, happy to be at his mercy and, when the fiddles finally stopped and I lifted my head, he planted a kiss on my gasping mouth.

The evening progressed quickly. We drank beer and apple cider to quench our thirst, we danced and laughed and we kissed. Liberated, I didn't care who saw me or what they might say and I forbade my mother from entering my thoughts. Eventually we found an empty sofa and I crumpled into the curve of its arm. Sweat was running down my temples and I had to loosen my belt.

'I can barely breathe,' I said. 'How did you learn to dance like that?'

Thomas was smiling again.

'Sailors just know how,' he said.

He settled in beside me and I allowed him to drape his arm across my knee as we watched the other dancers.

It was then that I saw Munch. He was sitting at a round table in the corner of the room, alone. An empty glass of wine sat next to a full one that seemed forgotten and ignored. I wanted to go to him, to tell him about my job, to tell him that things had changed and that tomorrow would be different, but his expression was stern and his arm was busily sketching shapes in a large book. I could not disturb him. Following the line of his eyes, I realised he was drawing the girl in the white dress. She was still standing apart from the others, rustling her skirt.

'Who *is* that girl over there?' I said, as much to myself as to anyone else.

'Over where?' Thomas straightened up.

'The one in the white dress, standing on her own.'

'Oh, that's Miss Ihlen, one of the admiral's daughters.'

'Ihlen?'

'Regine, the youngest,' he said, 'although they call her something else – Tullik, I think it is. They stay in Borre during the summer.'

'Yes,' I said. 'I've heard.'

'Looks like the madman has spotted her,' he laughed, pointing at Munch who was still sketching furiously, drawing the waves of her hair and the curve of her waist.

'Do you think he's mad?' I said.

'He must be. Haven't you seen his paintings?'

'I will be her housemaid tomorrow,' I said, changing the subject. 'I'll have to wait on her and serve her and clean that pretty dress.'

Thomas wasn't listening. He had already taken my arm and pulled me to my feet again. I surrendered completely and returned to the dance floor. I reeled and spun and followed wherever he led; but this time it wasn't Thomas I was looking at. I couldn't take my eyes off Tullik Ihlen, the girl Edvard Munch was so eager to draw.

3

Red

In looking steadfastly at a perfectly yellow-red surface, the colour seems actually to penetrate the eye. It produces an extreme excitement, and still acts thus when somewhat darkened.

Theory of Colours, Johann Wolfgang von Goethe

I arrived at the house just before seven. Mother, who had been awake all night fearing I would oversleep, was up at dawn laying out my clothes on the paint-speckled table and fetching water for the pitcher and soap to scrub me with.

'I think you should be on your way soon,' she said, tossing a flannel at me. 'Do your face, and behind your ears and I'll fix your hair.'

My head was pounding. I could still taste the remnants of the evening's beer that had drained me and left me thirsty. I still felt the kisses Thomas had pressed onto my face, still tasted him on my lips as I dragged the flannel over my mouth.

'What's wrong with you?' Mother said, jabbing my back. 'Straighten up. Ladies don't slouch like that – you'll have to learn.'

I endured her onslaught and, before the clock had even reached six, she pushed me from the hut, chanting orders and instructions in a loud whisper. Barefoot, and with a looser skirt, the walk through the forest to Borre would have taken me less than twenty minutes, but trussed up as I was and treading carefully in my effort to stay clean, by the time the church came into view the sun was so bright on the horizon I thought I might be late.

Unlike Åsgårdstrand, Borre was mainly flat and gently sloped to meet the sea. At its centre was the church, a few hundred yards from a dramatic Viking burial site by the beach. The enormous mounds where ancient kings had been laid to rest amongst their treasures always impressed me more than the stone-walled church and its ancient wooden beams.

The Ihlens' house was directly opposite the church on the other side of Kirkebakken. Chestnut-brown, with a wood-bound picket fence and a tiled roof, the building attracted the sun and shone like the houses in Åsgårdstrand. Mother called it the 'big house', but that was only in comparison to the rest of the huts and cottages that dotted that side of the road. The rectory by the church dwarfed the Ihlens' house and could have housed every person in the village. But none sat prouder or prettier than the Ihlens'.

I opened the gate and approached the front door, which was framed by four wooden pillars. Stepping up onto the porch, I ran my hand along the carved railings, not knowing whether to reach for the door knocker or wait until I was discovered. Two grand windows on either side of the door followed my movements like a pair of transparent eyes, chiding me for having the gall to enter by the front door. In a panic I scooted round to the back. I was met by the sound of hens clucking in a coop in the yard. I bent down to look at them and was just about to squeeze my finger through the wire when a voice called out from the house.

'You'd better get your apron on, if you're going to be touching Miss Tullik's hens.'

Startled, I leapt away from the coop and turned to see Fru Berg standing at the back door. Her bulky frame filled the rear entrance. A large tin tub dangled from her fist and a steel wash-board was clamped under her arm. She came striding out into the garden, calling to the hens, each of which had a perfectly normal human name.

'Coo-coo! Ingrid!' she called. 'Coo-coo! Margrete! Cecilia, you be sure to lay some eggs for me today, young lady; you gave us nothing yesterday, did you? And you, Dorothea, I've a good mind to pluck you and roast you for supper if you don't have any eggs for the admiral's breakfast.'

She continued to prattle to the hens as she laid her tub down by the well, where a pail was waiting to be filled.

'You ever cared for hens, Johanne?' she said, scooping up a fistful of corn from her apron pocket. 'You have to talk to them, you know – they understand every word, I'm sure of it. Don't you, Dorothea? There you are, good girl, give me some nice eggs now.' She tossed the corn through the feeding hatch and the hens raced for the grain, hammering at the ground with their beaks where it had landed. 'You'd better come in and get started then,' Fru Berg said. 'There's an apron hanging in the scullery there.'

I followed her into the house. The scent of lilac laced the air as I brushed past a bush that was ripening by the door.

'They'll be coming down for breakfast soon,' she said, pulling an apron from a peg. 'Here, put this on and I'll take you through.'

I hung up my shawl and looped the apron around my neck while Fru Berg went into the kitchen and began reciting a long list of chores and an inventory of cleaning utensils: linens, rags and polishes, which ones were best for which surfaces, and how long fabrics should be soaked and bleached, what time of day each meal was served and how that all changed if there were guests in the house. She showed me the basin, the stove, the stack of wood that fired it and an array of pots and pans. I tried to follow what she was saying but was too overwhelmed to focus. As she led me through the house I was distracted by the fine ladies and important naval officers watching me from their oval frames on the walls. The smell of coffee and pipe tobacco oozed from the walls, and the floorboards creaked as we crossed them. The whole house seemed to be breathing with renewed life, like an old lady who seldom has guests.

The rooms were simple but had sumptuous furnishings. The spying windows were dressed with swags and the floors were covered with richly patterned rugs. Decked in ferns and potted plants, the parlour was deep green like a jungle and had high-backed chairs and a round card table in the window. Along the wall a piano was ornamented with more family photographs in silver frames. In the dining room a white linen cloth had already been draped over the table, and Fru Berg hastened to smooth it out.

'Silverware's in the drawer over there,' she said, nodding at a dresser by the fireplace. 'You can set four places. Admiral Ihlen sits at the head, Fru Ihlen here, with her back to the window, and Miss Tullik and Miss Nusse on either side.'

'Nusse?' I said. 'She is a Miss?'

'Miss Caroline,' she said, 'they call her Nusse.'

I took the cutlery from the drawer and laid it neatly on the table. I couldn't help but think how much my mother would have admired it, with its curving handles and elaborate bevelled engraving. She would have loved the soft thud it made against the cloth.

'When you've finished that, you can come and help me with the breakfast. Ragna's off today, so I've got her jobs as well as all the laundry.' She hissed the words at me as though Ragna's absence was my fault. 'You'll have to work late and stay here tonight,' she said, before returning to the kitchen and leaving me alone.

As if prompted by the prospect of night, a yawn rose in my chest and I set it free under the watchful eye of a man with thick black whiskers sitting in a frame on the mantelpiece. Photographs made it hard to see into a person's eyes. They weren't the same as paintings. This man had a broad forehead, dark eyebrows and a deep cleft in his chin. He was wearing a double-breasted uniform with heavy brocades and holding a sword by his side. But his eyes were far away and he seemed to be concentrating on sitting perfectly still. There was no story to be told in the image. He was simply a man in uniform.

I quietly laid the plates out and straightened the cutlery around them, then found the salt and pepper pots and put them at the centre of the table. I crouched to hunt in the dresser cupboard for eggcups. While I was bent down I heard footsteps on the stairs and straightened myself up, jumping away from the silver like a thief. When the door swung open, I stiffened.

The woman who entered was small and portly but impeccably dressed in an olive crinoline skirt with a delicate striped bodice. Her hair was greying at the temples and piled on top of her head in a neat ball. She found me with clear blue eyes, almost translucent, that seemed to have caught the ripples of the summer fjord.

'Oh, hello,' she said. 'You must be Johanne?'

I bowed and curtseyed to her all at once, mumbling something about eggcups.

'I'm Julie Ihlen,' she said, 'the admiral's wife. Let me help you.' She came to join me by the dresser and gently rested her hand on the middle of my back. 'There's so much to remember in a new job, isn't there, dear?' she said. 'But don't worry, you'll soon find your way.'

Her voice was soothing and her tone was a treat, like whipped cream. Not even Thomas spoke to me in that way.

'I'm told you usually pick strawberries in the summer?' she said, opening a drawer and handing me some napkins.

'Yes,' I said. 'I sell them in town.'

'Maybe you can help us in the garden as well? We have rhubarb and gooseberries, and three good apple trees at the side. No strawberries, though.'

'I can bring you some seedlings from the forest,' I said. 'They catch on well in the right earth. Like the ones in—'

I cut the words *Munch's garden* from my throat and busied myself with the napkins, folding them into triangles and laying them on the plates.

A clock on the wall chimed and Fru Ihlen glanced at her wristwatch.

'I'll get the girls,' she said. 'We'll be ready shortly. The eggcups are in the cupboard, on the right.'

I finished the table and hurried back to the kitchen to find Fru Berg boiling eggs and brewing coffee on the stove.

'The hens have been generous,' she said. 'Here, come and spoon these out. I'll get the bread.'

She disappeared into the larder and clattered around, gathering condiments and preserves. I could hear her heaving and cursing as she stretched to the high shelves, asking questions that had no answers. *Where's she put the . . .? What the devil did she do with the . . .? Now where does she keep those . . .?*

She reappeared carrying a tray laden with jars and silver dishes.

'Put the eggs in that bowl and cover them with a cloth,' she said, 'and bring the coffee.'

With my hands full, I followed her back to the dining room. At the door she cleared her throat, then elbowed her way in. When I saw the family gathered at the table I hid behind Fru Berg, grateful for her size.

Admiral Ihlen was sitting at the head of the table. He was a lot older than his wife and had receding grey hair that was slicked back over his strong brow, and wild whiskers that grew straight out from his jaw like an untamed hedge. He was a mature version of the man in the photograph who had watched me yawn. I noticed that in life his eyes were deep and kindly, like the warm milky coffee my father would make and secretly heap with sugar.

One of the daughters had her back to us as we entered the room. She was dainty and poised, but I could not see her face. When I looked up to see where I should place the coffee I caught the eye of the other daughter on the opposite side of the table. She had red hair and clear blue eyes like Fru Ihlen's, but she had her father's strong eyebrows. She was unmistakably the girl from the dance, Tullik Ihlen. The flame of her wild hair lit the room and gave her pale complexion a yellowish tinge that made her eyes all the more striking. She smiled when she saw me and at once I tried to hide my face. Did she recognise me from the night before? Had she seen me dancing with Thomas, kissing him in full view of all the Kristiania guests? A thread of my mother's anxiety began to creep up my throat.

'Oh yes, everyone, this is Johanne,' Fru Ihlen said. 'She's come to help us for the summer.'

Fru Berg stood aside and I was exposed to the Ihlens' collective scrutiny. Caroline swivelled round in her chair. Her face was also a mixture of her parents', but her features were sharper, more pointed than Tullik's. It was clearly Fru Ihlen, rather than the admiral, who dominated their daughters' looks: the slightly slanted blue eyes, the straight nose and the pouty lips. All four of them looked at me and my skin flushed.

'You live in Åsgårdstrand?' said the admiral, his rigid face unchanging.

'Yes, sir,' I said, putting the coffee down beside him.

'Sandy-beach or pebbled-beach side?' he said.

'Pebbled-beach side,' I said, 'up on the hill opposite the Jørgensen farm.'

'I'd like to live there,' Tullik said, her eyes dancing with mischief, 'amongst all those painters.'

Caroline turned back to face her sister.

'What would you want with the painters in Åsgårdstrand?' she said, straightening the cutlery on either side of her plate.

Tullik didn't answer, but rolled her eyes as she helped herself to a slice of bread.

'I'm sure the views of the fjord are very inspiring from up there,' Admiral Ihlen said. 'Some of Herr Heyerdahl's landscapes are captivating.'

'I prefer his portraits,' Caroline said.

Fru Berg turned and looked at me. I stepped back towards the door, hoping the conversation would move swiftly away from Herr Heyerdahl and his portraits.

'Like the children he paints,' Caroline continued. 'The girls in the lane are very sweet.'

Tullik was pressing a slab of butter into her bread, stabbing at it with her knife to make it more malleable.

'They don't have the same depth as *his* paintings, though,' she said.

I gripped the sides of my dress. It was the way she said *his*.

'Whose paintings?' Fru Ihlen said.

Tullik continued to engrave the butter.

'Tullik? Whose paintings?'

Caroline shifted in her seat and flapped her napkin out by her side.

'Tullik,' Fru Ihlen pressed, 'whose paintings?'

Tullik's eyes were fixed on the butter. Now that it was more pliable, she began to spread it haphazardly around her bread. Then I remembered his hands from the night before, swirling around the page like the dancers on the floor, capturing the curves of Tullik's body and the wispy strands of her loose hair.

'Munch's,' I whispered.

Before I even realised the name had escaped my lips, Fru Berg was waving her arms and jostling me out of the room.

'Nils dear, do pass the coffee,' Fru Ihlen said, shooting Caroline warning signals with her sloping eyes. Seemingly unaware of the unfolding drama, Tullik continued to paint her bread with butter.

Fru Berg was trembling when we reached the kitchen.

'You can't mention that painter's name in this house,' she whispered. 'What were you thinking? You don't speak of him at home, do you? What makes you think you can speak of him here?'

'I'm sorry,' I said. 'I didn't mean for it to come out. It's just that Miss Tullik—'

'Miss Tullik nothing,' she snapped. 'You'll do well to say nothing, speak only when you're spoken to and get on with your work in silence.'

She banished me from the house and sent me out to tend to the hens. I was to clean out the coop, change their water, freshen up their hay and feed them. The job was hot and smelly. As the sun rose higher in the sky, the stench of stale droppings grew ever more potent as I raked and scrubbed, hunched over in the coop with the hens clucking and pecking at my feet. I made trips to the well, ducking in and out of the cage, careful not to let any of the birds escape. The mixture of water and vinegar I was using stung my nostrils and made my eyes smart.

Within minutes, the matter was settled. I hated cleaning. Stuck inside the coop with Dorothea and Ingrid pecking at my fingers, I noticed the scratches on my arms from Munch's garden. I didn't mind those scrapes. I would have suffered any amount of stings and thorns and scratches to pick my fruit. I yearned for those bushes and cursed my mother for sending me to the Ihlens, for trying to turn me into something I was not and would never be.

As my thoughts escalated I became more aggressive with the rake and found myself slamming the pail until the water sloshed over the edges. Lost in my anger, I almost hit a hen with the edge of a prong when a voice came chiming through the cage.

'He painted you, didn't he?'

I dropped the rake and smacked my hand to my chest. My heart was pounding in my neck.

'I didn't mean to scare you.'

When I looked up, I saw Tullik leaning against the coop.

'Miss Ihlen!' I said. 'I don't think I'm supposed to . . . I mean, I should really be getting on with this, I'm nearly done.'

'I'll help you,' she said. 'They're fine girls, aren't they? Aren't you, Ingrid,' she muttered to the hen, 'aren't you a fine girl?' She lifted the latch and climbed inside with me, gathering up the clucking hens in her arms, kissing them and lowering them back down again like children. 'Here, pass me that scrubbing brush,' she said, reaching for the bucket.

'Are you meant to do this?' I said, confused. 'I still don't know the rules. I'm sorry.'

Tullik Ihlen laughed a voluptuous, throaty giggle.

'Rules! Who cares about the rules? Who even makes the stupid things?' she said.

She unbuttoned her lower sleeves and rolled them up, delighting in the job that was the cause of my misery. She was wearing no apron or overalls, but she got down onto her hands and knees in her fine clothes and scrubbed the ground with the brush.

'I used to do all of this myself, when I was a little girl,' she said. 'I always kept hens. It was my job to look after them. I fed them and cleaned them and collected the eggs in the morning. It gave me such a sense of pride, such satisfaction. I don't see why I shouldn't do it now, but I don't know what happened. I turned twenty and all of a sudden everything I enjoyed was taken from me. Now I'm expected to sit quietly, say nothing and have no interests whatsoever. You're so lucky, Johanne, you still have your freedom.'

I raked a pile of fresh straw to the side and turned to face her. I wanted to weep.

'I love fruit the way you love these hens,' I said, drawing a strawberry shape in the dirt with a prong of the rake and filling in one side of it to make a shadow.

Tullik gazed up at me with her exotic eyes.

'You're the Strawberry Girl, aren't you?' she said. 'Herr Heyerdahl painted you – I heard Fru Berg say.'

'I was just a little girl then.'

'I hope I didn't offend you. I mean, what I said about Herr Heyerdahl's paintings.'

46

'No,' I laughed. 'I agree with you. He paints wonderful pictures, but they don't make me *feel* the same way as . . .'

'As Munch's?' Tullik's expression changed the moment she mentioned his name. She wiped her brow with her forearm and squinted up at the sun that was beating on my back. 'Do you know him?' she said.

'A little.'

'Has he painted you too?'

'Goodness. No!' I said. 'I'm sorry about earlier, Miss Ihlen. I don't know why I said his name. Out loud. I didn't mean to cause any trouble.'

'Don't apologise to me,' she said. 'I don't care. It's the rest of them. His name is like poison, salt in a wound in this family, after what happened.'

I didn't understand what she meant but, sensing our conversation had already gone too far, I didn't dare to ask. I laid the rest of the fresh hay and shifted to the other side of the coop. Tullik finished her scrubbing and threw the brush into the pail. We both bowed out of the cage and crossed the garden to the well to wash our hands. Tullik grabbed the pump and invited me to wash first. I rubbed my hands together under the cool water and splashed my dirty face and neck. When we swapped, I was about to start cranking the pump when Tullik laid her hand on mine to stop me. She glanced over her shoulder and looked back at the house, checking the door and the spying windows.

'It's my sister,' she whispered, 'she had an affair with him. They think I don't know.'

47

4

Crimson

*We are here to forget everything that borders on yellow
or blue. We are to imagine an absolutely pure red,
like fine carmine suffered to dry on white porcelain.*

Theory of Colours, Johann Wolfgang von Goethe

The room in my head was the one place in my life that adhered
to Mother's rules, being light and airy and free from clutter.
If I wasn't out roaming the forests where my mind was free
to wander with me, I would collect the thoughts that sparked
intrigue and sought solutions, siphon them off to that room
and store them there like insects in a jar. I'd return to them
later, picking them up where I left off, the way women did
with knitting.

My morning at the Ihlens' house quickly filled that place in
my head. Fru Berg kept me busy and each fresh task required
double the concentration. I was made to polish silver, mop
floors, dust shelves, air linens and help to prepare food. Every
second was laden with the fear that I would make another
mistake. I had already offended the Ihlens by breathing *his*

name out loud and I could not afford to flounder again. My mind was taxed to the limit, and any thoughts of Caroline Ihlen and Edvard Munch were quickly banished to be dealt with later.

Unaccustomed as I was to the inner world of the upper classes, the pattern of their day was wearisome to follow. The admiral was by far the easiest, busy with his papers and business affairs in his room at the back of the house. I only ever heard the rumble of his voice when the family gathered to eat, and once when he called out to Fru Berg to take a letter to the post office. Twice I took him coffee and delivered the pot and the cup in silence. His dark and regimental appearance unnerved me but he was never impolite.

The ladies' presence was far more obvious. Tullik and Caroline argued incessantly. Tullik was disconnected from the rhythms of the house and only gave in to her mother's demands under duress. Most of the time she seemed bored, sweeping listlessly about the house, wandering after the cat, reading books and tending the flowers in the garden. Caroline was staid and reserved and enjoyed finding fault with her sister. I could hear them shouting at each other upstairs, then there would be shrieking and the two of them would tear after each other like hot-tempered children, forgetting they'd ever grown up.

Julie Ihlen did her best to allay the bickering, but never raised her honeyed voice to the girls. *Now, Tullik,* she would say, *your sister's writing, come away now*. She drifted around them long enough to ensure peace was restored and then busied herself with her work: matters of the house, errands, meals, letters, and her involvement with a newly formed committee dedicated to the protection of animals. I overheard her telling the admiral that letters had arrived from Fru Esmark and Fru Schibsted suggesting a meeting to discuss the anti-vivisection laws, and that she might have to take a small trip back to Kristiania.

I was clearing away china plates in the dining room when the clock struck three and there was a rustle of activity in the house.

'Tullik? Are you coming?' I heard Julie call up the stairs.

'Let her stay here, if she wishes to,' said the admiral.

'Nusse! We're leaving now.'

There was a trample of footsteps on the stairs.

'She's not coming,' Caroline said. 'She'd rather fester here.'

'Then let her fester,' Admiral Ihlen said.

'But she must meet people – *socialise*.'

'There'll be plenty of time for that back in Kristiania,' the admiral said. 'Tullik,' he called, 'we're going to Aunt Bolette's.'

'Yes, Father.' I heard Tullik scramble to the top of the stairs. 'May I stay here? I'm reading.'

'Very well, dearest,' he said. 'We will send your aunt your best wishes.'

'I'm not lying for her,' Caroline said.

'No one is going to lie,' Fru Ihlen said. 'Aunt Bolette won't mind. Goodbye, dear.'

Tullik stomped back to her room without another word and for a second the house was silent.

Moments later Fru Berg appeared.

'It's calling hours,' she said. 'They've gone to Fru Nicolaysen's in Horten. We can sit for a while out the back. Come on.'

Fru Berg took a plate of bread and butter and two bottles of apple juice to the round table in the garden and we sat down together, dragging the legs of the iron chairs across the grass, gouging out clumps of earth with their feet. We were concealed by the admiral's shirts, hanging hand-in-hand with the girls' petticoats on the line. The lilac scent was intense in the afternoon sun and it curled around me, easing the tension from my neck and shoulders as I inhaled it. For the first time that day my breath found the top of my lungs.

'A quick refreshment before we start the dinner,' Fru Berg said. 'Ragna will be back tomorrow, thank the Lord. That means you can get on with the cleaning, I can do my washing out here and she can deal with the dinner.'

My hands were red and stinging from the vinegar and carbolic soap they had been introduced to. I swigged my juice from the bottle and pressed the cool glass against my skin to relieve the irritation.

'You'll soon get used to that,' Fru Berg said. 'Look at these!' She thrust her fists at me and opened her hands, turning them over to reveal chapped flaky skin between her fingers. 'They were soft as silk when I was your age,' she said. 'It's not pretty, but it won't kill you,' she laughed. She buttered a slice of bread and took a large bite that filled both her cheeks. 'Course it's not what I imagined myself doing,' she said, before swallowing, 'but grand plans are wasted on youth. What you want's a job, a steady pay – all the rest is just dreams.'

I thought of Thomas and his plans to travel the world: to sail to far-off places and return decked in jewels and riches.

51

I wondered how it was possible to dream a future so different from the present moment and somehow be able to link the two together through the passage of time.

'And then you get the likes of Miss Tullik,' she continued, whispering while chomping through her bread. 'Has all this, never has to work a day, and never will have to work a day, but is she happy?' She swallowed and shook her head at the same time. Picking up her bottle, she gulped back a long lug of juice, guzzling it like a drunkard. She stared up at Tullik's window and a look of bemusement crossed her chubby face. 'It's going to take far more than a husband and a nice house in Kristiania to make that one happy.' She wiped her mouth with the back of her hand and burped through her lips, satisfied with the conversation she had just had with herself and the conclusion she had drawn. 'All alone up there,' she said. 'Might want a bite to eat? Why don't you take her a bottle of juice? It's not good for her to be cooped up inside, just like those hens of hers.' She pointed in the direction of the scullery. 'There's a crate in the store cupboard,' she said. 'Take her a bottle. You know where to find the glasses.'

I finished my bread and collected my things.

'I'll just have another few minutes,' Fru Berg said, sending me away with a sweep of her hand, 'while it's quiet.'

She clasped her fingers together on top of her protruding belly and slid down in her chair.

I returned to the house and pulled out a bottle of apple juice for Tullik. It was silent inside and I barely breathed as I crept through the kitchen to find a glass. The cat, a plump old tabby, was watching me from her perch on the windowsill. I pursed my lips and whispered to her, *pusspusspuss*. She hopped down and began meowing at me and I regretted having disturbed her. The cat followed me from the kitchen and up the stairs, rubbing her body against the steps and twisting her tail around the railings.

I didn't know which room was Tullik's and I hovered on the landing for a moment, feeling lost and foolish, but the cat slipped past me and trotted to a room on my right and I waited with her as she sat and whined at the door.

'Really, Miss Henriette pussycat, can't you make up your mind?' Tullik said, opening the door. 'Oh, Johanne, it's you.' Her fiery hair was hanging loose about her shoulders and a book was swinging in her hand.

'I'm sorry, Miss Ihlen. Fru Berg wondered if you might like some apple juice?' I said, offering her the bottle and the glass.

'Thank you,' she smiled. 'Please, call me Tullik. Come in.'

I followed her into her room and put the juice down on her bedside table. Tullik's bedroom was both simple and chaotic. Simple in its decoration: plain walls, plain curtains, red rug. Chaotic in its arrangement: books piled, papers scattered, clothes strewn. It was dominated by a large wardrobe at the end of the bed. The bed, framed by carved wooden boards at the head and foot, was the same. Its simplicity was the crisp white linen; its chaos the assortment of blankets heaped at the end of it and the ill-fitting coverlet sliding to the floor. The thick mahogany wardrobe stood with its back to the wall, facing into the room like a guard. Solid as a mountain range, it seemed too heavy for the floor to hold. Above it, the roof sloped down to the open window where a pair of lifeless curtains hung. They were all that had shielded Tullik from Fru Berg's voice.

'How has your day been?' she said, as I poured her some juice.

'Quite hard,' I said, 'I don't think I'm a very good cleaner. And there's so much to learn.'

I bit my lip. I should not have criticised my own work in front of her, but Tullik just laughed her infectious throaty giggle.

'Well, this is one room you will never have to worry about. I don't like it to be tidy. There is an order to all this,' she said, waving a hand at the piles of books and loose papers scattered about the floor. 'I know where everything is. There's a system to it. Look at this,' she said, clearing away some papers beside her that were covered in illustrations and sketches. 'I try to draw sometimes but they never come out very well. They're just jottings really. Why don't you sit down, have a rest.' She patted the bed beside her and, seeing my hesitation, pulled my arm. 'Oh, come on, it's so hot today. My parents won't be back for hours, and what's old Berg going to say?'

Persuaded, I flopped onto the bed beside her.

'Those calls are so tedious,' she said. 'Mother enquires about my cousins and we have to go through the lives of all seven of them – and then it's our turn, and we have to sit there and listen to Nusse drone on about her wonderful fiancé and the wedding preparations.'

'Miss Caroline is engaged?' I said.

'Oh yes, to Herr Olsen. He's a doctor and a mycologist. That's a kind of biologist. He studies mushrooms,' she said. 'You're surprised?'

'Well . . . just a little, yes.'

'Why?'

'It's just – having been with a painter like Munch, to then, well, a doctor. It seems a bit . . . Forgive me, I am speaking out of turn.'

Tullik started laughing. Her giggle grew into a loud crow and she threw back her head. Her flaming hair rushed all about her, as though it was tickling her entire body.

Bewildered, I could do nothing but stare. Surely I'd insulted her? Who was I to make comments about the Ihlens? A simple fruit-picker, now a housemaid. My mother would have slapped me for my thoughtlessness and my cheek burned from an imaginary strike. But Tullik did not stop laughing.

'Forgive me, Miss Ihlen,' I said. 'But what's so funny?'

Eventually she caught her breath.

'Oh, Johanne!' she howled. 'You didn't really think I meant *Caroline* had an affair with Munch, did you?'

'You said your sister?'

'Yes, my *eldest* sister, Milly.'

Mother's voice came charging back into my head. *They have three daughters and they wear the finest clothes in all of Kristiania.*

'She was married to Carl Thaulow then – it was quite the scandal. They thought I was too young to understand, but I remember it,' Tullik said, as her laughter subsided and her eyes changed shape. Her whole face fell suddenly, as though she'd been struck, and her mouth, seconds ago animated with laughter, now drooped and paled. 'It was a horrible time,' she said, 'especially for Mother. All the talk, all the stories.

55

Endless gossip. It brought shame on us. That's what it's like in Kristiania. If you're not spreading gossip, you're the subject of it. Talk. Talk. Talk. It took its toll.

'Mother was distraught. They threatened to banish Milly, to send her to Aunt Bolette's in Horten with Grandmother Aars – anything for the humiliation to stop. But Milly was a married woman, so their threats were empty. She refused to go. She's married to another man now, Ludvig, and she has a daughter. She seems settled, and Mother and Father have put the whole episode with *that painter* behind them. They think I don't know about it, but there's nothing you can hide from sisters, is there?'

'Does Milly come to Borre in the summer too?' I said.

'Sometimes. She fancies herself as quite the actress now, though. Ludvig is a theatre man and they put on performances from time to time. She'll have you believe it's a demanding schedule, but it's nothing more than a hobby for her. Of course she gets restless out here for long stretches of time, although I won't be surprised if she turns up later in the season. A small group of the bohemians still comes over in the summer.'

'The who?'

'Bohemians. You must have heard of them? The Kristiania Bohemians?'

I shook my head as she leaned over to retrieve her book.

'I'm reading this,' she tossed the book into my lap. 'I have to hide it. It's illegal, so if I'm caught with it I'll probably be arrested,' she said, teasingly.

'*From the Kristiania Bohemians*,' I read the title aloud. 'Who is Hans Jæger?'

Tullik propped herself straight up against the wall.

'He's a friend of Munch's,' she said. 'Munch painted his portrait. I found this book at Milly's house. There are hardly any copies of it left. It was banned and Jæger was thrown into jail because of it.'

'Why?' I said. 'What is it about?'

She took it back from me and skimmed through the pages.

'Free love, free will, a free society. Freedom from rules and constraints. It's what they all believe in: Jæger, the Krohgs, Gunnar Heiberg; the artists, poets and writers. Milly used to meet them all. They gathered in packs at the Grand Hotel on Karl Johan Street, arguing into the night, setting the world to rights. She danced around the edges of it because it made her feel fashionable, but she doesn't have the depth. How could she understand?' Tullik pushed her hair back as though it had irritated her. 'What does she know about the passions that drive a painter? She can't appreciate art, not really. All she thinks about is hats and clothes, aesthetics. She doesn't know anything about real feelings. No wonder it didn't last.'

She snapped the book shut and slipped it under her pillow and I consigned it to the room in my head.

'You are staying here tonight, aren't you?' Tullik said, brightly.

'I think so.' I glanced down at my hands as the opportunity to paint slipped straight through my fingers.

'Then you must have Milly's room, it's the one opposite mine.'

I protested, but by the time the Ihlens returned, it had all been settled. Tullik insisted I take Milly's room even

57

though Ragna, the cook, slept in a box room downstairs at the back of the house. I was the youngest, an inexperienced housemaid, and my room was bigger and grander than both Tullik's and Caroline's. Milly's room was large and airy, filled with light that came sailing in through the front window overlooking the church. The walls were decorated in white wooden panelling and silky flower-print wallpaper. Pale-blue curtains hung at the window and were tied back with twisted golden ropes and tassels. Milly would be horrified to know that an interloper like me, a simple housemaid, was sleeping in her bed.

'She's never here anyway,' Tullik said, after my fifth objection. 'And if she brings Ludvig and Lila, they don't even stay here at Solbakken, they go to the Grand Hotel.'

'Solbakken? I thought this was Kirkebakken?'

'Solbakken is what we call this house,' she said. 'It's our little place in the sun.'

She tried to smile as she said the words, as if she were obliged to be happy here in Borre. But the corners of her mouth failed to rise and as she spoke I noticed the shadow of something dark flash across her eyes.

Ragna Thorsen was a young and skinny woman, so far from my expectations it was almost comical. In my mind she had been akin to Fru Berg: an ample-bosomed, rosy-cheeked woman with work-weary crow's feet and sausage fingers. But the woman who greeted me in the kitchen the following morning while I was cleaning out the ashes from the stove was a little sparrow who looked like she hadn't eaten in months.

'Glad to make your acquaintance,' she said, over the hurried chop of her knife. Her dark almond eyes followed her fingers like slaves and had to drag themselves away to meet mine, which they did only fleetingly, observing my face like an object, before returning to the onion at the centre of their world.

For the rest of the day, I crept around Ragna and spoke to her only at mealtimes when I helped her serve food. She rarely left the kitchen and, absorbed in her work, she hardly raised an eye as I came and went with my buckets and brushes. The silent cook seemed to communicate through the food she prepared, and I read the changing scents that filled the air as an indication of her mood. The morning was a symphony of smells that ranged from the pungent onion she chopped with such precision, to simmering vegetable broth, followed by the waft of strong coffee. After the Ihlens had eaten luncheon, Ragna's afternoon moved through the comforting hug of baking bread to the fresh, zesty tang of her juices and preserves. At times I was drawn to her with the sympathetic pull of potential friendship. During her bread-baking I was tempted to reach out to her. Perhaps I could pay her a compliment, tell her how delicious it smelled? But every time I plucked up the courage to approach her, I was quickly repelled by the acerbic sting of the vinegar and her stern face as she chopped and stirred.

I eventually concluded that she and I could become friends and decided that I would try to appeal to her with a friendly word or two at the next sign of baking. But before I had the chance to reach out to Ragna, Tullik set a gulf between us so wide that the friendship we might have had was killed before it had even been conceived.

It was mid-morning when Tullik came looking for me. I was at the bench in the scullery preparing the wax for polishing the parlour floor. Fru Berg had given me a brief demonstration and I was gingerly adding linseed oil to the beeswax. Ragna was shelling peas at the basin.

'Where's Johanne?' Tullik asked her.

I didn't hear Ragna respond, but Tullik found me when she came pacing to the back door.

'There you are! You must stop what you're doing at once and get ready,' she said. 'We're going to Åsgårdstrand. You can show me where you live.'

I wiped my sticky hands across my apron and stood there staring at her, my brain unable to cobble together her words and their meaning.

'I'm polishing,' I said, dimly.

'No, you're not. You're coming to Åsgårdstrand with me.'

Ragna clanged her colander against the basin and the tinny sound rang in my ears.

'Get ready!' Tullik said.

'But what about my work? There's so much to do.'

'I asked Mother and she said it was all right.' Tullik flashed me a smile and started towing me by my apron strings. 'Come on!' she said.

The blow that was to sever my ties to Ragna forever came when Tullik dragged me into the kitchen.

'Ragna, help Johanne clean this polish off her hands. She's coming to Åsgårdstrand with me.'

Ragna moved to a cupboard on the far wall and took out a rag and a bottle of clear liquid. She banged the two down on

60

the kitchen table without looking at me. The bottle wobbled precariously for a few seconds and I caught it just before it fell. My eyes almost melted from the fumes that hit me when I removed the lid.

'Rub your hands with it,' Ragna said, and returned to her peas.

The liquid stung my fingers, finding its way into all the tiny cuts and cracks in my broken skin. As I rubbed the cloth across my palms, my hands smarted and the stinging spread all the way up to my ears. I yelped and bit my lip. Ragna did not turn around or show any concern. She continued to systematically pop the pods and scrape the peas out with her fingertips.

Tullik was growing impatient.

'Come on – we can rinse it off at the water pump,' she said.

I rushed to the garden and flung my hands under the tap while Tullik pumped the handle. Fru Berg was sitting with her bucket, scrubbing something small and white at her washboard.

'What's this? What's this?' she said.

'My hands are stinging,' I said. 'Ragna gave me some liquid to get the polish off. Feels like nettles.'

Fru Berg scowled and threw the garment she was washing back into the bucket.

'Let me see,' she said, pushing the bucket aside with her foot and groaning as she heaved herself up. 'Has she given you turpentine?' She examined my hands. 'Good Lord above. You've reacted badly to that. I'll get some calamine and the oil.'

She returned a few minutes later and began dabbing my fingers roughly with a milky liquid. When it was absorbed she rubbed oil into my skin in a circular motion, which was meant to be soothing but her coarse thumbs scratched against my hands and made it worse.

'Can't have your hands idle now, can we?' she said. 'There's plenty to be done today, with all the floors, and those front windows need doing again.'

I shot a glance at Tullik, who raced to my defence.

'Johanne's coming with me to Åsgårdstrand today,' she said. 'It'll give her hands a chance to recover. I'll get her some balm at the chemist's while I'm there.'

Fru Berg's beady little eyes became so wide with surprise that, for the first time, I actually noticed their colour. They had always been black to me, but now I could see that they were hazel tinged with flecks of green. Fru Berg had been with the Ihlens since the girls were children and, unlike Ragna, she was not above speaking to them sternly.

'What about everything that needs to be done here?' she snapped. 'You can't take Johanne away today, Miss Tullik.'

I thought Tullik would see the impossibility of it and say *No, of course, Johanne has work to do – how silly of me*, then I would be released from their disagreement and free to return to my chores. But Tullik was insistent.

'I can!' she said, defiantly. 'I checked with Mother and she has allowed it. Now, if you don't mind, Fru Berg, we must go.'

The air flew out of Fru Berg's cheeks and her face deflated. I half expected her to wither like a dripping candle and collapse to the ground. She tried desperately hard to think of something to say, puffing up her cheeks again and again with varying degrees of strain. But she knew she was defeated. She could not contradict Julie Ihlen's decision and had no choice but to let us go.

'Well, don't be long then,' was all she could manage, but Tullik was already leading me away and Fru Berg's words became nothing but filmy bubbles, floating weakly skywards before bursting into the air.

5

Scarlet

The middle of this circle will appear bright, colourless, or somewhat yellow, but the border will at the same moment appear red. After a time this red, increasing towards the centre, covers the whole circle, and at last the bright central point.

Theory of Colours, Johann Wolfgang von Goethe

The sun was already high in the sky as Tullik and I crossed the road. We passed the church and headed down the lane towards the forest where the dark pines invited us into their shadowy world.

'It's so cool in the woods,' Tullik said, removing her hat and pulling the pin from her hair, 'so magical. Do you believe in fairies, Johanne?' She skipped between the trees with her arms outstretched, brushing her hands across the peeling bark. 'And trolls? And spirits? Do you think ghosts haunt these woods?'

The sun picked lines through the branches and illuminated her as though she were a drop of early-morning dew glistening on the silver pad of a birch. As the light caught her dress I could see the outline of her legs as she danced gracefully through the forest, twirling and sparkling like a veil of stars. Tullik was ethereal, a being not wholly of this world, moulding and shaping everything solid and earthly to fit her fantasy.

She continued to weave through the trees and then stopped abruptly behind a thick birch, clinging to the trunk of it and tilting her head.

'Did you hear that?' she said.

'What?'

'That noise. That cracking sound? Was it footsteps?'

'I didn't hear anything.'

'My father used to tell us stories about trolls and the huldre-folk,' she said, looking about her as though watching the imaginary creatures approach. 'I've walked these woods at dusk, when the sky is grey but not dark. I've seen shapes and shadows, moving like ghosts, seen yet unseen, among these trees. Have you, Johanne?'

'No.'

'And you don't hear that?' she said. 'It's getting nearer.'

I closed my eyes and listened but heard nothing, only the comforting slap of waves at the shore and the occasional caw of the crow.

'There's nothing there, Tullik,' I said.

She was still cowering by the tree.

'Check over there, behind me,' she said.

I walked towards her, probing the woods, but heard nothing out of the ordinary.

'Really, Tullik, there's nothing there.'

I thought she was playing make-believe, like a little girl. For a moment it was difficult to accept that she was almost five years

65

my senior, a young woman who had already turned twenty. As I approached her I could see that she was genuinely afraid and even when I reassured her, she would not let go of the trunk.

'Come on, Tullik,' I said, peeling her hands from the tree, 'there are berries over there by the path. Let me find some for you.'

She reached for my arm and gripped it tight, as though I was asking her to jump from a great height. Her eyes were fixed over my shoulder on the invisible evil that approached.

'It's all right,' I said, 'really, it's all right.'

'Don't let go of me,' she said.

'I've got you. I've got you, Tullik.'

She clung to me like a frightened child as I guided her back to the forest path. Stunned by this sudden change in her demeanour, I didn't know what to say. I led her to the side of the track where I reached into the leaves and plucked a ripe strawberry.

'Do you want to taste it?'

Immediately her face changed. The fruit vanquished the band of villains in her head.

'It's so sweet,' she said, throwing the strawberry into her mouth and becoming Tullik again. 'How did you know where to look?'

'Practice,' I said.

We dallied at the strawberry bushes and I took her down to the shore. There was no concept of time in Tullik's world. She seized every moment and stretched it or shortened it according to her will, allowing her instincts to lead her. We slipped out through the trees and walked along the coast, jumping across the stones, stopping to look at pebbles, gazing out to sea and pointing at ships on the hazy horizon.

The Nielsens' large white farmhouse appeared on our right as we emerged into Åsgårdstrand. On this side of the woods it was easier for me to associate myself with Tullik. Now we were in my territory, and in Åsgårdstrand I had never been bound by the restraints of employment. We continued along the path until it widened and joined Nygårdsgaten at the slope of the hill. The road was quiet. Its only occupant was Fru Book's pony hoofing at the dust in the shade. Fru Book was out weeding her garden and her head shot up over the fence when she heard us coming.

'Hello, Johanne,' she said, acknowledging me through the jasmine with an outstretched hand.

'Do you know everyone here?' Tullik said.

'Almost.'

'Where is your house?'

'Up there,' I said, pointing around the bend and up the hill.

'Can we go?'

'We don't live there at the moment. Herr Heyerdahl is renting it.'

'Herr Heyerdahl is living in *your* house?' she said.

'Yes. He rents it every summer with his wife and children.'

'Then we must go and meet him,' she said, stopping in the road, swinging her hat by her side.

'Why?' I said.

Tullik laughed.

'Why, Johanne? To see his paintings, that's why! To see him at work, of course!'

67

'The hill's terribly steep,' I said.

'So?'

She had already spun around and I had no choice but to follow her.

We trekked up the hill in the blistering heat, passing the gardens where rhododendrons and lupins were beginning to flower. The sun stretched its arms around us, making the climb ever more arduous. We had just rounded the bend and begun the final ascent when we met a woman carrying a basket, hurrying towards us. It was Mother.

'Johanne?' she shouted from several yards away. 'Johanne? Is that you? What are you doing here?'

Her gaze crossed from me to Tullik and back again, as a multitude of questions swept her face. *Was I being sent home? Had I failed the Ihlens? Had I done something wrong? Had I brought shame to my family?* For a moment I enjoyed her confusion. I could see she was struggling to find a reason why her daughter would be out at this time of day with a fine young lady from the city.

'This is Miss Ihlen,' I said. 'Tullik, this is my mother, Sara Lien.'

Tullik was as gracious to my mother as Julie Ihlen had been to me and held her hand out politely.

'Very pleased to make your acquaintance, Fru Lien,' she said, suddenly reeking of Kristiania society.

Mother was flustered by the attention and began her rehearsed Herr Heyerdahl lecture.

'Oh yes, hello, Miss Ihlen. I do hope Johanne is not causing you any . . . She isn't, is she? I was just on my way

68

to see the Heyerdahls. You know they rent our house in the summer? I thought I'd offer them some . . . But they have guests at the moment, from Kristiania. Do you know Herr Heyerdahl's work? He painted Johanne once, did she tell you?'

'Yes, in fact I was hoping to go and meet him right now,' Tullik said.

'Oh no!' Mother said, turning her disapproval on me. 'You can't go to the Heyerdahls' now, Johanne, they have guests. Didn't I say? Friends from Kristiania.'

'Then maybe I will know them?' Tullik said.

'They're mainly painters, I think,' Mother said, her eyes still on me. Her voice was tight, as though she was trying to swallow a reprimand aimed at Tullik. Knowing she was sinking fast, she turned on me again. 'But what are you doing here? Why aren't you at work, Johanne? I hope she hasn't—'

'She's doing a fine job,' Tullik said. She slipped her arm around my shoulders and a bolt of affection for her rushed through my body. 'I asked her to come with me today. My mother gave us permission. And we need to pay a visit to the chemist; Johanne needs some balm for her hands.'

'What's wrong with your hands?' Mother turned on me, accusingly. 'You have good working hands.'

'Turpentine,' I said, hoping the word alone would suffice.

'Then get some lavender balm,' she said, digging in her pocket. 'Here, I'm sure I have a few kroner. Or you can put it on our list at Herr Backer's.'

'No, no,' said Tullik. 'I'll get her the balm. She's our employee. We need some for the house anyway.'

Mother made an affected curtsey and moved closer towards us, herding us back down the hill.

'You should take Miss Ihlen to the pier, Johanne. Or go for a walk along the beach where there's movement in the air. You could choke up here. There's not a breath.'

'It's quite all right,' Tullik said. 'I'd like to see Herr Heyerdahl. I'm sure our visit won't be too much of an inconvenience.'

Mother had an odd look on her face. I had seen it before, in circumstances where she was desperate to argue but her surroundings, or the presence of others, kept her lip tightly buttoned. Like Fru Berg, there was nothing my mother could do to deny Tullik her wishes. She lifted her chin and forced an uncomfortable smile to her lips.

'Very well then, have a pleasant day,' she said, without making any further reference to me, or my hands, or my employment at the Ihlens'.

Tullik and I continued to climb until we reached the final stretch of road that led to our cottage. Both of us were wilting under the oppressive sun and had to stop and rest every couple of paces. Our eyes were pulled to the fjord and we stood there drinking it in, filling our bodies with the overwhelming sight of it, the immense blue that sparkled and stretched out into forever.

'No wonder the artists come here, with this view,' Tullik said. 'Who could fail to be inspired by it?'

'They tell me they come for the light too,' I said. 'Apparently it's quite peculiar here. The old farmers say it's because of the ancient bluffs that formed when the ice melted thousands of years ago. They say the shape of the landscape bends the light and that's why we're always bathed in gold. That's what the artists love about it.'

I lifted my face to the sky and allowed the light to wash over me. As my skin tingled in its heat I remembered what *he'd* said, about subjects in paintings, how they grow and change like life; how they *are* life.

'I can understand it,' Tullik said. 'It's truly captivating. But how do you manage in the winter? All the way up here in the snow and ice.'

It was impossible to imagine the winter at the present moment. My blouse and skirt were damp and sticky, and sweat was trickling down the small of my back. The sun's rays were beaming through every part of my body; my throat was dry, my brow clammy and my hands, still stinging from the turpentine, were now frying in the heat. I longed for the winter, just for a second of it. How wonderful it would be to throw myself down in the deep snow and breathe the clear cold air that froze my nostrils and reddened my nose.

'We walk,' I said. 'You get used to it.'

'On a hill as steep as this I would have to be pulled with a rope!' said Tullik.

'I think it must be something about living here,' I said. 'Our bodies seem to know exactly how to bend coming up the incline, and exactly how to lean going down it. There are very few places in Åsgårdstrand where people actually stand upright.'

We were just laughing about this phenomenon when I saw a man coming through our gate and out into the dusty road.

'Look at him then, Johanne,' Tullik said playfully. 'Is he a local? Is he bending at the right angle? Can you tell?'

I stopped to look at him properly. He was wearing a straw fedora with a black-and-white band and a dark jacket that hung low about his body. I couldn't see much of his face, but instantly I understood why my mother had been so guarded. The strong jawline and broad brow were unmistakable. The man approaching us was Edvard Munch.

'He's not from here, no,' I said. 'That's Munch.'

He was striding towards us, holding a cigarette in one hand and a sketchbook in the other.

'What should we say?' Tullik said, buzzing with energy.

'Don't say anything,' I said. In all my years of observing Munch I had come to know his mannerisms and the unusual way in which he interacted with people. 'You can't approach him. He walks about with his eyes half shut, like he's in a dream, not really paying attention. But then, if he sees something that interests him, he stops.'

'Do you think he'll stop for me?' she said.

I remembered Munch's fixation with Tullik at the dance, how he had sketched her so purposefully.

'I don't know,' I lied.

He was getting closer. He puffed on his cigarette and looked out at the sea. The dramatic fjord had captured his attention. The blue-violet surface was beckoning to him. He was studying it, committing the subtle details of it to his memory: the way the sunlight caught the waves and how the colour changed at varying depths. I had often seen him paint without ever looking at his subject. He lodged every image in his mind and could bring it to life in another time and place entirely.

Tullik dropped her hat.

'Oh, now look at me,' she said, slowly bending to pick it up, 'how clumsy.'

Munch was so close now that when his eyes returned to the road and he saw Tullik crouching in front of him, he had no choice but to stop.

'Excuse me, madam,' he said, halting.

Tullik raised herself up. She straightened her shoulders and pushed her hair away from her face.

'Sorry, sir, I dropped my hat,' she said, breathlessly.

Munch took a step back. His eyes opened fully and he removed the cigarette from the corner of his mouth.

'Johanne?' he said, tucking his sketchbook under his arm.

For a moment he wrestled with the same questions my mother had struggled with. He looked from Tullik to me and back again.

'This is Miss Ihlen,' I said, coming to his rescue. 'She is staying in Borre for the summer. I am working as her house-maid. Mother got me the job. That's why I couldn't come to paint with you – I'm sorry. Tullik, this is Munch.'

He held out his hand and Tullik reached for it gladly.

'Very pleased to make your acquaintance, Herr Munch,' she said. She tilted her head and smiled at him sweetly through the side of her mouth before saying the most startling thing. 'I believe you know my sister, Milly.'

Munch searched the road for an answer.

'Yes,' he mumbled, eventually. 'Fru Thaulow and I knew each other some years ago.'

'She's Fru Bergh now,' Tullik said.

'Of course, I had heard.'

'We were going to see Herr Heyerdahl,' I said, noticing the tremble in Munch's hand.

'Hans is entertaining the enemy. I had to get away,' he said.

Tullik laughed her infectious giggle.

'The enemy? You don't mean all those boring Kristiania guests, do you, by any chance?'

Munch's sad eyes ignited when she understood the reference.

'Boring, conceited,' he said.

'Self-absorbed, empty,' Tullik said. 'Sometimes the boredom drives me to distraction.'

Munch took a draw on his cigarette and looked at her as though she was an exhibit in a museum. He was puzzled by this flame-haired creature, delighted by her, curiously drawn to her as though she were something mythical, like a mermaid or a nymph.

'Have you been to the bathing house, Miss Ihlen?' he said. 'It's marvellously invigorating. I'm heading to the beach right now, as a matter of fact.'

'What a wonderful idea,' she said. 'Johanne, let's go and bathe!'

'But we don't have our bathing clothes,' I said.

'It's after twelve,' Munch said. 'The white flag will be raised, for women's bathing.'

'Then let's go and take a dip, Johanne. It will be refreshing.'

'But . . . '

A troupe of angry protesters paraded through my mind, buttressed by my mother with her condemnation and scorn: *Being seen with the Sinful Man? Encouraging Tullik's involvement with him, knowing how her family feels about him? Bathing without bathing clothes? Do you want to lose your job and your reputation in one day?*

'What about Herr Heyerdahl?' I said.

'Oh, he can wait,' Tullik said, waving her hand as though swatting a fly. 'And besides, he already has guests.'

She effortlessly twisted reality to fit her world and made a perfectly reasonable case as to why we should abandon our plan and instead follow Munch to the beach.

First it was Julie Ihlen, then Fru Berg, then my mother. Now it was my turn. I could not refuse Tullik or deny her these whims, despite my own better judgement. Reluctantly, I turned to meet my fate and trundled back down the hill behind Tullik and Munch. Her golden mane seemed to envelop him as they moved closer together, the upper halves of their bodies leaning towards each other as though pulled by an unseen force.

6

Ruby

*Thus, in physical phenomena, this highest of all appearances
of colour arises from the junction of two contrasted extremes
which have gradually prepared themselves for a union*

Theory of Colours, Johann Wolfgang von Goethe

As Tullik and Munch drifted naturally towards each other,
I was careful to stay a few paces behind them. Their conversation was not fluid but their silences were comfortable and
Munch seemed relaxed in her company. We reached the bottom
of the hill and passed the fishermen's huts. My heart pumped.
If anyone saw me, it would only be a matter of minutes before
my mother knew about it. I kept my head down and tried to
hide behind Tullik's delicate little body.

When we reached Munch's house I wanted to keep walking,
but Tullik and Munch stopped at the gate and I was forced to
linger there like a dog with its owner.

'You can walk through my garden if you like,' Munch said,
'take a shortcut to the beach.'

'Oh, how kind!' Tullik beamed, following him to the gate.

I scurried after them. At least we would be partially shielded by the trees, and being in the garden would be less conspicuous than out on the road. Passing through the gate, I found myself once again entering his forbidden world.

The paintings were still outside leaning against the studio wall. The dark lady was still unsettled by her shadow; the pregnant woman with the cherries was still forlorn. I noticed that more paintings had appeared. Scattered throughout the garden were canvases of differing shapes and sizes resting up against rocks and hedges, placed at random. Seeing the square blocks of colour merge with the plants and flowers surrounding them was like looking at an exhibition of nature.

'Oh, how magical!' Tullik said, as her eyes scanned the scene. 'An outdoor gallery!'

'I'm giving them the horse-cure,' Munch said. 'I leave them outside. It gives them life.'

Tullik wandered between the paintings, stopping here and there to view them, which she did intensely, agonisingly slowly.

Munch's eyes followed her with biting fascination. Apart from Inger, Tullik must have been one of the only women to take such relish in looking at his pictures. She showed none of the abhorrence expressed by the other Kristiania ladies and plunged herself into the paintings with open indulgence.

My own temptation got the better of me, and the grip my mother held on my conscience once again began to slip. I was drawn to a painting of a busy street at sunset. People were rushing towards me, as though running from the canvas, their faces filled with panic, eyes staring, startled and afraid. Against the rush of faces, in the middle of the road was a figure standing with his back to me, dark, thin. Apart. The lone figure was facing the inevitable coming of night, accepting its imminence, alone. Was the figure Munch? Was that how he saw himself?

Beside the street scene was a picture of a man I recognised. It was Jacob, the bathing-house attendant. His face was rough and weather-beaten. Munch had etched the years of Jacob's hard life into the canvas with relaxed precision, and the scattered, loose strokes of the brush brought the old man to life as his skin glowed in the yellow shine of a buttercup clump growing beside the painting.

Tullik was engrossed in a picture of a washerwoman; it must have been Fru Bjørnson, a substantial woman like Fru Berg, with thick arms and a determined posture. She took in washing and ironing from all over Åsgårdstrand. There appeared to be a sense of dignity and calm about the ordinary woman going about her work while Munch, the silent observer, stole a moment of her life.

Every single picture was a piece of life. The subjects were not posing, like models, and hardly seemed aware of the painter who was watching them. They were simply going about their business in their natural surroundings, undisturbed and real.

Tullik tipped her head from one side to the other as she studied the washerwoman and her daughter, Constanse, standing beside her in the picture. Then she returned to the studio, where her eye settled on the dark painting of the woman troubled by her shadow.

After a while, Tullik raised her hand like a pupil in a classroom. She turned to look for Munch, but found that he was already standing right behind her.

78

'What makes you paint like this?' she said.

'I try to paint life's unsolvable riddles, the things that perplex us,' he said. 'I try to paint life as it is lived.'

'People say it's not possible to paint the way you do,' Tullik said, lifting her hat to the painting before her.

'It's not easy,' Munch said.

Tullik laughed.

'No, no,' she said, 'they don't question your skill. They say it's vulgar, uncouth.'

'The truth can often appear vulgar, can it not?' Munch said. 'And lies can shine like beautiful stars.'

'Take this one, for instance,' Tullik said, pointing at the sketch of Jacob. 'He looks like a noble man, but he's just the bathhouse attendant.'

'Yes, I call him *The Native*,' he said. 'His life has a purpose and he knows what that purpose is. Not like the guests from Kristiania, the people at the hotel who are constantly trying to find new ways to pass their time. Where is their sense of purpose? Do they find it in newspapers and magazines, in restaurants, or during the promenade on Karl Johan? They accept Jacob's help when it suits them, without ever knowing that his life's purpose is being fulfilled just by serving them. Do you think they ever find real happiness, like the people here in Åsgårdstrand who find it in simple things like earning their keep?'

'The little people are the greatest people,' Tullik said, without looking at me. 'They may be little, but they don't care about the little things. And this woman, here,' she said, turning back to the dark lady and her shadow, 'who is she?'

79

'That's my sister, Laura,' he said, moving his hands, following the outline of Laura's body with his fingers. 'She is consumed by fear. She's always trying to escape her own shadow but cannot break free. Poor Laura, she suffers when people ridicule my art and mock me.'

'I can understand that,' Tullik said. Her hand brushed his arm in a reflex action that she herself was unaware of. 'I think I could be that way too.'

Munch did not answer but took a small piece of charcoal from his pocket. He began to sketch the outline of another woman around Laura's body and softly wove Tullik into the picture until there were two dark figures clinging together, seeking escape from their own shadows.

Tullik looked at the picture. She swept her hair back and returned her hat to her head in a similar act of completion.

'Come, Johanne,' she said, speaking to me but looking at Munch. 'Let's bathe.'

She held her arms up, pretending to fix her hat into place for longer than was necessary, inviting his eyes to roam her body. Even I was captivated as the sun lit her flaming hair and melted in droplets over her white dress.

'We'll see you at the beach, Herr Munch,' she said. 'Thank you for this most interesting exhibition.'

Munch lifted his hat as Tullik wandered dreamily away. We tramped through the long grass and past the outhouse, a tall sentry box at the bottom of the garden. Tullik howled with laughter as she scaled the wire fence, teetering as she straddled it, but still managing an undignified wave over her shoulder to the painter she knew was watching.

We walked past the Grand Hotel and the Kiøsterud house, then along the pebbled beach to the Central Hotel, another of the four hotels that housed the summer guests. The pier was humming with anticipation and a crowd had gathered at the far end, hungrily awaiting the arrival of the postal boat due in, bringing with it wages sent home from men at sea. A few sailors skirted the pier and a young man dangled his feet into the water, pulling a small rowing boat towards him with his toes.

The bathing house was surprisingly peaceful when we arrived. By now my clothes were sticking to me and I could not deny the enthralling temptation to dive into the water. Munch was right: the white flag was flying above the changing hut beside the boxy, roofless tent that shielded the female bathers from view.

'You see,' Tullik said, 'we don't need our bathing clothes, we'll be hidden behind the tent.'

'We can ask Jacob for towels,' I said. 'He gets them from the hotel.'

We strode out along the rickety wooden pier to the bathing area. A young girl sitting on the ramp was playing with a dog that barked enthusiastically as we passed. I tensed and quickened my pace to deflect the attention. Jacob was moulded into a deckchair on the veranda. The striped fabric of the chair sagged beneath his body and his hat was drawn down over his face, leaving only his whiskers and beard in view. He appeared to be sleeping, but at the clip of our heels he sprang from the chair as though it had been set alight.

'Ladies,' he said, readjusting his hat.

'May we borrow some towels?' Tullik said.

'And some bathing clothes,' I added.

Jacob raised his fingers to his mouth and punched a loud whistle into the air.

'Marie!' he hollered to the little girl with the dog. 'Run and get the ladies towels and bathing clothes.'

The girl jumped to attention and disappeared to the hotel.

'That's the granddaughter. She gets a few øre for helping out,' he said, scratching his wiry chin with his cracked old fingers. I looked at his face, noticing all the lines Munch had sketched with such care, now moving and changing shape as Jacob spoke.

Prompted by the mention of money, Tullik delved in her pouch for some coins.

'How long do we get?' she said.

'As long as you like,' Jacob said. 'It's quiet today. Visitors are at a music recital at the town hall.'

Marie came running back with her arms clinging tightly to a bundle that concealed her face. We took the towels and bathing clothes and Jacob unlocked the changing hut.

'Ladies,' he said again, showing us in with a crooked bow before returning to his deckchair.

Tullik undressed hurriedly, throwing her clothes onto the bench as though they were infected. Uninhibited, she stripped naked before me and I awkwardly averted my eyes from the flash of pale skin by my side. She reached for a towel and swung it around her shoulders, while I unhooked my corset and paused to enjoy the liberating release.

'I'm going in,' she said, ignoring the costume Marie had given her. 'Hurry!'

I looked at my bathing costume with its frilled sleeves and long pantaloons. Spurred by Tullik's lack of inhibition, I picked up my towel, wrapped it around my naked body and climbed down the ladder at the back of the hut.

There was a loud splash behind me as Tullik plunged into the water, followed by a spluttering and gasping sound as she came up for air.

'Woooo-hoooo!' she yelled. 'It's magnificent!'

I slipped my towel down into the railings by the ladder and lingered on the ledge for a second. Tullik giggled. Her lips were wet and gleaming and her hair floated around her like golden seaweed.

'Jump!' she said.

I gripped my nose, hopped into the air, then sank into the delightful coolness of the sea.

'Isn't it wonderful?' she said, when I popped to the surface. 'So bracing and refreshing!' She swam in circles around me as I pushed my hair back from my face and wiped my eyes. Then she flipped over onto her back and swam up and down in lengths from one end of the tent to the other, her arms stretching out purposefully over her head and her small breasts appearing at the surface. She continued to flip and turn, at moments disappearing underwater long enough to make me nervous. Then she shot up again with the water spraying around her, dripping from her face like liquid gold. It was as though she belonged to the sea, like Rán, the sea goddess we used to read about at school. All that was missing was the net she used to capture men who ventured out to the ocean.

'You know, Johanne,' she said, her eyes glistening in the sun, 'on days like this I could do something daringly adventurous, couldn't you?'

'Like what?' I asked.

'Oh, I don't know. Something bold and reckless.'

Our arms moved in circles by our sides as we faced each other while our legs kicked frantically below us to keep us afloat.

'Do you think Munch is at the beach yet?' she said.

Immediately I sensed the danger that tempted her. Something had spiked within her since the meeting with Munch. It strengthened her fearlessness and eased it up to an intrepid new level.

'Perhaps,' I said.

Her face shone like melting fire and she fixed her eyes on mine with an intensity I had not yet seen in her.

'I'm going to go and see,' she said, alive with excitement.

'What do you mean?'

She swam to the edge of the tent and lifted the oilcloth.

'Tullik?' I said. 'What are you doing?'

'Wait here. I'll be back,' she said.

She nosedived into the water and disappeared into its depths.

I swam to the wall of the tent and tried to raise the cloth enough to see through to the other side, but it was held firmly in place by ropes and wooden poles and I feared the entire structure might collapse all around me. Instead, I swam back to the ladder, pulled myself out of the water and up onto the ledge. I snatched my towel, chiding my own recklessness as I covered myself. At the corner of the tent I managed to slide my finger through a small gap in the oilcloth. Peeking out,

I saw nothing but the long expanse of sea gliding in and slapping against the rocks. Stretching onto my tiptoes, I pulled the gap wider.

'Tullik,' I whispered, frustrated. The thought of Nils Ihlen came to mind. I imagined being dragged into the admiral's office to face an interrogation. *Why had I allowed Tullik to swim away? Why hadn't I gone after her? How irresponsible it had been of me to let her go. Because of me, she had drowned.* Then, out of the corner of my tiny round window, I caught sight of a head materialising from the water. I held my breath. The head was sleek and cut through the waves like a dolphin. When it emerged a little more, I could see the long mop of hair attached to it and knew it was Tullik. I blew my relief out through my lips. *What are you doing?* She continued to swim diagonally towards the beach. *Where are you going?*

She stopped abruptly and began to crawl on her hands and knees. The water was so shallow she could no longer swim. With the depthless waves pooling around her, she came onto her side facing the beach, her shoulder and hip now clearly visible out of the water. Propping herself up on her forearms, she looked out towards the beach. Now her entire upper body and hips were exposed. One shoulder was slightly dipped and a curtain of hair fell forward over her arm. The other shoulder was gleaming white in the sun. The intense rays lit her breasts and the curve of her waist and hips. She stayed there for a few moments like a wild woman washed up with the tide, ethereal and golden, proud and unashamed. After a couple of minutes she gently lowered herself back into the water. As her skin slowly submerged, I knew that somewhere on the beach,

85

somewhere out of sight, a pair of sad eyes was watching her and a hand was dancing frenetically across a page.

Herr Backer did not question my association with Tullik. In his rheumy old eyes we were a pair of young girls out running errands together. Nothing in the world could have been more natural to him.

'Give it a few days,' he said, handing the lavender balm over the counter. 'And don't be going near any turpentine for a while. Some skins react worse than others. It's a good job you're not a painter, Johanne.'

'No,' I said, 'I'm not a painter.' *Not yet.*

Tullik took the balm and put it in her pouch.

We left the shop and came out into the town square where the hectic thrum of the market was in full swing. The cries of the traders slapped our faces and whipped our backs, some so loud they bordered on frightening. Tullik kept wincing and reaching for my arm.

'Do they think we're deaf?' she said.

'The ones that shout the loudest sell the most.'

'They won't have any customers if they scare us all away, though, will they?'

'Don't they have markets in Kristiania?' I laughed.

'Of course,' she said. 'Not that I'd be allowed to go to them. Only the maids are given that privilege.'

'I usually stand here,' I said, pointing to a lamp post opposite the Victoria Hotel. 'That's where I sell my strawberries.'

'I will come with you one day and shout at all your customers for you,' Tullik giggled.

'You might scare them away.'

'Good,' she said. 'Then I would eat all your delicious straw-berries myself.'

We drifted past the fish stalls, and the salt in the sea air became more potent. I hadn't been thinking about Thomas but suddenly he was in front of us, swiping his cap from his head and smiling at me with his twinkling eyes.

'Johanne!' he said, locking me in his glare like a blinkered pony. 'Are you buying? We have cod and mackerel.'

'No,' I said, 'we were just . . .' I guided his eyes to Tullik who, despite her damp golden hair and loud giggle, appeared to have gone unnoticed by Thomas.

'Hello, Miss Ihlen,' he said. 'Would you care to buy some cod?'

'Thomas!' I said. 'We're not buying anything!'

'Although we would love to,' Tullik gushed. 'But I'm afraid our dinner is already being prepared.'

'Are you coming home soon?' Thomas said, fixing his eyes on me again, unaware of his own tactlessness.

'Thomas!'

Tullik laughed again.

'There's another dance,' he said, determined to embarrass me, 'at the Grand. On Friday. Christian's playing. Will you come?'

'Thomas, really! This isn't the time to be—'

'She will,' Tullik said, folding her arms across her chest.

Thomas nodded firmly.

'Right then,' he said, returning his cap to his head as though he'd just agreed a fair price for a pallet of cod. I thought he might shake Tullik's hand. 'I'll see you there.'

Tullik tucked my hand into the crease of her elbow and pulled me away from the fish stall before I had time to say anything else. She didn't seem to notice the looks we were getting from the Kristiania ladies. If she did see their curious disapproval, it didn't penetrate her skin.

'*I'll see you there*,' she said, when we were out of the square and hidden away on a quiet lane. '*Who* was that?'

'It's just Thomas,' I said, shyly.

'Just Thomas? Just Thomas who?' she teased.

'Thomas Askeland.'

'He likes you,' she said. 'Do you like him?'

'I might.'

Tullik threw her arms around me and squealed.

'You might?' she said. 'Just might? How much is might? Is might a lot, or is might a little?'

'Tullik!' I said, enjoying her playful teasing. 'Stop it!'

'But you *might* like him,' she continued, squeezing me tighter until her forehead was almost touching mine. Beneath the rim of her hat and behind the drape of her hair, we were close enough to share the most intimate secrets. 'You might like him, a lot!' she said. Her plump lips skimmed my cheek and I felt her breath on my mouth as she goaded me seductively. 'You might *want* him,' she whispered. The outside world began to disappear as Tullik bewitched me with her soft teasing. 'You do want him,' she purred, 'don't you, Johanne?' Her tongue brushed her open lips as she drew me ever closer. Her hands were about my waist. We were concealed in the overhang of a jasmine bush whose delicate perfume was captivating, playing games with my senses. Locked in Tullik's world, I allowed her to pull me further, hold me tighter. 'You do want him – you do, you do,' she breathed, as her tone became husky and serious. Our breasts were cushioned together now, our skin sticky in the heat, chests heaving with fast-pounding breath. The fire of her touch enthralled me as the delicate lines between reality and fantasy began to blur. Her lips dusted mine again and lingered there for a split second, enough to ignite the burn and swell of desire between my legs. I was the only person in Tullik Ihlen's world and for that brief moment I knew what it might feel like to be truly loved.

As I opened my mouth to receive her sweet kiss, she broke into a peal of laughter and stepped back to release me.

7

Light

From these three, light, shade and colour, we construct the visible world, and thus, at the same time, make painting possible

Theory of Colours, Johann Wolfgang von Goethe

For the next few days at the Ihlens' I was caught between two worlds, the chasm between which was ever widening. Fru Berg became sterner with me, Ragna even more reserved. I rose early and dined alone. As my chores became standard and routine, they required less mental effort and gradually I was able to visit the room in my head while I worked. Analysing the treasures I had consigned there took the strain out of beating rugs and removed the drudgery from floor-mopping. This, and my growing friendship with Tullik, counteracted the resentment that Ragna was brewing in the kitchen.

At Tullik's request, I stayed at Solbakken every night. When I was finally released from my duties and weary to the bone, Tullik and I sat in her room whispering secrets long into the evening. We talked about many things, but mainly we talked about Munch.

'What did you mean,' she said, one night as we sat together on her bed, 'when we met him on the hill?'

'What did I mean about what?' I said.

'About this job? About it being the reason why you couldn't go and paint? Were you going to paint with him?'

'Oh yes,' I said. 'He saw my drawings last year and thought they were quite good.'

'You draw too, Johanne?' she said, scrambling closer to me and squeezing my arm.

'I try to. It's easier to say what I mean in drawings. But my mother doesn't like it. He gave me a book. I have to hide it from her.'

'Which book?'

'It's called *Theory of Colours*,' I said, surprised by the sound of the book on my lips. 'It's by a German man called Johann. His name's almost the same as mine.'

'Johann von Goethe?' Tullik said, excitedly.

'Yes. That's it.'

'But I have one of his books,' she said, jumping from the bed. 'Over here, in this pile.' She crawled to a tower of books on the floor by the window and began quoting a poem as she hunted. '*You can't, if you can't feel it, if it never rises from the soul, and sways the heart of every single hearer, with deepest power, in simple ways*. It's *Faust*,' she said, 'do you know it? Something, something, something, then, *Let apes and children praise your art, if their admiration's to your taste, but you'll never speak from heart to heart, unless it rises up from your heart's space*. Has he read *Faust* too?' she said. 'Does he have it?'

'I don't know,' I said, sounding hopelessly inferior. 'He just gave me the book about colours.'

'Then you must let him teach you,' she said. 'We will go to his house again. I will go with you.'

'I can't do that,' I said. 'I must work, here. And if my mother ever caught me at Munch's house I would be beaten. She thinks he's the devil.'

'She doesn't have to know, does she?' Tullik said, her eyes gleaming with urgent fire.

'That's what he said. But still . . .'

'Still what?' Tullik said. 'If it rises up from your heart's space, if your heart wants to paint, then paint you must. We will go tomorrow!'

'But how can I? There is so much to be done here.'

'I will think of something,' she said, tapping the cover of Goethe's *Faust* as though it contained all the answers.

Tullik was the youngest of the Ihlen daughters and, as such, the admiral and his wife enjoyed indulging her.

'I told them I needed you to help me pick out fabric for a new dress,' she said when we were out of the woods in Åsgårdstrand.

'Wouldn't your Kristiania friends be better suited to that task?' I said.

'Oh, they're so tedious,' she said. 'Mother knows I have no time for them. She likes you, and as long as your work gets done when we return, she doesn't mind you accompanying me.'

The chores would pile up and Ragna and Fru Berg would be furious, but with the sun bringing the summer to life before my eyes, I immersed myself in Åsgårdstrand without another thought for cleaning or soap. The clematis had begun to flower and roses clung to fences, framing doorways and windows with their enthralling perfume. Nature had started painting, and so must I.

'We can't just go into his house,' I said as we approached Munch's hut.

'Why not?' Tullik said.

'You have to be invited. He needs to be . . . I don't know, *in the mood* for guests.'

'Then we must make him in the mood,' she said, removing her hat and ruffling her hair. 'Come on!'

We passed the front door of the hut. Munch never used it. It remained closed to the road for the entire summer, encouraging passers-by to keep on walking. Tullik stopped at the gate and turned back to face me.

'Well?' she said, taking my hand. 'Are you ready?'

How could I ever be ready to enter Munch's garden?

'Hello?' Tullik called, before I could stop her. 'Herr Munch? Are you home?'

He was sitting at an easel at the back of the house. His palette was hooked over his left thumb and a bundle of newspaper sat on the ground beside him. The package contained tubes of paint. He liked to carry them around like that. The painting he was working on was of a man on a bridge looking out into a swirling, violet fjord. Soft tones of blue and brown and black dominated the lower half of the picture. The man on the bridge in the foreground was wearing a dark coat like Munch's and a fedora like Munch's. Two figures in top hats

93

and black suits walked away into the background. The wavy sky was colourless; it had not been painted yet.

The sorrow of the painting made me step back and clutch my chest. I could have taken Munch in my arms right there in his garden, so great was the ache that radiated from him.

'Tullik,' I whispered, 'we should go.'

She dragged me closer to him, despite my resistance, and at once she was all around him like the scent of the roses.

'We were just passing,' she said, as he looked up. 'Is it an inconvenience?'

To my astonishment, Munch left his easel and returned his brush to a jar on the ground.

'Miss Ihlen,' he said, 'it's you.'

'Yes,' she smiled, 'we came to say hello.'

Munch turned to me and I looked at his sad blue eyes apologetically.

'Johanne,' he said, 'there's a canvas waiting for you in the studio. I'll get it. While you're here, you may as well . . .' His voice drifted away and he shaped the words into the air with his hands. 'I'll ask Inger to make some coffee.'

He took the painting of the man on the bridge down from the easel and disappeared into the studio. Tullik hung her hat on the back of his chair and wandered around the garden, looking at the other canvases scattered amongst the plants.

'Prime it with chalk,' Munch said, coming out of the studio with a canvas under his arm and handing me a stick of white chalk. He put the canvas on the easel and motioned for me to begin. 'Just rub it on – that's right,' he said. 'I've been mixing this paint with cadmium pigments. They give the most vibrant

94

colours, especially yellow. Look at this,' he said, showing me a bright-yellow liquid in a jar. 'Do you want to try it?'

When I'd finished priming the canvas, he handed me a brush.

'Go on,' he said, 'the canvas is jute; feel the texture of it. It will absorb paint quickly, so layer it on.'

Lacking inspiration, I gazed out at the garden. Tullik was meandering by the fence, looking intently at the paintings leaning up against the stones.

'Paint not what you see, Johanne,' Munch said, handing me his palette, 'but what you *feel*.'

I dipped the brush into the yellow liquid and slapped it onto the canvas, moving it around, smudging it in with the thick horsehair bristles.

How do I feel?

How does this feel?

The shape of the sun appeared on the canvas before me. Without thinking, I added yellow waves, like the waves of Tullik's hair reaching out from the sun. Tentacles of fire.

'Look for the light,' Munch whispered. 'Yes, that's it. Let the brush move how it wants to.'

My brush began to move faster, skimming across the canvas in short strokes, making the sun's tendrils move and pulsate with life.

How do I feel?

Spirited. Vigorous.

How do I feel?

Happy. Joyful. Free. I feel free.

'Look for the light,' Munch whispered again.

I mixed red in the palette and lined the curves of the sun's fiery limbs with crimson.

How do I feel?

Purposeful. Alive. I feel alive.

My brush flicked faster and faster across the jute canvas, creating more waves and arms and branches from the sun at the centre. In some places the paint was sparse and the canvas showed through, in others great dollops of cadmium yellow coagulated to make ridges of fire. Burning. Vivid. Electrifying. Curling. Whirling. Radiant. I continued to paint. Stroking, dabbing, listening. It was as though I was having a long conversation with myself. The garden around me blurred and time was suspended. My emotions, my feelings, came pouring from me in an expression I had never been able to utter in words. The daubs of yellow were fuelled by my affection for Tullik, the time she almost kissed me in the jasmine. Her full lips. Her hair. Then Thomas, dots of uncertainty. Munch. Sweeping, curious waves. I lost all awareness of where I was and could barely feel my body or hear my own thoughts. It was only when Inger Munch appeared at my shoulder that I finally sat back and looked at what I had done.

'It's very vibrant,' Inger said. 'I didn't know you could paint so well, Johanne.'

I shuffled out of the chair and placed the brush on the stand.

'I didn't know I could paint at all,' I said.

'Would you like some coffee?'

I looked to Tullik for instruction. She was standing in the middle of the garden with Munch. His head was bent and his hands clasped behind his back. Tullik was leaning towards him and they were talking quietly.

'Edvard!' Inger shouted. 'Coffee!'

'Hmm?' he said, turning back towards the house. 'What is it, Inger?'

'You wanted coffee?' she said.

'Right, very well then,' he said. His jaw tightened.

Tullik and Munch looked at my painting before joining Inger at the table.

'You have wonderful insight, Johanne,' Munch said. 'But your story is not yet complete. I will leave it here for you to come back to.'

'It's marvellous,' Tullik said, but she wasn't really looking at my painting. Her eyes were fixed in study on Edvard Munch's face. 'There's a dance tomorrow,' she said, 'at the Grand Hotel. Maybe that will inspire her to paint more? Don't you think so, Herr Munch?'

'As long as she paints what she feels, inspiration can come from anything at all,' he said, easing Tullik's chair back, inviting her to sit down beside him.

My father used to say that there were many ways to enter a forest. You could run into it with enthralling expectation, never knowing what discoveries you would make; you could walk into it, talking and laughing with friends, oblivious to the subtle sounds that surrounded you; you could stroll into it, hand-in-hand with a lover, seeking sanctuary and a stolen moment alone; or you could creep into it, silently, noticing the very breath of nature, communing with it through a magical and inexplicable osmosis.

This was how Tullik and I entered the forest the following evening. We crept along the path, aware of each other's presence, but belonging only to the woods. The early-evening light, muted and tired, stretched the remains of the day out through the branches of the trees, thinning it like gossamer, delicate and elegant in the final moments of its dance. Unannounced, the rush of the stream came racing past us, flowing to the sea with a tumultuous bubble and thrash. On high, the birds made their aerial chorus: meaningful songs of survival, of love. The breeze caressed us as it caressed the plants and the leaves, surging through the forest, racing on to where it was bound. The unmistakable backdrop of the sea and the flow of the waves, lazy and hypnotic, could be heard from time to time through breaks in the trees. That was where I found my comfort, in the fjord that had provided for me since the day I was born.

I was wearing one of Tullik's dresses. She said I could borrow it for the dance, that Thomas might like it. It was a beautiful pale-lemon gown, embroidered with tiny fans and delicate knots on the sleeves and hem, so minute and complex it was as though it had been crafted by the hands of fairies. I could not even begin to imagine the hours of work that must have gone into this exquisite dress, a work of art that had been tailor-made for Tullik. The fabric flowed around my skin, cool and fluid like a pitcher of cream. It smelled of jasmine and of Tullik's musky hair.

Tullik's own dress was stunning in its simplicity. An effortlessly stylish silvery-white gown, it hung like a waterfall and tied with a silk charcoal band at the waist. It had a modern scooped neckline and she wore no jewellery, leaving her décolletage bare. The most eye-catching part of Tullik's outfit was of course her flaming hair that hung in wavy tresses about her shoulders.

The night was balmy and in our fine clothes we were like two young starlings about to take flight. The forest grew louder as we entered its depths. I listened to the murmur of its secret messages as they fluttered through the sway of the never-ending trees. The mutterings high above our heads spoke like warnings. Tullik was subdued. Her playfulness had been supplanted by melancholy and I walked alongside her in silence, sensing the branches of the trees watching me.

Somewhere in Fjugstad forest the spell was cast and Tullik and I emerged again in Åsgårdstrand as equals, if only in my own mind. Walking along Nygårdsgaten, Tullik awoke from the spell and spoke to me for the first time since leaving the house.

'What a beautiful evening,' she said. 'If God were a painter, He would spend His summers here, marvelling over the fruits of His creation, allowing them to inspire Him and fill His senses. That's if there is a God. Do you believe in God, Johanne?'

It was a question I had never been asked before, and something I had never truly contemplated. God was someone I met on Sundays in Borre church, someone who didn't like the house to be untidy, didn't like Munch or his paintings. I had never felt the urge to question His existence.

'Yes,' I said. 'Doesn't everyone?'

'Christ said, *God is in me. I am in God. The Father is in me. I am in the Father.* Isn't that just what you or I could say? It would be just as true for us, wouldn't it?'

Her questions perplexed me. I tried to think carefully and form a meaningful answer, but my mind was not in the mood for thinking and my thoughts were like heavy freight. All I could feel was the fjord and the waves and the sound of the night. Then I remembered something from the book.

'Goethe says, *If the eye were not sunny, how could we perceive light? If God's own strength lived not in us, how could we delight in Divine things?*'

'Precisely,' she said. 'I wonder what Edvard thinks?'

Edvard? When had she started calling him Edvard?

'If he is here tonight, I will ask him,' she said.

We passed the huts and Munch's cabin without stopping. Tullik's eyes twitched towards his house, and when it was out of sight she looked back over her shoulder several times, pulled by invisible strings.

When we arrived at the Grand Hotel it was already throwing its light and its gaiety out into the sea like a flamboyant dancer. Music greeted us in the foyer, where a flourish of colour seized our eyes as the Kristiania ladies came into view. They were fussing and fawning over each other with insincere compliments and overblown flattery. Tullik ignored them and deliberately set herself apart, preferring to align herself with me, the housemaid.

'Let's go downstairs and see if we can find Thomas,' she said. 'He'll be looking for you.'

She led me by the arm and we went down the sweeping staircase, following the sound of the fiddlers' jig. When we entered the dance I was not as anonymous as I had been the last time. Countless pairs of eyes were on us, pinning us to the door. They zigzagged backwards and forwards between Tullik and me, all of them wondering why we were together. The local towns-folk eyed me disapprovingly; *who did I think I was, dressed in my finery with my new Kristiania friend?* The Kristiania guests were no better, throwing daggers at Tullik for her disassociation from them and her open friendship with me.

'Let them stare,' she said. 'Who cares what anyone thinks?'

We swept boldly in and Thomas was soon at my side.

'Johanne! You're here!'

'I told you she would be,' Tullik said. 'Aren't you going to dance with her?'

'Of course.' He reached out for me and I floated into his arms. We spun onto the dance floor and soon I was submerged.

'You look fine,' Thomas said, pressing his lips against my neck.

He twirled me and spun me around in his arms, and again, I was lost in the rhythm of the dance. We whirled around like the paint on my canvas. Quick brushstrokes, flicking, flicking, feeling something new and vibrant. I closed my eyes and saw yellow, gold, lemon, corn, bronze and tinges of crimson like the arms of my sun. Faster and faster I felt the painting grow within me and I happily merged with it, just as I had merged with the trees in the forest.

We continued like this, spinning and twirling, dance after dance. Yellow, bronze. Yellow, bronze. Yellow, bronze, crimson, gold. I didn't even think about Tullik until the music faded and Thomas was handing me a glass of beer.

'You're dancing like a city lady now,' he said. 'What happened?'

'I had a good teacher,' I smiled. 'But where's Tullik?' I said. 'Have you seen her?'

'I've seen no one but you,' he said. 'Or hadn't you noticed?'

I craned my neck, searching the dancers and the clusters of guests mingling at the side of the room.

'We promised Fru Ihlen we'd go back together, that we wouldn't be too late.'

'She'll be here somewhere,' he said, taking my hand and pulling me back towards the dance floor.

'No,' I said, remembering Tullik's melancholy mood. My head jerked from side to side as I peeled myself away from Thomas and searched for her flaming hair.

I left him by the fiddlers and hurried through the crowds, with voices booming all around me. Men in waistcoats and shirtsleeves lifted glasses of beer and clinked them together with uproarious laughter while women tittered in groups. They huddled together, exchanging jokes and gossip, devouring wine and champagne with unquenchable thirst. I cursed their merriment. *Where was Tullik?* I scoured the lounge, then ran out into the hall. When I didn't find her there I darted through to the dining room, only to find it dark and deserted.

'I've lost her,' I said to Thomas when I returned. My voice a thin thread.

'She's a grown woman, Johanne, what does it matter? She can take care of herself.'

'But we promised Fru Ihlen,' I said. 'I don't know why she would desert me. I can't think where . . .' Before I had finished the sentence, I had already found the answer. 'I have to go,' I said. 'I have to go to Nygårdsgaten.'

'Then let me come with you,' he said.

We left the hotel before the dance had ended. My hurried steps kept me a few paces ahead of Thomas as we scaled the hill of Havnegata and turned into Nygårdsgaten.

'Why is this so important?' Thomas complained.

'It was her mood. She was different,' I said, not expecting him to understand.

'Why do you care what mood she's in?'

'I care, that's all.'

'Why? You're with me tonight,' he said, reaching forward and taking my hand. 'Why should you care where she is?'

'She's my . . .' *Friend*. I wanted to say *friend*.

'Employer,' he said. 'But you're not at work now, Johanne. Come on, let's go back to the dance.'

'I have to find her first,' I said, shaking him free and rushing ahead again. 'To make sure she's safe. You don't know what she's like.'

I heard him groan and thought he would leave, but he followed me, keeping a tense distance between us.

When I reached the gate to Munch's garden I stopped and waited for Thomas to catch up with me.

'What are we going in here for?'

'Shh!' I said. 'And don't let yourself be seen.'

The windows were incandescent with a subdued light: the fading remnants of candles. The garden was quiet and the only sound was the faint rush of the evening breeze. I lifted the latch on the gate and felt the cool metal beneath my fingers. Peering into the garden, I saw the startled faces of the people in the street still rushing from the painting in terror. Beyond them was a flame of red hair. Tullik was standing with her back to me, facing the painting of Laura Munch with her shadow. I was about to go in when I heard the back door open and close, followed by footsteps on the porch. I released the gate and sprang backwards, stepping on Thomas's toes.

He slipped his arm around my waist and we stayed there, crouching together at the gate.

'I had to come back,' I heard Tullik say. 'I had so many questions.'

Munch answered in his gentle voice.

'Of course,' he said.

'Do you believe in God?' Tullik said, laying the profound question out before him as though she were offering him a drink.

'Why do you ask?' he said.

'It's just, it would sadden me if you didn't. Not because of your lack of faith, but because when I look at your pictures I see something so spiritual, so beautiful, something that could only come from God.'

Munch moved closer towards her.

'It's true,' he said. 'I have questioned God. I prayed for my mother and my sister, Sophie, but my prayers were ignored. Where was God then? My father was so convinced our prayers would save them, even in their final breaths. I prayed for him at the end too but God didn't spare him, either. Does that mean God does not exist? I don't know. I have been faithful to the goddess of art and she has been faithful to me. It is the soul you see in these paintings. A true artist uses their art to express the soul's journey, to express that which cannot be answered by the intellect. Do you read Dostoevsky, Miss Ihlen?'

'Tullik. You must call me Tullik, if we are to be friends.'

'And are we to be friends?' he said. Their bodies were moving closer, their voices weakening in the night air.

'Yes,' she said, breathlessly, 'yes, we must.'

'Won't you walk with me, Tullik? The evening is so mild.'

When I heard their footsteps approach the gate I shoved Thomas backwards and the two of us stumbled into the lane by the houses next door.

'They're coming out,' I said, crouching behind the hedge.

Thomas could not have been less interested.

'Can we go back to the dance now, then?' he whispered. 'Now that you know she's safe?'

'No,' I said, 'I can't lose her again.'

Tullik and Munch came out into the street and began to walk towards Fjugstad forest.

'Come on,' I said. 'We must follow them.'

'Into the woods?' Thomas's interest was suddenly roused.

'Yes, into the woods.'

Careful to keep our distance, Thomas and I crept behind them as they edged closer to the forest. Their bodies were almost joined as they walked. Tullik's silvery-white dress was like a shadow in the sunset and her hair a silky veil that wanted to protect them. She leaned her head towards Munch's shoulder and eventually, at the hungry gape of the forest's mouth, he slipped his arm around her waist and the two figures merged into one.

A red glow burned through the trees as the forest was cast in Tullik's light. The dark depths of the pines shone auburn as they embraced the pair, entering the forest in *that* way, the way of lovers.

'Come,' said Thomas, swift in his gait, 'who cares about Miss Ihlen or crazy-man Munch? Tonight you are mine, Johanne Lien.'

8

Cerise

All nature manifests itself by means of
colours to the sense of sight

Theory of Colours, Johann Wolfgang von Goethe

Afraid and excited, I took Thomas's hand and rushed towards the woods. The breeze was exhilarating as we surrendered to the cover of the branches.

'Come to me, Johanne,' he whispered, leading me off the path and into the ruddy darkness of evening.

He kissed my neck and then his big hands were in my hair. Twining it around his fingers. Tugging. His mouth engulfed mine quickly. Hot and hard. Red. Cerise.

He pressed himself against me as we kissed and touched me as he pleased. His hands were on my breasts, hips, legs. Down, down beneath my hem and back up again. Tracing lines up my inner thighs. His caresses brought longing. The blossoming of desire. Ruby. Scarlet. I was ready. Soon my hips were moving on their own. Rising. Falling. Inviting his hand. But he did not touch me. Not yet. He replaced his fingers with the hard bulge of his groin. Pushing. Pulsing. Pleasure. Crimson. Fuchsia. Gold.

Perhaps it was wearing Tullik's dress, or simply the budding of love in the forest, that made me so loose. I hooked my leg around him. Again he lifted my dress, my petticoat. This time his hand touched me, softly, where no one had ever touched me before. He groaned and delved. Stroked. Circled. He slid his finger through my wetness, then pushed it firmly in. I gasped, and let him do it again and again.

A surge of guilt hit me like a slap. Indigo. I pushed him away.

'No,' I said. 'No, Thomas, stop!'

He froze and bit the air as though in pain.

'I can't. Not now. I'm too young. I'm not ready. I'm sorry,' I said, smoothing the ripples of my fear from Tullik's beautiful dress.

He moved away from me and slumped against a tree. When he found his breath he turned and smiled.

'Johanne, why don't you marry me?'

'Is that a proposal?' I said.

'Yes.'

'I'm too young to get married. I'm only sixteen.'

My hand twitched up to my shoulder and felt for the fabric.

'Engaged then? We could get engaged. You do like me, don't you?'

'Yes,' I said. Alone, I would have wept.

'So why that look on your face?'

'I just hadn't thought that far ahead yet,' I said, hitching the edge of my sleeve up and pulling it towards my neck.

'You don't have to answer me now,' he said, taking my hand and kissing my fingers, 'but think about it.'

I swung his hand in mine childishly, scared by his seriousness and scared of what I had done. It was getting darker and I was afraid. Again, I had lost Tullik.

Drawn to the comforting slosh of the sea, I suggested we go to the beach. A pale moon was rising through the smooth chop of the waves. There was something pure about it that urged me into its embrace. We passed the muttering stream and found a gap in the trees where the path curved away from the thicket and down to meet the shore. It was here that I found them, alone amongst the pines.

Tullik was standing with her back to the water. Her face was lifted to the sky, her eyes half closed. Her hands were clasped behind her back and her chest was pressed out. The subtle moonlight found flecks of gold in her hair and on her dress. Her lips were poised as though waiting for a kiss. Munch was watching her, studying her. They did not speak.

The sea stretched out behind Tullik, a flat expanse of blue violet. The rocks peeped out from the shallows and dotted the surface, stirring and making faces. Between the tree trunks the moon flashed luminous and yellow, a wide golden column across the blue water.

Munch pushed his sleeves to his elbows and went to her. He began arranging her hair, teasing some of it forward over her shoulders and letting heavier strands fall behind her back.

'You look like a mermaid,' he said.

Tullik stretched her neck out and lifted her chin further; her parted lips were begging to be kissed. Munch slipped his hand behind her head and softly pulled her mouth to his. Only then did Tullik release her clasped hands from behind her back. She wrapped them around his body and returned his kisses. I watched as Munch, powerless, was gently sucked into Tullik's world.

By the time I made my presence known to Tullik the forest had cast another spell, the consequences of which I could not yet know, but the promise of its colossal power was immediately palpable. The summer sky was as dark as it was ever going to be. Unable to produce a cloak of blackness in which the stars could shimmer, it settled for an insipid lavender that challenged the moon to work twice as hard.

The arrival of voices and laughter in the woods told me the dance was over. Fresh bands of revellers came and went, some drifting drunkenly to the water and splashing like fools in the sea. I sent Thomas home. We had spent the evening strolling in Tullik's radius, keeping a safe distance, as I was anxious not to lose her again. I didn't mean to spy but couldn't help myself. I was close enough to witness the growing fervour of their kisses, the way he touched her, how she succumbed and returned his passions. Something about their exploration and hunger for each other fascinated and excited me.

When Tullik saw me over Munch's shoulder, she gently released him. Munch strolled sheepishly out to the beach and Tullik came skipping towards me. Relief and fear mixed in my stomach as I saw that her melancholy had vanished and she was restored to her usual self, full of fire and danger and life.

'Johanne,' she said, beaming the widest smile, 'surely it can't be time to go home yet?'

'It is. We promised your mother. And you left me at the dance – I've been looking for you.'

'I was going to come back,' she said. 'I didn't know what time it was and it was such a lovely evening.'

Again, Tullik had stretched the time to suit her world.

'The dance is over now,' I said. 'We must go home.'

'All right,' she said. 'I'm coming.'

She turned back to Munch, who was standing at the shore.

'Edvard!' she called. 'I have to go now.'

'Let me take you home,' he said, scrambling across the pebbles.

They walked behind me to the edge of the woods. Something sank in my chest as I left Fjugstad and returned to Borre a housemaid once again, Tullik's employee. In her dress I felt like a fraud. I forged on ahead, up to the church, and waited by the ancient doors. The church made me nervous, as if it had seen Thomas's hands on me and already knew my sin. I waited until Tullik and Munch were closer, then meandered across the road to the sleeping house. The windows were dark and the house looked vacant, although I had the feeling that someone was watching me. Tullik and Munch lingered at the church sharing whispers and kisses, pretending to leave, then clinging to each other again and again.

I let myself in at the back door and hurried up to my room. With a guilty pleasure I hid behind Milly's plush curtains and watched the new lovers as they prolonged their goodbye. I didn't know why they intrigued me. Perhaps it was the feeling that Tullik, with all her fire and pluckiness, held the key to unravelling the mystery of *him*.

111

I was already in bed when she floated into my room.

'Johanne,' she whispered, 'are you asleep?'

'No,' I smiled. 'Come in.'

She climbed into bed with me and sank her head into the pillow. Her hair spread around us like ribbons and brought with it a waft of the fresh night air.

'He's going to paint me,' she said, turning to face me, propping her head on her hand and slipping her arm around my waist.

'I have no doubt,' I said, remembering how he had sketched her and studied every curve of her body at the dance.

'He said he would start tonight, under the moon while the sky is clear. Oh, Johanne,' she gasped, 'he kissed me!' She rolled onto her back and pulled her hair out to the sides, dragging her fingers through it repeatedly. 'He kissed me,' she said again, abandoning her hair and touching her lips, feeling the kisses that still lingered there. 'And he touched me,' she said, taking my hand and holding it to her breast, 'here.' She stared up at the ceiling and was silent. 'There's a sadness about him,' she said, after a while.

'Yes,' I said. 'Something haunts him.'

'It's a sadness I could spend a lifetime loving, but never be able to appease,' she said.

Although she had a sense that Munch's sadness could not be loved away, I knew as we lay there staring up at the elaborate cornicing on Milly's ceiling that nothing was going to stop Tullik from trying.

On Sunday evening I was sitting at the uneven table, picking at a speck of paint with my nail. Mother was spooning gravy

112

over Father's and Andreas's potatoes. Seated at the lowest of the odd chairs, I was small again, I was the Strawberry Girl. I hid there in the Painting, allowing the conversation to match my painted age. The last thing I wanted to talk about was Tullik.

'The berries will ripen this week,' Mother said. 'You can pick them on your way home and sell them at the market. They should fetch over two kroner for a pound. And don't forget the Heyerdahls. I said you'd take them some. Oh yes, and that reminds me: did I tell you he was entertaining the Sinful Man? Did you know that, Halvor?'

My father had lost interest at *two kroner for a pound*.

'Hmm?' he said, cleaning the excess gravy from his knife, wiping both sides on his potato until the silver gleamed.

'The Sinful Man! At the Heyerdahls'. Poor Christine, she must have been going spare, trying to keep him away from the children.'

Andreas wiped his mouth with his sleeve to cover a smile and I attacked another fleck of paint with my thumbnail.

'He was painting the children?' Father said, only hazily following the story.

'I certainly hope not,' Mother said. 'I turned away when I saw him. In our garden! Think about that, Halvor. I hope they didn't let him inside. The house could be infected by now – by his filth. The doctors do warn against it, you know, Halvor? I'll have to give it a proper good clean when the autumn comes.'

Father slid another potato back and forth through a few drops of gravy to clean his plate.

'Anyway, I walked away,' Mother continued, 'of course I did. And who should I meet coming up the hill but this one, with her mistress.'

'Tullik's not my mistress,' I said, jumping from the Painting, leaving the little girl behind me.

'Oh, really?' she said, welcoming me into the conversation like a sparring partner. 'So what is she then?'

'She's my friend,' I said.

'Ha! Did you hear that, Halvor? Miss Ihlen is Johanne's *friend*. Don't you dare, my girl, don't you dare!'

'Don't dare what?' I said.

'Halvor!' Mother screeched, her face flaring hot and furious. 'Did you hear that? The cheek! Tell her, Halvor! Tell her!'

Father's plate was clean. His fork was licked, his knife was licked. Every drop of gravy was gone and there was nothing left to polish. He slotted his knife into his fork, making a triangle of defeat on his plate.

'Tell her!' Mother yelled.

'I think what your mother means, Johanne, is that it's probably safer for you to know your place with the Ihlens. You are a housemaid: no more, no less. There's a line between employee and employer that should never be crossed, for when it is, a multitude of complications will arise.'

I thought about Ragna and the turpentine and the sting returned to my hands.

'Tullik's friendly towards me, that's all,' I said.

'And it isn't *Tullik*,' Mother raged. 'It's Miss Ihlen, to you.'

'Just be careful, dear,' Father said, picking up his empty plate. 'Andreas, dishes.'

We cleared the table in silence. Mother continued to fume, taking out her rage on the table, setting about it so vigorously I thought she would rub away the specks of paint and smooth the wood down to the grain.

'Not on the Lord's day, Sara,' Father said, returning to the table with a pot of coffee and his pipe. 'Not on the Lord's day.'

Andreas and I escaped to our room and closed the door.

'I'm on the bottom,' I said, as he dived onto the bottom bunk.

'No, you're not. You don't live here,' he said, playfully.

'You want me to wake you up before dawn,' I said, 'squeaking about on that bed? Come on,' I tapped the top bunk with my hand. 'Up you go.'

'Gah!' Andreas stood up reluctantly. As he walked to the end of the bunk, his foot caught on a loose floorboard and he tripped. He flew at me and I caught him in my arms.

'Damned thing,' he said, half angry, half laughing. 'That's the third time I've done that this week.'

'Can't we nail it?' I said.

'Too big a job,' he said, kneeling on the floor. 'Look at it, they're all loose.'

One by one he lifted the floorboards from the middle of the room and rattled them all the way across to the window.

'We'll just have to be careful,' I said, ruffling his hair. 'I'll get a mat to cover it.'

After everything that had happened since my employment at the Ihlens' I ached for my brother, for his youth and his simplicity. He kicked off his boots and climbed to the top bunk. I changed into my nightgown and crawled into the hard bed below him. Above us the Andersens' baby cried.

115

Andreas wriggled around in his bed and punched his pillow.

'Is it true?' he said, when he finally settled.

'Is what true?'

'That Miss Ihlen posed for Munch, on the beach?'

'Where did you hear that?' I said.

'Markus and Petter said they saw her,' his head appeared over the side of the bunk, 'and they said she was . . . you know?'

'No, I don't know,' I said. 'And don't believe everything Markus and Petter tell you.'

'But is it true?' he said, grinning at me.

I found it hard to conceal anything from my brother. We had shared too much, suffered collectively at the hands of our mother for too many years, but this was a rumour I had to quash, for Tullik's sake and mine.

'I wouldn't know,' I said, 'but I doubt it. Those boys have vivid imaginations, that's all.'

'But they said they saw her after too, with wet hair; they said it must have been her.'

'Let them think what they want,' I said, sounding exactly like Tullik.

'Did Munch paint her, though?' he said.

'How would I know?'

'Just that you talk to him, don't you?'

'No!'

'You do sometimes.'

'Sometimes. Hardly ever,' I lied.

Munch and I had met many times before: along the lanes, on the beach and in the forest where I searched for fruit and herbs from morning to night. I trailed him, shy and gawky, intrigued

116

by the paintings he left out in the open, the way they spoke to me. Sometimes he'd see me sketching close by and come and offer words of advice. He never sounded like the other adults, though. He spoke as an artist, of shadow and light, colour and perspective, and he expected me to understand.

'I won't tell anyone, you know,' Andreas said.

'Tell anyone what?' I said, blankly. 'How can you tell them nothing?'

He rolled back onto his bed with a grumble.

'Thomas was here yesterday,' he said.

'And?'

'Brought Mother some fish, but she told him she didn't need it. Then she argued with Father because he couldn't understand why she'd turned down a good bit of cod.'

'Did he say anything?' I said, as guilt crept across my chest: the forest, his hands, his proposal.

'Who?' Andreas sounded bored.

'Thomas.'

'Anything like what? Like, *May I marry your daughter?*'

I kicked the bottom of Andreas's bunk.

'Stop it!'

'You will marry him, though, won't you, Johanne?'

'How do I know who I'll marry?' I said.

'You can marry crazy-man Munch, for all I care,' Andreas said and twisted over in his bunk, making the slats creak.

He continued to twist and turn for most of the night, squeaking and creaking like a wheel in need of grease. Sleep held her hand out to me for hours at a time, but I could never seem to grasp her for long enough to sink into a dream. The morning found me quickly and just as I teetered on the cusp of my hundredth attempt at sleep, Mother was in the doorway calling me to awaken, while Andreas snored on.

'He's been doing that all night,' I whispered, tripping on the loose floorboard. 'And that bed squeaks at the slightest movement.'

'Stop complaining, Johanne. I expect you'll sleep tonight after a good day's work.'

I had not told my mother about Milly's bedroom, or my luxurious sheets and curtains, how I slept like a queen at the Ihlens'. If Mother had known, she would no doubt have complained to the Ihlens about it herself. I wondered how long it would be until Fru Berg started talking.

I dressed hurriedly. When Mother returned to the stove, I slid my hands beneath the mattress and retrieved the book. I stroked its grey canvas cover and ran my fingers over Goethe's name on the spine, before casting it into my pocket.

'Remember to look for strawberries this week,' Mother said, pushing a cup of coffee at me as we sat at the table. 'If you get your jobs done quick enough you might be able to get to the market, or at least sell door-to-door.'

'Yes, Mother.'

'More guests are arriving this week. The *Horten* and the *Jarlsberg* are running double service: eleven forty-five and ten past six. The hotels are filling up, so there'll be plenty of buyers. Come on now – hurry up, we don't want you to be late.'

I picked my boots up at the door but didn't put them on. I walked faster barefoot and wanted to feel the cool rub of the stones along the beach as the sun came up.

Outside the morning belonged to the birds, mainly gulls, gliding and squawking. They wheeled over the bay, scouring the beach for morsels of food. Hooked beaks and black eyes crossed overhead as I ran down to the shore, searching for new pebbles and shells amongst the rocks that parried the waves.

The pungent tang of the sea air laced my nose and throat as I followed the curve of the coastline and headed towards the woods. Hardly a soul moved at this hour: a few fishermen pushing off by the pier, a man loading bait under the watchful eye of the birds. I passed them without a sound, hopping expertly over the rocks. I spied a terracotta rock speckled with unusual white markings and stopped to pick it up. It was coarse and heavy, nestled amongst grey pebbles and white stones. I put it in my pocket and moved on.

The beach diminished as I approached Fjugstad forest. Trees and shrubs grew thick on my left and forced me to the water. I paddled in the cold tide as it came to meet me. The beach was sandier now and slimy clusters of brown seaweed stuck to the soles of my feet and lodged between my toes. Clumps of thick grass sprouted through the sand and soon I was at the path that led into the forest.

I was stamping my feet at the base of a tree trunk when I became aware of a presence, a subtle change in the air around me. When I looked back towards the sea I saw a man sitting on a large boulder further along the shore. It was Munch. Something called me to him. A sadness sprang from nowhere and plunged through my chest. I thought I might weep. It would not have been right to go to him, although that's what my body was urging me to do. My feet wanted to run, my arms wanted to reach out, but I had to resist and dig my toes firmly into the moss and twigs of the forest bed.

His very presence held me spellbound and I was rooted to the spot like the trees that surrounded me. I kept looking at him with longing and pain, unable to break away. Then, with a swift twist, he turned and caught me looking at him. His reaction was not what I had expected. He threw me a wave and I waved back, then he beckoned me to him and I began to run.

He jumped from the rock and came springing towards me, sketchbook in hand. He was not wearing a hat and his wavy hair was messy, blown about by the sea breeze. I did not know how long he had been sitting there, but I'd often seen him in strange places at an odd hour and it was possible he'd been there all night. His expression was determined and serious.

'Johanne!' he called, still some paces away. 'I was just thinking about you.'

I stopped running and waited for him to reach me.

'And here you are! Have you ever experienced that? You think about someone and then a few minutes later they appear? It happens to me often. Do you think there's something in it? That we have a kind of mystical power? Do you think that's possible?'

His sad, heavy eyes fell on me, almost begging for the answers. The ache in my chest expanded. I smiled but felt horribly simple.

'I felt you before I saw you,' I said, honestly.

'Then you have it too,' he nodded, and seemed reassured by my answer.

I saw beauty in his face. It was in the slope of his sombre blue-grey eyes and the curve of his voluptuous lips; the perfect Cupid's bow that sat below his moustache and the strong cleft in his chin where each side of his jaw met. He was arresting: masculine yet vulnerable.

'Are you going to the Ihlens'?' he said, pulling the familiar sketchbook from under his arm.

'Yes.'

'Would you take a picture to Tullik?'

'Of course.'

He took a loose page out of the pad and it flapped in the breeze.

'I'll roll it up,' he said, before I had a chance to see it. 'Come, I'll walk to the church with you.'

We strode through the woods and I was comfortable with him, barefoot, my boots hanging from my hand.

Munch didn't make much small talk. He was either silent or talked in an endless flow of thought that came pouring from him as though he had been saving it all up. This gush of thought was like a spiritual bleeding, a catharsis it was impossible to take part in. All I could do was listen.

'It's not finished yet,' he said, handing me the sketch, 'but I'd rather paint a thousand decent unfinished pictures than a single bad completed one. Wouldn't you? So many artists these days think a picture is only finished when they have filled in as many details as they possibly can and it's all glossy and neat, covered in a brown gravy glaze, but one single brush-stroke can be seen as a completed work of art if it is done with feeling. More details, added to make something more realistic, only make a picture false. What could be more real than a feeling? There's nothing more realistic than that, is there?'

His hushed voice became excitable and feverish as he spoke, his hands waved around as though he was painting, even though there was no brush or canvas, only the visions in his mind.

'One must paint true observations – the true feelings in what is being painted. You see things at different moments with different eyes; differently in the morning than in the evening. The way you see also depends on your mood, doesn't it?'

I knew his questions were not directed at me but at himself, so I stopped trying to find answers and merely listened to his chain of thought.

'Moods change. Thoughts change,' he said. 'The outer life and the inner life are connected. Our outer world changes according to our inner feelings. That is what I must convey. Just as Dostoevsky penetrates into the realms of the soul with his words, so I must penetrate the same realms in my art.'

We had reached the doors of the church and the sun had begun its climb, its forehead peeping up over the trees in the distance.

'I must go now,' I said.

'Can you tell her I'm here?' he said. 'I'll wait, under these linden trees, or in the woods. I'll wait.'

'I'll tell her, yes. Goodbye, Munch.'

I left him alone to find answers to his unanswerable questions.

Ragna was boiling eggs when I arrived. She didn't look at me, but eyed the roll of paper in my hands and pursed her lips as though I had said something offensive.

'Good morning,' I said, with deliberate charm.

'Mmm-hmm,' she said, staring into the pan with the concentration of a scientist about to make a shocking new discovery.

She had not started the coffee yet and breakfast was still a while away. I leapt up the stairs and rapped on Tullik's bedroom door.

'Yes?'

'It's me,' I whispered.

The door swung open. Tullik reached for my arm and pulled me in.

'You're back!' she said. Her face was radiant. She hugged me close, as though she had not seen me for several weeks.

'I have something for you,' I said, handing her the scroll. 'It's from *him*.'

Tullik gasped and snatched the picture out of my hands. She took it to the window and carefully unravelled it towards the light.

'Look!' she said, inviting me to join her. 'Come and look at it!'

The sketch was made in a combination of pencil, pen, charcoal and paint. It was of a woman, obviously Tullik, standing between the trees in the forest with the fjord in the background. Munch had sketched Tullik first in pencil, then outlined her in black pen. She was standing with her hands behind her back, her chin lifted, her chest pressed out, exactly as she had been a few nights ago. Tullik was at the centre of the picture, with tree trunks behind her to her left and right. The trunks were sketched in charcoal. Some were filled in with smears of dark paint. On the left there was a gap in the trees where Munch had

123

drawn the column of moonlight stretching across the water. It was messily filled in with yellow. Above Tullik's head was a row of branches, some of which had been smudged with green. The yellow moon and the green branches were the only colours in the otherwise black-and-white picture. Out on the sea Munch had drawn a tiny rowing boat where the outline of three figures sat, unaware of the beauty hiding in the trees.

'I will treasure it,' Tullik said.

'You'd better hide it somewhere,' I said.

Tullik opened her enormous wardrobe and beamed at me.

'They don't go in here,' she said, tucking the picture away behind a swish of coats and dresses.

'He's waiting for you,' I said, 'outside.'

Another gasp.

Tullik grabbed my elbows.

'Tell them I've gone to pick berries,' she said, 'or to get some air. Tell them anything, Johanne. I must go to him.'

Her eyes were a vivid gleam of fire, hot with a danger she could not resist.

9

Blue

*They are like two rivers which have their source in one
and the same mountain, but subsequently pursue
their way under totally different conditions*

Theory of Colours, Johann Wolfgang von Goethe

Munch was a wanderer. He had the ability to tuck himself
away, to blend, chameleon-like, into his surroundings where
he could silently observe. He was not approachable but he had
always fascinated me. He painted. He sketched. He did the
things I wanted to do. Communicated in shapes and colours,
like me. As a child I would find a spot some distance away and
sit with him, although we were always apart. He knew I was
there. We sensed each other.

Gradually I started to move closer and he didn't seem to
mind. I observed him, while he observed life. Sometimes he
would rip a page from his sketchbook and let me draw with
him. I sketched shells and stones, the boats on the fjord, simple
drawings that allowed me to talk. Still we hardly spoke. Then
last summer I met him one day on the beach. It had rained

and the sand smelled fresh like mud. He had no jacket and was sheltering under the fallen branch of a tree that had been tipped by the wind.

Seeing him, I stopped.

'Hello, Johanne,' he said, pulling me towards him with a rare smile. 'Come here. I have something for you.'

His attention scared me, but I followed his instruction. He was holding a book in his hands.

'Take it,' he said, 'you should study it.'

In silence, I accepted it.

'You think about colour and light and perspective, don't you, Johanne?'

'I draw,' I said, lost.

'Then read this book,' he urged. 'It's by Goethe – look, his Christian name is Johann, almost exactly like yours. Read it. Study it. It will help you understand light.'

I flicked through the book, noticing the occasional diagram: circles, stars, chequered patterns, triangles.

'And nature,' Munch said. 'It will help you understand nature.' He stood by my shoulder and turned to one of the first pages. 'There, read that,' he said, 'go from *Nature speaks to other senses*.'

I cleared my throat. I was not a strong reader.

'*Nature speaks to other senses*,' I began, '*to known, misunderstood and unknown senses: so speaks she with herself and to us in a thousand modes.*'

'Go on,' Munch said.

I gripped the book and held it close.

'*To the attentive observer she is nowhere dead nor silent; she has even a secret agent in inflexible matter, in a metal, the smallest portions of which tell us what is passing in the entire mass. However manifold, complicated, and unintelligible this language may often seem to us, yet its elements remain ever the same. With light poise and counterpoise, Nature oscillates within her prescribed limits, yet thus arise all the varieties and conditions of the phenomena which are presented to us in space and time.'*

I barely understood the words I had read but had a sense that they were in some way magical, that this man, Johann, had understood and been able to unravel the very secret of nature itself.

I was spellbound.

I hid the book under a pile of handkerchiefs in Milly's top drawer. Nestled in its back pages were the only two drawings I had ever managed to conceal from my mother, pictures of the coast and the bay, the first sketches I was ever proud of. Along with Munch's sketch in Tullik's wardrobe, the hidden book was the first of a series of secrets and deceptions that Tullik and I would conceal. As the strawberries ripened and the season began to flourish, so too did Tullik's passion and Munch's creativity. Tullik began to disappear for long stretches of time. In the afternoons she avoided calling hours altogether and drifted off to the forest, claiming she needed the air. Whenever I could be released from my duties she took me with her, using me as a foil. She protested to her mother that the Strawberry Girl must not be denied her berries and insisted we pick fruit together in the forest. But when I went off to sell my wares at the Victoria Hotel, Tullik went to meet Munch. Ragna and Fru Berg were infuriated by my absences, but Tullik was delighted and that was all that seemed to matter to Fru Ihlen.

One afternoon Tullik returned from the forest and found me in the garden hanging washing on the line. Her cheeks were flushed and her hair was tousled. She had made no attempt to tidy it.

'Inger has returned to Kristiania,' she said.

'Why?'

'It's Laura. She is very ill. Hardly even talking any more.'

I thought of the woman in the painting, dark and grey. So Munch's youngest sister had finally succumbed to her shadow.

'They're sending her to Gaustad,' Tullik said.

'Where's that?'

'It's a hospital, for women. At Ekeberg,' she said. 'Edvard says she will receive proper treatment there. Maybe they will be able to help her.'

'How long will she be there for?'

'They don't know. Inger and their Aunt Karen will talk to the doctors. It will probably be indefinite.'

Although this was apparently bad news, I couldn't help but sense an element of achievement in Tullik's eyes.

'They must be very worried,' I said.

'Oh, terribly. Poor Edvard. He will of course need a companion to offer some comfort. I can't allow him to wallow, can I?'

After that, Tullik's disappearances became lengthier and more frequent. She always returned with a sketch. All of them were of her. We found an old cut of black fabric in Caroline's cupboard and tacked it to the back of Tullik's wardrobe with pins, making a false back behind which we hid the sketches. Shielded by her fine gowns and coats and dresses, Munch's drawings lay hidden in their silent scrolls.

Tullik tested the limits of her freedom and began staying at Munch's until late in the afternoon, sometimes even missing dinner.

Then one night she didn't come back at all.

'That's the third time she's missed dinner,' Caroline said, as I cleared the plates from the table.

'Where could she have got to, Nils?' Fru Ihlen said, tapping her lips with her fingers.

'You know what she's like,' said the admiral, 'enjoys a good wander, an adventure in the woods. Just let her be. She'll be back soon enough.'

They moved through to the green room to take their coffee and I returned to the kitchen to wash the dishes.

'You know where she is, don't you?' said Ragna, who was scraping leftover jam back into the jar.

'No,' I said. 'How would I know where she is?'

'You and her,' she said, shaking her head, 'it's not right.'

I ignored her and continued with my chores. I dried the china and returned it to the dining room, removed the table-cloth and took it out to shake it in the garden. I swept the floors and wiped all the surfaces and even polished the cutlery. The hours dragged slowly by and still there was no sign of Tullik. I tried to busy myself with tasks, cleaning everything twice to fill the time. I started on my chores for the next day to avoid going to bed, unable to settle without her. Eventually, when the clock was drawing towards midnight and there wasn't a chore left in the house, I climbed the stairs and went to my room.

I stood at the bedroom window straining my eyes to see if I could see her, inspecting every shadow. I scoured the landscape – the edge of the forest, the churchyard and the length and breadth of Kirkebakken – but there was no trace of her. Downstairs, the Ihlens were heavy in discussion. Caroline was angry, Julie anxious. I could not hear their words but the tone of their voices, the rises and lulls in their conversation and the deep growl of the admiral told me that they would not rest until she was home.

I heard the parlour door swing open and then there were footsteps on the stairs, followed by a knock at my door. Without waiting for me to answer, Fru Ihlen came hurrying in with Caroline at her heels.

'Oh, you're still awake, Johanne,' she said, momentarily searching the bed, then finding me at the window. 'I hate to trouble you, dear,' she said, 'but Tullik's still not back. The two of you are close, aren't you? Do you know where she might be?'

'No, I don't know,' I said. 'Perhaps she's with friends in Åsgårdstrand?'

'Not until this late, surely?' she said.

'You *do* know, don't you, Johanne?' Caroline said. 'You know where she is.'

'Really, I don't,' I said, holding a blank expression, determined to protect Tullik. 'She didn't tell me where she was going.'

'Would you mind going to look for her, dear?' Julie said. 'I wouldn't normally ask, but we are so very—'

'Of course,' I said, speaking out of turn. 'I'll go.'

I reached for my shawl and rushed down the stairs to where the admiral was waiting for me with a lantern. His penetrating stare told me to hurry and I fled from the house by the front door.

The night was cloudy and the air had turned surprisingly cold. I clutched my shawl about my chest with one hand and held the lantern in the other. The forest was an inky-blue darkness. No longer my friend, it had become threatening. The crack of twigs beneath my feet coupled with the pained cries of the crows above me and the endless sighing of the trees urged me to run. As the lantern swung in my hand, an amber glow pooled around my feet, but I could not see further than a few yards ahead of me. Although I knew every bit of the forest, it now seemed foreign to me, hostile, as though it was trying to expel me.

I was relieved to see the Nielsens' farmhouse looming on my right, even though the house was dark and the animals were quiet. I chose Nygårdsgaten over the beach as I would only risk being seen by my mother if I crossed in front of the fishermen's huts. Being found there at this hour was a circumstance I did not care to explain. Creeping along the street like a house-breaker, I held the lantern low by my side. I could have walked down Nygårdsgaten blindfolded and had no need for the weak glow of the oil lamp.

When I reached Munch's house, fear slid its icy hands about my throat. *What if Tullik wasn't there? What if she was genuinely lost? What would I say to him? What would I say to the Ihlens?* I opened the gate and stood motionless for a while, holding my breath to listen. A murmuring sound was coming

131

from the back of the house. Approaching, I recognised it as the sound of voices. Barely audible at all, they were rippling softly like the distant waves of the ocean. I leaned against the house and inhaled deeply, gathering strength, ogled by the panicked stares of the people rushing from the painting. Terrified of what I might find, I inched my way around to the back.

They were sitting on a bench in the garden, coupled together at one end of it. Tullik was wrapped in Munch's arms with her cheek raised to his face. He was whispering to her, pressing words onto her neck and into her ear. Her eyes were closed and her expression was serious. A dark bottle and two empty glasses stood at their feet. They were so involved with each other that I didn't want to interrupt. I felt a fool, standing there watching them in the middle of the night with my lantern hanging by my side.

'Tullik,' I said, plainly. 'It's time to go home.'

Her eyes snapped open and she searched the darkness for my voice.

'It's me, Tullik,' I said, stepping closer. 'I've come to fetch you. It's time to come home now.'

Munch jumped from the bench and held his arm out to me while Tullik roused herself with a shake of her head.

'I do apologise,' Munch said. 'We must have lost track of time.'

'What time is it?' Tullik said, scrambling to her feet.

'It's after twelve,' I said. 'Your parents are worried.'

'Oh,' she said, vaguely. 'Yes, Edvard, I must go.'

They kissed. I tried to avert my eyes but could not turn away. I had never seen such intensity: how they gripped and possessed each other. Finally, Munch let her go and she came reeling towards me like the loser of a fight.

'Would you like me to walk with you?' Munch said, as I cradled Tullik in my arms.

'No,' I said, fearing we might be seen with him – another circumstance I did not care to explain. 'I know the forest like my own hand.'

Tullik was cold and her shoulders were sloping and rounded beneath my arm.

'We must hurry,' I said. 'How long have you been sitting out like that?'

'I don't know,' she said, stumbling as I moved her. I could smell a cloud of alcohol about her head.

'Have you been drinking, Tullik?'

'A little. Just a bit of port that Edvard brought back from Germany. He uses alcohol to blur the edges.'

'Edges of what?'

'Life,' she said, absent-mindedly.

Dulled by the port, Tullik was unaware of the trouble she was in. She had floated over into her world without a care for the reality she had left behind. Time was stretched. Edges were blurred. But what did it matter if passions were being followed?

'Wait, before you go,' Munch said, 'the painting, Tullik. I want you to have it.'

He accidentally kicked over the empty glasses as he crossed to the steps at the back of the house. Tullik rushed to pick them up again, standing them neatly on the grass.

Munch reappeared with a canvas under his arm.

'Here it is,' he said. 'For you. It *is* you, Tullik. Your voice, as it was in the forest. Take it. It's simply called *The Voice*.'

Tullik took the painting without looking at it. She kissed him on the cheek and he patted her back, as a father might pet a child.

'Go on now,' he said. 'Go with Johanne. Goodnight.'

I helped Tullik with the painting and we carried it out into the street. Without studying it, I recognised it instantly as a painted version of the first sketch Munch had given her – Tullik in the forest. I saw the brown lines of the tree trunks and the pearly-white shine of Tullik's dress in the moonlight. I clasped the painting in my arms and let Tullik carry the lantern as we dashed back through the forest.

'Where are we going to put this?' I said.

'It'll fit in the wardrobe, won't it?' Tullik said.

'Tullik, your father is waiting for me to return with you. How are we going to pretend you have been anywhere but Munch's house, when we arrive carrying *this*?'

'Oh. Yes, I see,' she said, suppressing a giggle. 'We'll have to hide it somewhere until morning. The church. We'll hide it there.'

'It won't be open at this hour,' I said.

'Then we'll hide it in the graveyard. Slip it behind a gravestone. You can retrieve it before Ragna and the others wake up,' she said.

We emerged from the forest and stole up the path that led to the church. Tullik walked ahead with the lantern and I ambled behind, pacing gracelessly with the canvas in my arms. Solbakken's windows were glowing with candlelight. Julie and the admiral were waiting. We veered off the path to avoid

134

the clear view from the house and slipped round the back of the church, creeping around its walls with a fearsome tread, afraid we might awaken the dead.

'Here,' Tullik whispered. She had drifted out amongst the graves and was pointing at a wide gravestone below the linden trees. 'Will it be concealed here?'

I gave her the canvas and we leaned it up against the back of the grave, turning it on its end so that it was a similar size to the stone.

'The leaves hide it well enough,' Tullik said. 'It's only until sunrise.'

We walked away. Like the deceased all about it, the painting was in God's hands now.

The admiral was waiting at the door, standing erect the way I imagined he would on a ship.

'Regine Ihlen, where have you been?' he barked. It was the first time I had ever heard him call Tullik by her real name.

'Hello, Father,' she said, 'sorry I'm late.'

'Where was she?' he said to me.

'In Åsgårdstrand.'

'Where in Åsgårdstrand?'

'She was already on her way home,' I lied. 'I found her at the far side of the forest.'

'Get to bed, both of you,' he said, bundling us inside and slamming the door.

I darted to my room and ran to bed without changing into my nightdress. Sinking into my pillows, I wished I was in the bottom bunk with Andreas. I longed for my simple life, the fishermen's hut and the loose floorboards that needed mending.

I slept only fitfully and as soon as the room became light I jumped from Milly's bed and ran barefoot from the house. Slipping through the fresh morning dew, I raced to the churchyard and found *The Voice* exactly where we had left it. Crossing myself, I thanked the Almighty as I retrieved the painting and carried it back to the house, where the Ihlens were still sleeping.

My first goal was the scullery. I leaned the canvas up against the workbench and closed the back door, then tiptoed into the kitchen to listen for Ragna. Not a sound. Taking the painting up in my arms again, I fled to the hall and sneaked up the stairs, my cold wet feet making odd patterns on the steps.

I burst into Tullik's room uninvited. Astounded, I found the curtains drawn back. She was already awake and standing by the window. Her hand was raised to her mouth and she was biting her left thumb.

'Thank God, you found it,' she whispered, turning. 'I've been waiting. Thinking. Thinking about the painting.' Her face was pale and her eyes were dull, red-ringed and weary.

'It's here,' I said, 'we must hide it.'

Tullik leaned the painting against the wardrobe door and we both stared at it for a while. The long column of moonlight reflected on the water shone golden in the dimly lit room. It illuminated Tullik's dress in the painting and the auburn shine of her hair. Delicate lines of gold.

'Do you think it is me?' she said, returning her thumb to her mouth and gnawing on her cuticle.

'What? Of course it's you. It's exactly as you were that night.'

136

'But do you think it looks like me?'

'It's your very image. Who else could it be?'

'You don't think it looks like Milly, do you? My sister?'

I had only seen photographs of Tullik's eldest sister in silver frames on top of the piano. In some pictures she was just a child and her resemblance to Tullik was only vaguely etched in her mouth and eyes, but in more mature photographs the likeness was more pronounced. Despite Milly's ornate costumes and hats, the characteristic Ihlenness of all three sisters – the sloped eyes, the long nose, the pouting lips – were unquestionably evident in all of them.

'You're being silly, Tullik,' I said. 'You *know* it's you. Munch even said so himself. He said it's you, your voice – don't you remember?'

'But it could be her, couldn't it? It could be Milly. The dark shadows of the eyes, they look like hers, don't they?'

'Tullik, this painting is of you. It's just as you were in the woods. Now, we need to hide it.'

Tullik bit the hangnail free and a tiny pool of blood surged to the surface of her thumb. Sucking it, she opened the wardrobe doors with one hand and reached through her clothes to unpick the pins. When she had freed the black fabric and moved the sketches clear, I lifted *The Voice* and leaned it against the back of the wardrobe. We pulled the fabric up again and quickly pinned it in place. The painting was concealed. The secret was safe.

At the breakfast table, Julie, Nils and Tullik did not appear to be speaking to each other. As I moved about them, laying things out and clearing things away, I could have cut the tension in the room with the butter knife. There had been no mention of Tullik's misbehaviour the night before and no indication as to any punishment.

A letter was lying on the table. It was addressed to Caroline. 'When did this arrive?' she said, picking it up and sliding her knife across the top of the envelope.

'Fru Berg brought it in,' Julie said. 'I think it's from Milly.'

'Yes! It is!' Caroline said, unfolding the paper. She sipped her coffee, then read it aloud:

'My darling Nusse,

We are coming to Åsgårdstrand to celebrate Sankthansaften, so be sure to light a fire for us! We are taking the Jarlsberg on Saturday. Tell Mother not to worry about accommodation; we won't stay at Solbakken, we'll be staying at the Grand Hotel. Lila is very excited and I have bought her a special new outfit for the occasion, which is simply precious. The new summer fabrics are a breath of fresh air and the ladies on Karl Johan have already been admiring us during the promenade. Lila is adorable in her ruffed sleeves and her little parasol. Everyone says she is a miniature version of me. Of course I have invested in a new hat for the summer, which you will see when we arrive.

Send my love to Mother, Father and Tullik,

Your loving sister,

Milly'

Caroline refolded the letter and slid it into her pocket. 'She's coming on Saturday. That's tomorrow!' she said.

138

When no one replied, Julie Ihlen dabbed the corners of her mouth with a napkin.

'That's wonderful, dear,' she said, pursing her lips. 'I'm afraid I will not be here for Sankthansaften.'

'But, Mother,' Caroline said, 'why not?'

'Kitty and Thrine have called a meeting in Kristiania. I must return for just a few days. Fru Esmark is writing an article for *Aftenposten*. The organisation is becoming official. It will be known as the Norwegian Women's Society for the Prevention of Cruelty to Animals.'

'But you'll miss the bonfire on the beach,' Caroline continued, ignoring her mother's achievements. 'There's always music and dancing. It'll be fun.'

'That's excellent, my dear,' Admiral Ihlen said to his wife. 'You ladies are doing a fine job. Now, as for you girls, the three of you can go to the beach together,' he said, 'and you will *stay* together.' He threw a stern glance at Tullik, who was slouched to the side with her chin propped in her hands. She had not explained her whereabouts from the previous night, but from the look on her face, she was still there in Munch's garden. Perhaps Julie Ihlen had seen that look before on the face of her eldest daughter? Perhaps she'd seen the look of Edvard Munch in Milly's eyes too? Whatever it was she saw in Tullik's face scared her. She refused to look at her youngest daughter and kept dabbing at her mouth.

When breakfast was over, Tullik returned to her room. I did not see her again until late that evening when I was sweeping out the ashes. Everyone else had gone to bed and the house was creaking softly to the ticking of clocks.

'Milly's coming,' was all she said.

As I turned to face her, she slumped into a chair and stared intently at the surface of the kitchen table.

'So I understand,' I said.

'What if he sees her? What will happen then?'

'Milly's married,' I said, emptying the ashes into a bucket.

'That didn't stop her before.'

She looked at me. Her eyes were glassy and afraid.

'He loves *me*,' she said.

'And do you have any cause to doubt him?'

'I suppose not,' she said, picking at the skin on her thumb.

'So what does it matter?'

'You don't know what she's like,' she said. 'She hates to see anyone else happy, to have things – whether it's pretty dresses or hats . . . or love, it's all the same to her.'

'She is your sister, Tullik,' I said, wiping my hands on my rag. 'Surely she would not wish you to be unhappy.'

Tullik laughed; blue, empty and bitter.

'Edvard said she humiliated him and I have no doubt that's what she'll want to do to me too.'

'She doesn't have to know about you and Edvard, though,' I said, 'does she?'

'I wish she did,' Tullik said. 'I wish they all did.'

She scraped her chair back and left me to my cleaning. I heard her heavy tread on the stairs as she returned to her room.

Danger again. Crimson. Ruby. Danger.

Sankthansaften was our midsummer-night festival. The old farmers said that the Vikings who occupied the shores of

Borre used to celebrate the summer solstice by lighting fires to give power to the sun. It was a time of renewal and magic, and people believed that holy places had extra power that night. Invalids and the sick still came to Borre to drink from the freshwater spring all night, hoping that the water's healing properties would cure them. But the church had turned the festival into a celebration of the birth of John the Baptist and our bonfires were lit to ward off witches and evil spirits. For Tullik's sake, I hoped it would work.

I was dismissed early. The Ihlens took the carriage to Åsgårdstrand pier where they were to meet Milly and Ludvig from the *Jarlsberg*. Forced to go with them to greet her sister and say goodbye to her mother, Tullik was miserable, her fire extinguished. She would not be let out of their sight for a second.

I walked back through the forest deliberately slowly. It was fresh and moist and the scent of grass and clover filled the air. Flies buzzed about my face but I did not swipe at them. I had learned that it was futile to fight against nature, so I let them be. I let everything simply be. Nature was beginning to flower, already building to its blossoming crescendo, and the woods were carpeted with purple hyacinths and tall amber lupins. Juicy bright rosehip berries hung in the hedgerows and the wild roses were starting to unravel their floppy pink petals.

The pebbled beach was a hive of activity with the arrival of the steamship, the fishermen coming in early, and the women making preparations for the festival. Children were gathering flowers for the wreaths they would wear in their hair, and dry logs and sticks for the bonfire that was being built on the sandy beach where we would eat and dance. I saw Jacob's granddaughter Marie laden with flowers, running to the beach with her little terrier yapping at her heels. For a moment I envied her. I envied her bare feet and her short sleeves and the innocence of her heart, not yet confused by emotions she could not understand.

When I reached our hut I found my mother carrying a heavy pot of water.

'Oh, good, you're here, Johanne,' she said, by way of a greeting. 'You can help me carry this.'

I took a side of the handle and together we went in.

'I'm making a fish stew for tonight. You can fillet the cod for me, if you like,' she said, pointing at a plateful of fish on the paint-specked table. It was not an offer, but an order. 'The knife's there.'

'That's a lot of fish,' I said, rolling up my sleeves and pulling on an apron. 'Where did you get all this?'

My mother was unusually silent. I thought she hadn't heard me.

'Mother?' I said. 'Where did you get all—'

'Your father accepted it from *that* . . .' She paused, lighting the stove and stoking it with her breath. When she turned around her face was red. 'Your father accepted it from Thomas,' she said. 'He thinks he can buy his way into this family with a pallet of fish. Well, I certainly hope you'll make him work harder than that, Johanne.'

I smiled to myself as I dug the knife into the shiny silver scales. It was the closest my mother would ever come to giving Thomas her blessing.

10

Mixing

Yellow demands Red-blue, Blue demands Red-yellow,
Red demands Green, and contrariwise

Theory of Colours, Johann Wolfgang von Goethe

Julie Ihlen had a twin sister. Her name was Fredrikke Vilhelmine Regine. Tullik was named after her. Julie's twin died when she was just twenty-three years old. I had seen pictures of her in the frames that hung in the hall and the portraits I cleaned on top of the piano. Seeing Milly and Tullik together for the first time was like looking at Julie Ihlen and her twin, despite the fact that Milly was a full twelve years older than Tullik.

Of all the Ihlen daughters, it was Milly who resembled Julie the most. She was an exact replica of her mother. They had the same turquoise translucent eyes, the same straight nose and the same full lips. Her features showed not a hair of the admiral. The only difference between mother and daughter was that the occasional solemnity that crossed Julie's face cast itself on Milly as haughtiness. She stood straight, with her chin up and her nose in the air, moving along the beach from one poised and seemingly rehearsed position to another.

The bonfire was lit and the beach was ablaze with flames and the copper shine of the setting sun. Milly's showing off was lost on the Åsgårdstrand locals, who were dancing in circles, joining hands and pulling each other round in reels to the tune of the fiddlers seated on the grassy mound.

Milly was wearing a white dress that folded in swathes across her chest and ballooned at the sleeves. An assortment of jewels hung from a choker at her throat, which emphasised her long neck. She was impossibly thin and her waist, like Tullik's, was tiny. Her yellow hair was piled beneath a tilting straw hat crammed with flowers and hung in waves down her back. I was helping my mother wash dishes when I saw them approaching. Tullik was a striking sight in a crimson dress with her wild hair flaming like the midsummer bonfire. From behind her sister, Milly looked down her long nose at me without lowering her chin.

'So this is the housemaid who's sleeping in my bed,' she sniggered.

'No, this is Johanne,' Tullik said. 'She's my friend.'

I was instantly intimidated by Milly. There was nothing that endeared me to her, like Tullik, or their mother.

'Hello, Fru Bergh,' I said, shakily. I found it mildly amusing that Milly's new married name was so similar to their servant's.

Before Milly had even looked at me, I was forgotten.

'Well, are we going to stand here and wash dishes all night or are we going to dance by the fire, Tullik?' she said.

'You can do what you like,' Tullik said.

'Well, you know I'm not allowed to let you leave my side while the others have gone for their walk, which is tedious for you and for me, so why don't we . . .' She looked over my shoulder and screwed up her eyes to bring something behind me into focus. 'Oh, look!' she said, breaking into a smile. 'If it isn't darling Edvard! I must go to him. Come, Tullik.'

Tullik spun round. She reached out to my waist and pushed me aside, stretching her neck for a clearer view.

'What do you want to speak to him for?' she said.

'Oh, we're old friends,' Milly said, already walking away.

'Fru Lien,' Tullik said to my mother who had been pretending not to listen, 'may Johanne be excused for a while? I'd very much like her to come with me.'

Mother was horrified.

'Oh, let the young ones go and enjoy themselves, Sara,' said Fru Jakobsen, who was scraping plates into an old tin tub beside us. 'We can manage here. Off you go, Johanne, go and dance.'

Mother and I stared at each other and that strange look appeared on her face. Her lips rolled inwards and she wanted to say something, but the circumstances would not allow it.

'I won't be long,' I said, as Tullik dragged me away.

Munch was sitting on the edge of the grassy mound with his sketchbook propped on his knees and a bottle of beer between his feet. His wrist was bent forwards and he flicked his pencil around the page in large swirls, then moved in on one section more closely, sketching tightly backwards and forwards. He was unaware of the people around him and didn't even look up when a little girl almost lost her balance and reached out and grabbed his shoulder for support.

'Hello, Edvard,' Milly said, smiling like Tullik did, from the corner of her mouth.

'Edvard,' Tullik said. 'It's me.'

He lifted his face from the sketch. When he saw the two sisters standing in front of him, he dropped his sketchbook and his pencil rolled into the sand.

'Milly,' he said, shyly. 'You're here.'

Milly giggled.

'Yes, darling. I'm here. Won't you come and dance with us?'

'You know I don't dance,' he said.

'Then walk with us for a while,' Milly said, cocking her head and looking down the sides of her nose at him. 'It's such a beautiful evening.'

Munch stood up and Milly offered him her hand.

He took it.

Tullik was incensed. She gripped my arm with hands like crab pincers.

Milly squeezed her hand into the fold of Munch's elbow and led him away from the beach towards the pier. She twittered away to him quietly and he tipped his head to listen.

Munch dissolved into Milly's conversation and they walked on, forgetting we were even there. Their steps trampled Tullik's heart, and when we reached the end of the beach she stopped dead and allowed them to walk away.

'He didn't even look at me,' she said. 'I hate her.'

'Maybe he was just trying to protect you, Tullik,' I said. 'So that your family wouldn't find out.'

'He ignored me,' she said, her voice quivering. 'All because of *her*. I hate her. Why did she have to come here?'

I guided her towards the shore, where the water was unmoving and we found a rock to settle on. Across the fjord I could see the faint glowing light from the bonfires that dotted the coastline of Bastøy. Our own fire was still roaring, sending sparks high into the air.

Tullik gnawed at her thumb.

'They went into the forest, didn't they?' she said.

'I don't know. I didn't see.'

'Maybe they went up to his house?'

'Do you think Milly would have done that? With her husband just—'

'She only cares about herself,' Tullik said. 'It was the same with Carl. He was powerless to stop her from doing as she pleased.'

'Were they married long?' I said.

'Ten years. I was only nine at their wedding. She was twenty-one. She always used to brag about how terribly good he was, letting her do whatever she liked. There were other men too, not just Edvard; there were actors, writers. That's why she liked the idea of the bohemians. Their lifestyle gave her permission to do whatever she wanted.'

'And what about this marriage, with Ludvig?'

Tullik raised her palm towards the pier.

'Where is he now?' she said. 'And where is she?'

We sat there in silence on the shore with the festival going on all around us. Tullik was a fuming ball of fire in her red dress. She clenched her teeth and ground them together, huffing and sighing. She threw stones at the water with the force of a warrior. When she could no longer contain her anger, she sprang to her feet and strode back towards the pier.

'Wait! Tullik!' I said. 'Where are you going?'

'You don't have to come with me,' she said, 'not if it will get you into trouble.'

'Wait,' I said. 'I'm coming.'

She marched ahead of me without speaking, heading for the path along the shore. Her elbows pumped at her sides as she passed the Central Hotel and the bathing house, then the Kiøsterud house and the Grand Hotel. She didn't stop until she reached Munch's garden. Heedlessly yanking her dress after her, she cast herself over the fence, pulling and tearing her skirt in several places.

Tullik stormed up the garden through the gallery of paintings that had so charmed her the day we went swimming. Now she hurried past them without giving them a second glance. The house looked abandoned. The door was open but there were no lights, no candles at the window.

'Edvard!' she shouted, charging up the back steps. 'Edvard? Are you here?' She banged on the door and the window, but there was no reply. 'Very well, I will stay here and wait for him,' she said, letting herself in.

I followed her inside. The hut was a dim collection of three connecting rooms. It was dark and cluttered and smelled of cigarette smoke and turpentine. Tullik lit a candle and rooted around for a glass on a shelf that was packed with tubes of paint.

'Tullik,' I said. 'You can't stay here. Your parents—'

'Who cares about them?' she said, disappearing into the kitchen.

As my eyes adjusted to the glow of the candlelight, small details began to emerge: the low roof, the thick floorboards and the brown flowery wallpaper. Canvases were strewn about the floor and easels lined the walls. The bed came out into the room, perpendicular to the wall. It was covered in a grey bedspread with a golden trim. At the foot of it sat a small folding table covered with a pipe and packets of tobacco.

Tullik reappeared with a bottle of port. She poured herself a glass and sat down on the bed.

'Tullik, do you really think you should be—'

'Oh, stop it, Johanne!' she snapped. 'You sound just like the rest of them. Shouldn't do this, shouldn't do that. I've had it with them! From now on I will do exactly as I please. If Milly can do so, then why can't I?'

Her outburst silenced me and I lingered in the doorway for a moment, before moving back outside and sitting down on the steps.

In the distance I heard the cries of the dancers and the music from the beach. Mother and Thomas would be wondering where I was. I had promised Thomas a walk to the forest later to pick herbs. It was common for girls to pick herbs at midsummer. Tradition said that if a girl could pick seven different herbs on midsummer night's eve and put them under her pillow, that night she would dream of her one true love. Thomas joked that a girl like me could easily find a hundred different herbs in Fjugstad forest, but now I might not even find one. The festivities would continue long into the night and it could be hours until Munch returned.

I sat there thinking about Sankthansaften and the evil spirits, wondering if they were in the air tonight and if that was what had hexed Tullik. On the beach they were singing songs of dishonest folk, the wicked and the cowardly. The old folk songs told tales of lazy farmers and loose women. The songs were meant to teach us the merits of moral virtue and lead us in the footsteps of the faithful, which made me think of Milly and her lack of conscience. The bonfire's flames were still licking the sky and I willed them to banish whatever had possessed my friend.

Peering back into the house, I saw that Tullik was now lying on Munch's bed, staring up at the ceiling with her hands clasped at her breast. I didn't want to disturb her but couldn't leave her there either, so I waited on the steps for Munch to return. At first I looked out at the paintings, finding outlines of figures and shapes in the darkness. Some shone clearly: a large painting of Inger in a luminous white dress, sitting on a rock at the shore. Others, like Laura and Tullik staring at their shadow, disappeared entirely in the gloom.

I leaned my head against the hand railings and stared emptily into the garden. Then I noticed that the studio door was ajar, open like an invitation. Tullik was still lying on the bed. She had turned onto her side and was facing away from me. She wouldn't notice. No one would. I sneaked over to the studio and let myself in.

I was met by the painting Munch had been working on in the garden, the man on the bridge looking out into the fjord. Munch had added some colour to the lower right half of the picture, a muddy green, layered on in feather-like strokes and aggressive dark-blue dashes like scratchings on the man's back.

What struck me the most, though, was the sky. Above the boats in the bay and the distant mauve mountains, Munch had added a blaze of fire, a white-yellow flash covered in angry vermilion, a red that had grown incisors and lacerated the sky. The glow from the flaring heavens lit the man's face and highlighted his hat and collar as he stared, eyeless, into the fjord beyond.

The ache returned to my chest and I leaned closer to study Munch's brushstrokes. They moved quickly, as if painted in a panic. The intense reds and yellows were a battle waged by two painters, arguing and fighting for space on the canvas like gods in combat for power. The lonely figure gazed out in despair, knowing the overhead battle could not be won.

Without thinking I picked up a brush. I lifted the painting down from the easel and searched the studio for my own. I found it propped against the wall in the corner, the bright sun with snake-like arms whirling like a talisman. The paints and palette were easy to find, scattered about the room in disorganised clusters. I lit a candle and grabbed a palette. Blue. I needed blue. My fingers rummaged through the tubes and grasped everything dark. I squeezed dollops of oil paint into the palette and lifted my painting onto the easel.

Sad.

Heavy. Aching. Dull.

Indigo. Ultramarine. Dark like the depths of the ocean.

Darkness all around me. Shadows. Long and mournful. Sinister. Black.

Tullik drunk. Lying on the bed.

Sorrow. Sorrow like nature. Cawing crows. Squawking flocks.

Umber. Charcoal. Smearing, thick. Curdling. Condensing.

Tullik. Wading through the swamp. Seeking. Gasping. Drowning.

Tullik. Lost in the marsh. The doomed black pits of her heart.

Paint dribbling, spilling like tears.

'Johanne, what in God's name are you doing here?'

I dropped my brush, sending paint splattering to the floor. Heat rushed in my chest, my mouth was suddenly metallic and dry. My hands trembled and the palette hung limply on my thumb.

'Johanne? Are you painting?'

I turned.

It was Herr Heyerdahl.

His burly frame filled the doorway and he had me trapped.

'Don't tell my mother,' I blurted.

He laughed.

'Does Edvard know you're here?'

'No,' I said. 'But he gave me this canvas, to practise on.'

'Who's the woman?' he said.

'The woman?'

Did he mean me? Had he finally allowed me to grow beyond the Painting?

'In your picture,' he said, pointing over my shoulder.

'Oh, no one in particular,' I said, surprised to find that a forlorn figure had appeared on my canvas. Her back was turned away from the sun.

'It's really rather good,' he said, 'the contrast.'

I returned my painting to the floor and cleared away the paint and brushes.

'Edvard sent me up for a bottle of wine. There's music and dancing,' Herr Heyerdahl said. 'Don't you want to join us? He said the house was open, that I could just let myself in.' He began to walk away.

'Miss Tullik is there,' I said, running after him, 'she's waiting to see Munch.'

'Edvard's down at the beach,' he said, opening the cabin door.

'Tullik!' I shouted. 'Tullik! Herr Heyerdahl is here.'

She was sitting on the edge of the bed, hunched over, drinking.

'Pleased to meet you, Herr Heyerdahl,' she said. Her lips were dark, stained by the port. Her hair messy and rough.

'Hello, Miss Ihlen,' he said, lifting his hat. 'I am acquainted with your sister, Milly. I met her several times a few years back.'

'How unfortunate for you,' Tullik drawled.

Herr Heyerdahl pointed into the kitchen and mumbled something about a bottle. I looked at Tullik, but her head sank and she turned away.

'This is the one he was after,' Herr Heyerdahl said, returning to the room, holding up the wine as though inviting us to inspect it. 'Munch is at the beach,' he said to Tullik. 'Would you like me to fetch him?'

'No,' she said. 'I will wait for him here.'

'But it could be hours before—'

'I'll wait,' she said.

'Very well,' he said. 'Johanne, would you like me to accompany you back?'

I looked at Tullik.

'Go,' she said.

'Tullik, I'll stay with you if you like.'

'Just go,' she said, reaching for the port and pouring herself another drink.

With Herr Heyerdahl I was a child again, I would always be his Strawberry Girl. Afraid of Tullik and unable to help her, I walked back down the garden with the painter whose picture would never let me grow up.

Herr Heyerdahl did not ask any questions, despite the obvious tension at the house. He talked about Åsgårdstrand and how wonderful our cottage was, how he'd been productive since his arrival. I listened to him talk but thought only of Tullik.

We crossed the fence and walked along the path, past Kiøsterud and the Grand Hotel. When we reached the bathing house, I saw Caroline approaching us. Ignoring Herr Heyerdahl completely, she thundered at me, waving her arm.

'You!' she shouted. 'Johanne! Milly said you and Tullik went running off, the moment her back was turned.'

'That's not true,' I said, 'they walked away to the—'

'Are you calling my sister a liar?'

I shook my head.

'Where's Tullik?' she said. 'Where is she? You know where she is, so don't lie to me!'

'I don't know,' I said, feebly.

'You don't need to,' Caroline said. 'I'm sure I can guess. Come with me.'

She took my arm and marched me brusquely away, leaving Herr Heyerdahl, stunned, on the path.

'In here,' Caroline said when we reached Munch's garden. She pushed me over the fence, then mounted it herself,

154

wavering and cursing the wire and the post. Caroline walked ahead of me up the hill. Startled by every painting, she let out a string of gasps and shielded her eyes with her hands.

'Tullik!' she shouted, looking around the garden.

When she reached the house she stood there with her hands on her hips, staring out into the darkness.

'Tullik! I know you're here somewhere. Come out! Tullik? Where are you?'

'I'm here,' Tullik said, appearing, dishevelled, in the doorway.

Caroline turned.

'I knew it!' she said. 'This is where you've been sneaking off to every day.'

'You brought *her* here?' Tullik said, looking at me, her sloping eyes heavy with disappointment.

'She didn't have to,' Caroline said. 'I know you fill your head with pathetic notions about artists and bohemians. I knew you were coming here. What are you looking for, Tullik? Excitement? Attention? Are you hoping this man will paint you?'

Caroline couldn't have known that Munch had already painted her sister and sketched her several times.

'Edvard loves me, and I love him,' Tullik said, as the fire returned to her eyes.

'Don't be such a stupid little fool!' Caroline spat. 'Edvard Munch is a madman and a drunk. Everyone knows that. He doesn't love you – he loves Milly.'

Tullik put her hands on her hips and lifted her chin.

'That's not what he says when he's kissing me,' she shouted, 'when he's making love to me.'

155

'You little whore!' Caroline screeched. 'You're just as delusional as he is. If you've allowed him to kiss you, then you've fuelled all his fantasies about Milly. It's not you he's making love to, it's not you he even cares about – it's her. They had a love affair. There, now you know. He's obsessed with her. But he couldn't have her, so now he's using you as a poor man's substitute.'

'What would you know about love anyway?' Tullik sneered. 'I bet you haven't let Olav touch you. I bet you've never even kissed him. You're as frigid as a nun.'

Caroline lurched up the stairs and flew at her sister, but Tullik was unmoving.

I ran after them.

'Get out of here, you simple girl,' Caroline shouted, swiping at me with her arm.

I tried to move between them, but Tullik already had her hands on Caroline's shoulders and was pushing her back down the stairs. They clawed at each other, pulling clumps of hair and baring teeth, hissing violent cerise like a pair of tormented cats.

'Stop it!' I shouted. 'Tullik! Tullik! Let her go!'

They continued to wrestle. Savages. They would kill each other.

I wailed at them in my desperation, but neither of them listened. All I could do was call out their names and keep shouting.

Then there was a gruff voice behind me and I heard someone running up the hill.

'She said "Stop it! Stop it!" That's enough!'

I turned to see Thomas striding up the garden. His face was fixed in a grimace and I cowered away from him. I'd been gone for ages, missed the dancing, missed the walk to the forest. I'd let him down. I thought he might strike out at me, but he strode right past me and waded in between Tullik and Caroline to prise them apart. The women were wafers in Thomas's strong arms and he peeled them off each other as though they were infants.

'You ought to be ashamed of yourselves,' he said.

Caroline backed away, wiping her face and tidying her hair, affronted that someone like Thomas had seen her openly brawling with her sister. She pushed her shoulders back and cleared her throat.

'Tullik, come with me, we will settle this at home,' she said, in her best Kristiania voice.

Munch wasn't coming and Tullik knew it. She left the hut and closed the door. The two sisters walked silently past us then Caroline stopped and glared at me.

'Our mother will not know about this, about *any* of it,' she said. 'Do you understand?'

I nodded.

Tullik's face was wet with tears. I watched her with a pain in my heart. My lips rolled inwards and I wanted to say something but the circumstances would not allow it.

'Come on, Johanne,' Thomas said, his voice softening as he curled his arm protectively about my shoulders. 'You have herbs to pick tonight. You promised me a walk, remember?'

I threaded my arm around him and we drifted to the front of Munch's cabin, coming out into a moonlit Nygårdsgaten and heading, once again, into the woods.

Palette

Both are general, elementary effects acting according to the
general law of separation and tendency to union

Theory of Colours, Johann Wolfgang von Goethe

Milly stayed in Åsgårdstrand for three more days. She brought her husband, Ludvig, and her daughter, Lila, to Solbakken for tea every day and I waited on them in pastel shades of silence. The little girl was so royally dressed it seemed difficult for her to relax in the heat. Tullik played with her from time to time and made polite conversation with Ludvig, who was amiable enough, but she did not speak to Milly at all.

Julie returned from Kristiania to a house full of friction. She was unaware of Caroline and Tullik's fight, but still seemed afraid of what she saw in Tullik's face. She appeared to be bracing herself, as though she knew something sinister and damaging, a hurricane, was on its way.

After luncheon on the third day, Fru Berg and I were hanging sheets on the line when I overheard Caroline and Milly whispering in the garden. They were sitting at the iron chairs by the table. Milly was perched on the edge of her seat, her back poker-straight and her chin erect. Her face was shaded by the brim of her hat.

'Well, you have to try to stop her,' she said to Caroline, who was leaning towards her with her hands laced in prayer in front of her lips. 'It's silliness. Childish silliness. He can't be interested in her, not really.'

'Of course he isn't,' Caroline said. 'But you know what she's like, with her fancies about painters and artists.'

'The man can't get over me,' Milly said casually. 'It's so tiresome.'

'Mother's only just recovered from all of that, and she's glad to see you happy with Ludvig now. Imagine her shame if Tullik had an affair with the same man. It seems we're never to be rid of this mad painter.'

Milly laughed, then pressed a gloved hand to her mouth.

'It's not funny,' Caroline said. 'Can you not imagine the shame it would bring to this family?'

'I'm sorry,' Milly said. 'I just find it so amusing . . . He's still besotted with me, isn't he? He adores me. And he thinks he's getting a piece of me through my little sister. How terribly pathetic. You must put an end to it, Nusse, darling, before she starts believing his lies.'

Milly opened her parasol and paraded the few steps to the back door as though she were stepping out on Karl Johan during the promenade.

'Ludvig, darling, it's time to go,' she called. 'Lila, sweetheart?'

Caroline gave me a hard stare as she pushed her chair under the table.

'Get on with your work,' she said, looking down her nose at me, as Milly did.

An event was made out of Milly's departure. There was endless unnecessary fuss as she and Ludvig stepped into the carriage, throwing kisses into the air like the king and queen, creating a stage for themselves on the wagon. Lila was wedged in beside Milly like an accessory: a pretty flower or a piece of jewellery. She waved neatly, like her mother, her fingers bound up in lacy gloves.

When the fanfare was finally over and the last sound of the horses' hooves echoed away on the road, I was confronted by Ragna in the kitchen.

'We need milk,' she said. 'You'll have to get some from the dairy at the rectory. Take this can.' She thrust a tin can into my hands and pointed to the front of the house. 'You do know where the rectory is, don't you?' she said, speaking slowly, as though I were an imbecile. The question didn't merit an answer, but I nodded.

'Of course,' I said, swiping the can from her hands.

'And don't be long. I've a lot to catch up on, after this visit.'

I welcomed the break from the house. The atmosphere had been cumbersome in Milly's presence, and Tullik and I had not spoken since Sankthansaften. I had been into her room only to clean and dust around her. Every time I entered she buried her face in her book, a thick novel called *Devils*. She did not speak to me and spent hours in solitude while her two older sisters colluded against her.

I collected the milk from Isabel Ellefsen at the dairy, a girl my age with a plump figure and strong arms. Our mothers were acquainted and I had seen her at church on Sundays, although we had never spoken to each other much before.

'How do you like it at the admiral's?' she said, pouring the milk into the can with expert steadiness.

'It's fine,' I said.

'They're a good family, you are lucky to work for them.' She leaned closer towards me and dropped her voice to a whisper. 'Just watch that Ragna,' she said. 'She doesn't miss a thing.'

I thought it a strange thing to say, coming from a dairymaid who could not have known Ragna well.

'Comes over here, those dark eyes darting everywhere,' she said, screwing the lid onto the can. 'Is it any wonder she hasn't found a man to marry her? Tries to be all meek and mild, but I'm not convinced. My sister said she was engaged once. He left her for another. Escaped before it was too late, and you can understand why. Just you watch her. There's something those eyes aren't telling you.'

I wanted to ask her a hundred questions, but knew I could not be caught gossiping at the dairy. I hadn't considered why Ragna was not married, and couldn't possibly imagine her being engaged to anyone, or in love with anyone for that matter. Isabel handed me the milk as though she was raising a glass, proposing a toast to our conniving.

'You watch her, Johanne,' she said, 'because you know she's watching you.'

I took the milk and hurried out, wondering if Isabel genuinely knew something about Ragna or, more worryingly, if she knew about something Ragna might have seen. Me. Graveyard. Canvas.

When I reached the church, Ragna was in the front garden picking mint. On the other side of the street, below the linden tree, a man was lingering in the shade.

'No,' I whispered. 'Not now, Munch. Not now.'

I clung to the wall of the church and waited to see what he would do. He was leaning against the tree trunk and looking up at the house, holding a long tube, a scroll. He seemed lost and abandoned and a cold sadness spread across my chest. I wanted to run to him, but was afraid Ragna might see me, so I tried to get his attention by swinging the milk can. His eyes were fixed on the house, scrutinising every plank of wood, every hammered nail, every roof slate and every pane of glass for the thing that had been stolen from him. It looked as though he would wait there forever until it was returned.

While Ragna was hunched over the herbs I sprang out from the church and waved at him. When he saw me, he came rushing over.

'Johanne!' he said.

'Shh!' I held my finger to my mouth and beckoned him around the back of the church. When we were out of sight he handed me the scroll.

'Please will you give this to her?' he said. 'I can't work without her. She has not come for days. I can't paint. I can't think.'

'You expected her to come?' I said. 'After . . .'

'After what?'

His sad eyes darkened and he pressed a hand to his chest.

'Milly,' I said.

The single word was irrelevant to him and he rushed on without a thought.

'I cannot work without her and if I cannot work I cannot live. You must take this to her. Please, Johanne, you must bring her back to me.'

It was impossible to ignore his desperation. He was gasping. Tullik was the air he needed to breathe. Perhaps he had only been protecting her the other night on the beach? Perhaps he had kept his feelings for her concealed so as not to expose their affair to her family? Whatever the reason for his behaviour, I could not question him now. I took the scroll solemnly from his hand.

'Tell her I'm waiting here,' he said. 'I will wait by the tree as long as I have to.'

Ragna had returned to the kitchen and met me with a suspicious glare.

'Where've you been? I only asked you to go to the dairy.'

'Sorry,' I said, handing her the milk, 'I was talking to Isabel.'

'And I was waiting,' she said.

Her eyes flitted across my body and I flinched. She stared at the scroll of paper, unravelling it with her eyes. She knew. She knew it was a *sinful* painting from the *Sinful Man*.

'I have sweeping to do,' I said, rushing away from her, 'on the upstairs landing.'

Caroline was with her mother in the parlour and the admiral had retired to his office. Fru Berg was buried in clothes and sheets at the mangle and I could only guess that Tullik was in her room.

Henriette the cat guarded the door.

I stepped over Henriette's tail and knocked.

'Tullik,' I whispered, 'may I come in?'

163

She did not respond.

'Tullik,' I said, a little louder, 'I have something for you.'

The door finally opened and Henriette slid inside, brushing against Tullik's legs with a soft meow.

'What is it?' Tullik said. Her hair was hanging loose. She had been sleeping.

'May I come in? I need to talk to you.'

She walked back into the room and allowed me to follow her.

'Here,' I said, closing the door behind me. 'I have this for you.'

I handed her Munch's scroll.

'What is it?' she said.

'I think it's a painting. It's from *him*. He's waiting for you.'

'I won't see him,' she croaked.

'I don't think he will leave until he sees you,' I said.

'What about her?'

'It's like he doesn't even know her name.'

Tullik hesitated for a moment, then snatched the scroll from me. She closed her eyes and cleared her throat before opening it.

The woven paper uncurled in her hands and when it became too big to hold she laid it on her bed.

The painting was haunting.

A soft watercolour-and-ink sketch, it was of Tullik, in the water, on the day she swam out naked and lay before him at the beach. He had painted her as a mermaid, her lower legs curling up softly into a tail. His signature column of moonlight lit her pale skin and her luxurious auburn hair hung down over one shoulder and rested in waves over the other. It was Tullik, in all her ethereal and elegant beauty, a tantalising vision, a mythical creature born of a summer night.

Tullik's eyes flew hungrily across the sketch.

'Is it me?' she said, tears appearing.

'Of course it is,' I said, 'exactly as you were that day.'

At the foot of the page were the words *E Munch, Mermaid 1893*.

'My poor darling,' she said. 'Where is he?'

'At the linden tree.'

'Then help me get ready. I must go to him.'

She hurled herself at her wardrobe and pulled several dresses from their hangers.

'Which one, Johanne?' she said. 'Which one?'

'Any!' I said. 'You're beautiful in all of them.'

'Am I? Do you really think so?'

'Of course I do,' I said, pushing her hair from her shoulders.

She chose a light-cream summer dress. Her hair flowed down her back and she pumped a fresh-smelling perfume around her neck and behind her ears.

'Tell them I've gone for a walk in the forest,' she said, 'if they ask.'

I bowed myself into her deception and once again became the keeper of Tullik's secrets.

When she had gone I stared at the painting for a while. Tullik's beseeching expression beckoned me to her, drawing me into the sea. Her submerged hands and her curving tail seemed to make her helpless. *Come*, she said, *come and embrace me in this moonlit water*. My fingers traced lines around the tips of her hair. The thick strands of it floated like orange seaweed on the water's surface. The bright shine of the moon bronzed her skin and set fire to her hair. She was living fire, living, breathing, liquid gold. The essence of life itself.

June joined hands with July in a feverish pact of steaming intensity. Temperatures soared, bringing the hottest summer in living memory. While most of us withered, Tullik blazed in the heat. Her skin warmed to a soft tan, her hair was even more glorious than ever, glowing with golden streaks where the sun had bleached it. Her very soul was scorching with life and thrill and danger.

The heat made the admiral and Fru Ihlen apathetic. They moped about the house with great effort as though they were constantly sedated. Caroline was no better, lolling from one room to the next in an endless search for shade or the last gasp of a breeze. Fru Berg was beside herself with irritation. Her puffy cheeks shone as red as apples and she was forever wiping her brow with her forearm, unable to ebb the tide of perspiration that rolled from her temples. But Ragna was resolutely alert. Like a lizard, her senses piqued in the heat. Her black eyes were as sharp as ever and her attention unbending. She followed my every move as I lied and hid to uphold Tullik's charade.

We lied about musical recitals and bathing afternoons. We lied about dances at hotels and dances on the beach. We lied about walks in the forest and fruit-picking, and all the while Julie and the admiral lapped up our lies as though they were the sweet nectar of the flowering honeysuckle. As long as Tullik did not stay out too late they did not ask any questions and for a while, as she had vowed, Tullik did exactly as she pleased.

Then the bohemians arrived.

Of all people, it was my mother who informed me. The Sunday-evening announcement was made at the dinner table.

'The barbarians have arrived,' she said. 'I heard them all night.'

'Hmm?' Father said, puffing on his pipe. 'Who?'

'Those people,' she huffed, 'at his house. They came in from Kristiania a few days ago. Up all night with their devilish revelling and drinking. It's a disgrace.'

'Who are *those people*?' I said.

'You don't want to know, Johanne,' she said. 'You should keep away from that kind of sinfulness. We don't want it spreading. These friends of his are a sorry crowd. Lowering standards. You make sure you steer clear of them. Goodness knows, I might have to find a job for you in the city, send you to Kristiania. Borre won't be far enough away. It seems like Herr Heyerdahl is the only one with any decency.'

They were probably writers and painters. Tullik was bound to find them irresistible, and I knew that sooner or later I would be caught up in a lie about a dance or a walk and find myself amongst the very people my mother feared the most. Then what? Would she really banish me? Send me off to Kristiania? After dinner I rushed from the hut and ran straight out to the rocky shore where the sea was calling me. Kicking off my shoes and peeling off my stockings, I hopped and ran to the waves. I lifted my skirt and waded into the water. Tilting my face to the call of the ocean, I inhaled the setting sun, the salty

167

air that spat against my skin and the sound of the gulls winging above me. I stayed there for a long time, trying to find a way to avoid the unavoidable.

When I eventually turned back, the sky had become dark and I searched for my shoes in the shadows. My stockings would never be found. I couldn't even remember where I'd cast them.

'What are you doing, Johanne?'

The voice came from the rocks ahead of me.

It was Thomas.

'Looking for my shoes,' I said. 'I came out for some air.'

'It's been so hot,' he said, 'the women are suffering in the heat.'

'It grips you tight,' I said. 'Even down here by the sea there's hardly anything to grasp onto.'

'Will you walk with me?' he said, grinning and offering his hand.

'Only for a short while.'

We headed out along the steam pier and stopped halfway to lean against the railings. Even at night, when it was tired, Åsgårdstrand was beautiful. The hotel windows were aglow against the balmy summer evening. Lanterns hung along the veranda that stretched across the back of the Grand Hotel. Some were hung in trees and made pretty patterns from the dark branches. The boats bobbed gently in the harbour at our feet and the only sound was of the water swaying and sploshing against the harbour walls.

'Have you thought any more about that proposal?' Thomas said, nuzzling against my neck.

'Only that I'm too young,' I said.

'It's not a *no*, though?'

'No,' I said. 'It's not a no.'

Talk of marriage was like an invitation for my mother to join us, with all her consternation and her shaking head.

'I should be getting back,' I said, stepping away from him.

'My father's letting me take the boat out alone next Sunday,' he said. 'Do you want to come with me, on an adventure?'

'I doubt my mother would allow it,' I said.

'Does she have to know?'

I had become such a seasoned liar that I should have slipped easily into a new lie, but I found that my appetite for deceit was waning and I baulked at the thought of more lies; the thoughts I had to think, the tales I had to tell, the tracks I had to cover. A murky spiral. Brown. Dark umber. Gooey and black.

'I can't promise anything,' I said.

We sauntered back past the hotels and along the track towards the fishermen's huts. The peace of the evening was shattered when we passed Munch's garden. A woman was squealing with laughter. I looked over the fence and saw her join hands with a man and dance in circles up and down the hill. The shadowy presence of men with cigarettes loomed around them and I heard the sound of glasses clinking and corks popping. One man was singing, another clapping.

'I see crazy-man Munch has guests again,' Thomas said. 'Went on all night last night, from what I heard.'

I stood and watched as the couple spun back down the hill towards us.

'They're making up the rules as they go along,' Thomas laughed. 'Maybe we should be more like them?'

I wanted to agree with him. I wanted the freedom that spilled from Munch's garden. I wanted a taste of it, even though it was tainted. It carried a danger whose consequences were too great for me to bear and yet I was drawn to it, sucked in by its allure. I wanted to join the dance that whirled beneath the trees, for Thomas to take my hand and twirl me through the paintings that were scattered about the hill. With nature growing up all around it, immersed in the sun and the moon and sea, it was not a dance of destruction, but a dance of life.

I wanted to join the dance of life.

12

Ultramarine

As the upper sky and distant mountains appear blue,
so a blue surface seems to retire from us

Theory of Colours, Johann Wolfgang von Goethe

Swirling green. Emerald. Jade.

Exploring. Tentative. Moving. Crawling. A touch of cyan. Opening the prism.

Tullik. Wandering. Hands reaching out. Hands retracting. Away from the sun. Into the unknown.

I follow. Curious. Inquisitive.

Afraid of the garden. Afraid to go out there. I hear their voices. Deep and dark. Laughter rough. Scratches like sand. I hear their glasses. The chime. The knell. Blue. Cyan. They come to me.

In paint I hide.

A man is behind me. Humming a tune.

In paint I hide.

'Are you going to hide yourself away in here all afternoon, Johanne?'

I circled my brush in the jar of turpentine before turning.

He sucked at a pipe. On his breath, alcohol.

'I like it in here,' I said. 'I like painting.'

'She's a beauty. Haunted. And with her back towards the sun? Is she hiding from something too?'

'I don't know,' I said. 'I'm just practising. Munch lets me borrow his things.'

'I like it.'

The man had an extraordinarily long nose and his hair was receding, not even starting until some unseen midpoint high up on the top of his head. His pointed chin was inclined as he studied my painting. Scrutinised it.

'I'm sorry, Herr—'

'Delius, Fritz Delius.'

He spoke Norwegian through a thick accent, clipping my language in places, rounding it and hollowing it out in others.

'Perhaps Tullik and I should be getting back?' I said.

'Oh, nonsense! You'll stay a while longer. Let me get you a glass. Something to help you hear the notes.'

He held his arm to the studio door, where a shaft of light was pouring in. I stepped into the light where the motes were dancing and he followed me out.

'Jens!' he called to a man in the garden. 'Johanne needs a drink. Worked up a thirst. Been busy painting.'

Jens, a small man with a dark beard and moustache, disappeared into Munch's hut. Munch and Tullik were sitting with a third friend at a table in the middle of the garden. He was an odd little Danish man with a prominent nose, an inwardly

172

sloping chin, tiny ears and a high wave of dark hair. He moved his arms elaborately as he spoke.

'Come, Johanne,' Delius said. 'Come and sit at the table. We were talking about light.'

Tullik was pinned to Munch's arm. Barely moving, she listened intently to the conversation.

'He's stealing my play, Delius,' the Danish man said.

'Surely not, Helge! The man's a painter.'

'The idea I had, *Dansen Gaar, The Dance Goes On*!' the Dane continued. 'My character, the artist, he says, "*My picture shall be called* The Dance of Life! *There will be a couple dancing in flowing clothes on a clear night through an avenue of black cypresses and red rose bushes. The earth's glorious blood will gleam and blaze in the roses, Claire. He holds her tightly against himself. He is deeply serious and happy. There will be something festal about it. He will hold her to him so firmly that she is half sunk into him. She will be frightened – frightened – and something will awake inside her. Strength is streaming into her from him. And in front of them is the abyss.*"'

'Life's dance! What a marvellous idea!' Delius said. 'I can hear the overture already. Send your play to me, Rode. I would like to read it.'

'Does anyone know where the absinthe is?' Jens said, returning from the hut.

'Here,' Munch said, lifting a bottle from under his chair.

'Well, fill her up then. She's empty.'

Jens handed Munch a glass and he poured a green syrupy liquid to the brim.

'There, Johanne,' Delius said, 'down the hatch.'

I waved the glass away, but he insisted.

'Come on, Johanne,' Tullik said. 'It'll help you paint.'

I took the glass from Herr Delius and sipped at the surface. The green liquid passed through my lips and I gulped it down quickly as the strong aniseed taste coated my tongue and snaked down my throat. My eyes fired and I forced my mouth to smile.

'There!' Delius applauded. 'Just what the doctor ordered.'

'So, Munch,' Jens said, ushering me to the table. 'What's this? You're painting a dance now?'

'I have some ideas. Not just a dance, but an entire frieze. A frieze of life. A study of life and love and death.'

'I can hear it spinning, climbing and falling,' Delius said, sitting down beside me, 'and it must be played out here, in this beautiful landscape of yours. Here, in this dramatic country. Deep in the mountains and the fjords. How I wish I could stay here forever.' He lifted a glass and gulped down the green aniseed liquid. 'Here in Norway, my second home. Or is it my third? Or my fourth?'

'England is your first home,' Jens said. 'Or is it Germany?'

'Or Florida, perhaps? said Delius. 'Perhaps America is my home?'

'But you are headed to France next,' Munch said. 'Is that not home for you too?'

'Then let the world be my home,' Delius said, 'and Norway – let Norway be my soul.'

The drinking continued and the conversation blurred. From the scraps I understood, I deduced that Fritz Delius

174

was an English composer of German descent. Munch had met him through mutual friends in Paris and, from the way Munch referred to Delius's letters and postcards, it seemed they had maintained a regular correspondence. Helge Rode, the Dane, was a poet and writer. The occupation of the third man, Jens Thiis, remained unknown to me, but he followed their thoughts and seemed to know a lot about art, quoting the names of foreign painters I had never heard of. They were all friends with someone called Gauguin, whose name was mentioned frequently.

Their conversation regarding Rode's play and the idea surrounding the dance of life continued sporadically throughout the afternoon. I held onto it, without mentioning that the same concept had just occurred to me the day before. Poetic, soulful thoughts about the earth's blood, then Munch's own blood sinking into the earth and fertilising the flowers, circled the table like prayers, then splintered into coarse jokes about prostitutes in the back streets of Paris.

I followed the metronomic tick of their voices. Dulled by the absinthe, I tuned in and out according to topic and volume. One particular wave of sedation was broken by Munch.

'This force, flowing between man and woman,' he was saying, 'you have it the wrong way round, Rode. It is not the man who holds the woman tightly, but the woman who holds him. The woman clasps the man, grabs onto him. And the abyss that lies before him, it is the abyss into which one is thrown by the arms of love.'

Tullik smiled at him proudly, not quite understanding the warning in his words.

The sun's rays intensified as the afternoon wore on and I withered and dizzied in the heat. My eyes saw double, my lungs were tight, my stomach nauseous from the drink. We had been there for hours, against my will, against my judgement. Tullik had forced me here under the cover of another lie. I was about to drop to my knees and beg her to leave, when Munch stood up abruptly and ordered us all to go.

'I must work,' he said, scraping his chair back and slamming his glass down on the table with a loud smack. 'You can go now. All of you.'

At first his friends laughed. Helge poured himself another drink.

'No, Helge. I *must* work, and cannot if I am not left in peace. Please, leave now.'

The three drunk men peeled themselves from the table. Delius wobbled unsteadily to his feet.

'We hear you, we hear you,' he said, patting Munch on the shoulder as he staggered away. Helge Rode and Jens Thiis followed ruggedly behind him. The three of them wandered off down the garden, commenting incoherently on the canvases that lined their path.

When they had gone, Tullik sidled up to Munch and slipped her arm into his. She stretched her neck up and puckered her lips for a kiss.

'You too,' Munch said, pulling his arm free. 'I must work. Don't you see that? Go!'

Tullik stumbled away from him as though she had been slapped.

'Edvard, darling . . . won't you let me—'

'Go!' he shouted.

'Edvard?'

'Get out!'

Exasperated, he turned from her. He had to escape. Her presence was contaminating, suffocating.

'But . . . Edvard?'

I reached for Tullik's arm and gently guided her down the hill.

'It's time to go home now, Tullik,' I said. 'We've been gone all day. Your parents will be getting worried.'

'What if this is my home now?' she said, yanking her arm away from me and going after him.

'It isn't, though, Tullik, is it?'

'What if it is?' she said. 'What if I can do whatever I please? What if I can go wherever I like – be anyone I like? What if my home is right here, with Edvard and our friends?'

'Come, Tullik,' I said, 'he needs to work.'

'What would you know about it?' she said, spitefully. 'You're only a maid.'

Her words stung. She was drunk.

'Tullik, please, leave him.'

Munch was setting up his easel and laying out paints in his newspaper parcels. Engrossed in his process, he had already forgotten we were there.

'Tullik,' I whispered, 'it's time to go home.'

She gazed up at him, watching him, willing him to lift his sad eyes and see her. He squirted some colours into his palette and hooked it around his thumb, then lifted a large canvas onto the easel. It was the man on the bridge below the swirling skies. Munch's brush dabbed at the wavy, unsettled waters of the fjord. Immersed in his paint, he was gone.

My fingers were stained with jade-green oil paint. I didn't notice it until we got home. My main concern had been getting Tullik to her room without anyone seeing she was drunk. I couldn't use turpentine, so I found soap in the kitchen and took a scrubbing brush to my hands. I scraped at my skin until my fingers were a deep shade of purple. But the paint held.

I returned to my work under Ragna's vicious glare. She saw the specks of green on my skin and raised her eyebrows. Her thin lips curved down. She was disgusted with me, repulsed at my behaviour: stepping over the lines, neglecting my duties, and now this, painting.

'Miss Tullik missed dinner again. Why?' she said, her eyes dark with interrogation.

'She is tired,' I said. 'She retired to her room, for a nap.'

'There's a smell of aniseed in the air,' she said.

'Is there?'

'Where were you today?'

'Åsgårdstrand.'

'Where in Åsgårdstrand?'

'Seeing Tullik's friends. Ladies from the city.'

'You don't fool me,' Ragna said, taking a knife from the drawer and tightening her grip on the handle. 'I know where you go. It would only take a word to the admiral. Fru Ihlen, no, she could not bear the shame of it; but the admiral, he will stamp it out, before its evil spreads. You start advising Miss

Tullik. Advise her against this path, Johanne, or soon she will lose everything. They won't suffer this a second time.'

'Why would she listen to me? I'm only a housemaid.'

Ragna didn't say anything else. She took a dishcloth and wiped the blade of the knife with it, sliding the serrated edge between her thumb and fingers, perilously close to the skin. I did not look at her again, but felt her gaze lashing my back as I left the kitchen and climbed the stairs.

Tullik was lying on her bed face-down with her head and shoulders hanging off the edge, staring at the floor. She had taken Munch's sketches out from the back of the wardrobe and scattered them about the floor. *Mermaid* was unravelled. A book at either end held it flat.

'Tullik, what are you doing?' I said, gathering up the pictures. 'Anyone could come in, at any minute. Do you want them all to know you have these?'

'What if I do?' she said.

She rolled back on the bed and looked up at the ceiling. Her eyes were two dark wells of grey.

'He does love me, you know, Johanne. It's not what you think.' She started picking at her thumb cuticle again. 'He's an artist. He needs room, that's all.'

'Of course,' I said.

'But then, does he? I mean, does he know what love is? Does he know how to love? He needs me to show him – that's it. We will go back again tomorrow.'

'Is that really a good idea, Tullik? If he's working?'

She sat up on her bed and leaned against the wall, digging her nail into her cuticle and peeling back the skin.

'I can show him better than Milly did,' she said, biting at her thumb. 'She knows nothing about him. Look at her,' she said, pointing at Munch's sketch of *The Voice*, Tullik herself in the woods. 'Look at her, with her dark eyes and her hands clasped behind her back. She didn't know how to seduce him. She didn't know how to *love* him, did she, Johanne? What does Milly know about life? Nothing. Look at her, hiding in those trees, trying to enchant him. And there, in the water. What was she thinking? She can't love him. Not the way I do. Not with her soul. My soul and his are connected, don't you see that, Johanne? Joined together.' Her thumb was bleeding and she sucked it clean. 'It's not me,' she said, waving at the pictures as though they were waste paper. 'It's not me. It's not me!'

'Tullik, Tullik,' I said, gathering up the scrolls and returning them to the wardrobe. 'Of course it's you. He said so himself. And they look like you. Here, in the woods – I was there. I saw you, exactly as he sketched you. And here, in the water. I was there that day. What is this all about?'

She was crying now. Pulling at her hair. Tugging. Twisting. Making loops round her bloody thumbs.

'You're hurting yourself, Tullik,' I said. 'Won't you lie down and get some rest?'

'I will go to him again tomorrow. You will come,' she said. 'You will see how he loves me, just as I love him. He doesn't love Milly, he loves me.'

'Shh now,' I said, closing the wardrobe door, then easing her down to her pillow. 'You must rest.'

'He does love me, doesn't he, Johanne?'

'I'm sure he does, Tullik.'

She slumped on her side and finally released her hacked thumbs from her own onslaught.

She frightened me. She was just as I was painting her, moving away from the sun and into the dark unknown, falling into the abyss that Rode and Munch had spoken of.

It was late morning when she found me in the garden, beating the rugs from the parlour.

'Are you ready?' she said, tying a wide-brimmed straw hat in place with a bow under her chin.

'Tullik, I'm busy,' I said. 'I have all my jobs from yesterday and Fru Berg needs help with the laundry today. She's doing the beds.'

'It can wait,' she said, 'all of that can wait. It's not important, is it?'

'It is, for your mother and father. They hired me to do it.'

'But you must come. I've told Mother we're going to the beach.'

'When am I to get my chores done?' I said.

'You hate your chores.'

'That's not the point.'

'But you are *my* housemaid, so you must do as *I* say,' she said, reaching for my hand. She was trying to be lighthearted, but I wasn't in the mood. I wanted to warn her about *him*. How could I make her understand? He needed space to work. Another visit now would distract him too much. He needed time to develop the motif.

'He will be working,' I whispered.

'So I will let him work.'

'But he needs peace to work. You don't—'

'I don't what?' she said. 'I don't *understand*? Why? Because I'm not a painter? Because I'm not a painter, like you? Is that why I don't understand?'

'No, Tullik,' I said. 'That's not what I meant.'

'Then get ready,' she said. 'I'm waiting for you.'

Fru Berg was sitting by the chicken coop. Her arms were submerged in the tin tub. The cloudy water came up past her elbows.

I tried to cross the garden unnoticed, but she caught me at the scullery door.

'What's this? Where are you swanning off to now?'

'Miss Tullik wants me to go to Åsgårdstrand with her,' I said. 'I can finish the rugs later.'

'You will finish the rugs now,' she said, her cheeks puffing and reddening.

'She's coming with me,' Tullik said. 'She's my maid, not yours.'

'She has work to do, Miss Tullik.'

'And it will be done,' Tullik said.

'Will it be done today?'

'Of course.'

'Can you promise me that?'

'Of course,' Tullik said, without a care for whether or not the work would be done.

My heart dropped to the pit of my stomach. No matter what time we returned, I would still have to heat the irons on the stove and press the linen, beat the rugs and dust the house and mop the floors. When would I ever sleep?

Tullik led me away like a prisoner. Fru Berg rearranged her cap and shook her head as she returned to her tub. In the kitchen Ragna was watching us. Her black eyes followed me and her arm circled menacingly as she mixed something in a bowl out of sight. Like a witch brewing a potion, she cursed us, smirking as she stirred, knowing that she held our fate in her arms. Ragna was catching up with us. The deceit could not continue.

13

Yellow

This is the colour nearest the light. It appears on the slightest mitigation of light, whether by semi-transparent mediums or faint reflection from white surfaces.

Theory of Colours, Johann Wolfgang von Goethe

I picked a handful of redcurrants at the edge of the woods. Gleaming like marbles with a gold and crimson sheen, they were irresistible. The summer had reached its pinnacle, the height of its power, and the warm scent of flourishing fertility laced the air. In the woods I forgot about Tullik and Munch, and Ragna and Fru Berg. I saw nothing and felt nothing but nature, the rich and plentiful gifts of the forest, nothing but Åsgårdstrand, my home. Nestled in the steep hills, lit by the bright sunshine, here at the fjord's edge the summer sang its fecund chorus.

Tullik marched ahead of me and did not stop until she reached Munch's gate. He was already outside, working at three different easels. We crept around the house and I waited at the back stairs while Tullik went to speak to him.

'Edvard, darling,' she said, 'may I talk to you?'

He turned from his canvases. One was the man in despair, standing on the bridge by the fjord; another was a different version of the same motif. It was sketched out in the same dimensions, but the figure on the bridge had become more abstract. The third was not a canvas but a piece of cardboard, a sign that Munch was running out of money. On it he had sketched the outline of the motif, the wavy sky and fjord and the bridge, but in this one there was no figure at all and the lower half of the painting was still empty. He was thinking. Developing.

'Johanne has picked redcurrants,' Tullik said, sweetly. 'Would you like some?'

'I'm working,' he said, greeting her with an awkward kiss on the cheek. 'I shall have more guests on Sunday. The Krohgs are arriving. They will want to come and paint.'

'Christian and Oda?' Tullik said, eyes ablaze.

'That's right. You must meet them. You will meet them,' he said, waving his brush in the air.

'I will go inside now,' she said. 'I do not want to disturb you. Johanne and I will make redcurrant juice – there are more berries here in your garden.'

He mumbled something incoherent. Before he returned to his paintings, he hesitated. 'Johanne may paint, if she wishes.'

Tullik scowled at me.

'She'll make juice first,' she said. 'She is the maid, after all.' She snatched the redcurrants from my hand and climbed the stairs to the back door. 'Go and find more, Johanne,' she said, 'enough to make juice.'

185

I crossed the garden, finding a spot of shade by the hedge where the redcurrants hung. I took as many as I needed, gently plucking them from the bush and dropping them into my apron pocket. I stretched and bent, moving steadily down the garden. When I came to the end of the bush I reached around to pick my last bunch, a small cluster dangling on an outer stem.

'Johanne! What are you doing in there?'

Fru Jørgensen was standing on the other side of the hedge, talking to a neighbour.

I clung to the redcurrants, unable to let go. My face flushed and the heat spread, my own skin becoming berry-red.

'I followed the hedge. I was looking for redcurrants,' I said, as absent-mindedly as I could.

'You're in Munch's garden,' she said. 'Does your mother know you're in there?'

'Oh no,' I said. 'I didn't realise. I just followed the hedge.'

A voice came calling from behind me, a lick of fire I was incapable of stopping.

'She's picking fruit for me,' Tullik said. 'She's my maid. I ordered her to do it. Is there a problem?'

Fru Jørgensen felt the slap of Tullik's snobbish Kristiania tongue.

'No,' she said, insulted. 'I own this property and lease it out to Munch. Is he aware that you're taking fruit from his garden?'

'Perfectly aware,' Tullik said, rudely. 'Come, Johanne. We're all getting thirsty.'

Fru Jørgensen was livid. Her mouth was a tight fist. There was nothing I could say in my defence, no appeal I could make to her. Word of this would reach my mother quickly, before the sun dipped in orange ripples on the fjord. In the morning I would be thrown onto the *Jarlsberg* and sent to Kristiania to seek salvation from this odious sin.

'I said Johanne could paint,' Munch said, as we walked back up to the hut. 'Your painting is there in the studio where you left it, Johanne,' he said. 'It's very good. You are painting what you feel, not what you see. This is the only way to paint. Tullik, you can make the juice. Let Johanne paint while she is here.'

I thought Tullik would attack me. She came striding up to me, hands stretched out towards my neck as if to strangle me. She reached for the cord of my apron and ripped it from my body, ruffling my hair as she pulled it off.

'Very well,' she said. 'I will make the juice.'

The studio was hot and the mix of oil paint and turpentine was suffocating, but I could not risk being seen in the garden again and set up my painting in a space at the far end of the room, safely out of sight. In my picture the woman with her back turned towards the sun was wading out through a green shadowy quagmire into a darkness I had not predicted. It had created itself when my brush touched the canvas. In contrast to the fireball of the sun, the dark green had a murky depth that sucked the woman under. She appeared to have no feet, nothing to stabilise her. I needed to work on the sky. Patches were still bare, and blank canvas peeped through the holes.

The sky was not blue. It was amber. Tinted by the colour of Tullik's hair. Tainted. Layers of copper, cooling behind the sun. Spewed like lava from a volcano, settling. Hardening.

Tullik footless. Sinking beneath the smouldering air. Threads of her hair catch the sun's fire. Their flames stretch up like fingers, joining the waves of the sky. Merging. Tying. Knotting together. Golden. Yellow. It is Tullik who links it all together: the sun, the sky and the darkness of the earth. It is Tullik. Sinking.

She appeared at my shoulder.

'I can't make juice,' she said. 'There's no strainer, no muslin. He doesn't even have a bowl. And now Delius has arrived and they're drinking absinthe, so I doubt redcurrant juice will interest him.' She came to stand beside me and slipped her arm around my waist. 'It's me, isn't it? In your picture?'

'I hadn't really thought about it,' I said.

'It is me. I can see it,' she said. 'I'm sorry I was mean, earlier. I just need to be with Edvard. My heart is so heavy, my mind so insistent. I don't want to need him, but I do. I love him like breathing. I fear I might go mad if I am not with him. We are joined, you see, Johanne. Our souls. They're tied together like threads. Just like my hair, here,' she said, pointing at my painting. 'Joined. Forever. Up there in the sky and down there in the earth.'

I put my brush down.

Tullik drew me closer in.

'I must be with him, Johanne. Or I shall be mad.'

I could hear Delius laughing in the garden. The heat rose and a spinning panic encompassed me. Long afternoons. Strange talk that made no sense. Sun. Intense. Absinthe. Dizzying. Work to be done. Mother. I must get away from him. I must get away, or *I* shall be mad.

188

'Tullik, I think we should go back. I still have all that work to do, and Fru Jørgensen has seen me here. There will be talk.'

'Oh, let them talk,' Tullik said, 'if that's what amuses them. We will stay.'

'There will be consequences, for me,' I said. 'I cannot stay.'

I packed away my brushes and palette and went out into the garden. Delius and Munch were standing at the three easels.

'Johanne!' Delius called.

I flinched. Was Fru Jørgensen still there? Could she hear him? Who else could hear his deep voice calling my name? My mother? Andreas? Thomas?

'Herr Delius,' I said, quietly. 'May I speak with you?'

Delius smiled and strode up the garden, swinging his long arms and spilling his drink. He towered above me and I squinted against the sun as I looked up at him.

'I need to get back,' I said, shading my eyes. 'I have a lot of work to do today. But Tullik wants to stay here, with Munch. Can I ask you to see that she gets home safely? And not too late? She's so . . .'

I wanted to say *troubled* or *disturbed*, but stopped myself as it felt like a betrayal. But then Herr Delius seemed to say it for me, as if he knew, as if they all knew about Munch and the consequences his friendship brought.

'Poor Tullik,' he said. 'He can't possibly know the effect he's having on her.'

'You see it too?'

'We all react to his paintings, Johanne. I do. Don't you? They affect each of us in different ways. His illness – this

189

anxiety, this fear that he feels is so necessary to his work, and this endless search for absolute authenticity. It takes a robust soul to withstand it.'

I wiped beads of sweat from my brow and wondered if anyone could walk Munch's path with him. Even those who loved him?

'You can trust me,' Delius said. 'I will bring her home. But we will see you on Sunday, won't we? Christian and Oda will be here.'

'It's church on Sunday,' I said.

He continued to grin at me as if I'd made a joke.

'Then the Lord can come too,' he said.

I smiled politely and walked away, leaving Tullik, alone, in Munch's garden.

The afternoon's chores were long and brutal. It was dinner time when Tullik returned. She joined the others at the table but made little conversation. She was drunk. Again.

Caroline had received a letter from Milly. It was lying open beside her plate. Fru Berg strained to read it while she laid out the bread. Caroline did not read it aloud, but responded to its various points by periodically making remarks.

'For heaven's sake,' she said, followed by, 'Oh dear, the poor thing,' and later, 'Of course, she would.'

'Nusse, darling, do tell us Milly's news. Don't just keep it to yourself,' Julie said, as she daintily sipped at her soup.

'She says the Krohgs are coming to Åsgårdstrand.'

'Oh,' Fru Ihlen said, dabbing the edges of her mouth.

'The Krohgs are friends with Munch,' Tullik said boldly, 'and Jæger.'

'Jæger. That lunatic,' Caroline said. 'You know that he would rather we kill ourselves than live within the sacrament of marriage? Perhaps I should mention that to Olav?'

'Why?' Tullik said. 'Do you think he would rather commit suicide than marry you?'

'Tullik!' Admiral Ihlen said, raising his eyes.

'Oh, it's all right, Father,' Caroline said. 'She's only pretending to support that view because she knows no one will ever want to marry her.'

'Girls, really! That's enough,' Julie said. 'What else does Milly say, dear?'

'Oh, just that the ribbons on Lila's new bonnet were too tight, and Ludwig has a recital at the National.'

'Well, isn't that fascinating?' Tullik said, throwing down her napkin. 'Isn't that just the most interesting thing? Doesn't it make you want to ponder the entire meaning of our existence? Think about it, Mother! The ribbons on Lila's new bonnet were too tight. What could it mean? What could it *really* mean?'

Julie patted the edges of her mouth again.

'Tullik, are you quite well?' she said. 'Perhaps you should go and rest.'

'Rest!' Tullik said, leaping to her feet. 'Rest from what? From this demanding life we lead? From this taxing and stimulating conversation?'

'Tullik!' the admiral shouted. 'How dare you speak to your mother in that way? What's got into you? Go to your room at once and lose this disagreeable manner.'

191

Tullik's mouth opened wide and she laughed. She stared at their three incredulous faces with hard condemnation and laughed at their ignorance.

Fru Berg ordered me back to the kitchen. She took me by the elbow and dragged me outside to the hen coop.

'Where has Miss Tullik been all afternoon?' she said, hurrying the words from her mouth before anyone saw us. 'Tell the truth now.'

'I don't know,' I said.

She puffed out her cheeks.

'Those people they were talking about in there,' she said, dipping her jowly chin towards the house. 'Has Miss Tullik been with them?'

I looked into the hen coop and watched Dorothea and Cecilia peck at the ground. I said nothing.

'Your mother's told me how she hears them at night. At his house. Even ladies. Dancing, drinking, screeching. If Miss Tullik is mixed up in this, there will be talk.'

'What kind of talk?' I said, nonchalantly.

'The kind of talk that would finish Fru Ihlen . . . and the rest of this family.' She moved her weight from one foot to the other and with her free hand swiped a mosquito from her brow. 'It's your job to see that there is no such talk. I won't have Fru Ihlen suffering any shame. She's a fine lady. You're close to Miss Tullik. You talk to her. You tell her to stay away from Edvard Munch and those friends of his.'

'Why is it my job?' I said.

'You have her ear.'

'She is not obliged to listen to me. I'm just a housemaid. I'm the one who serves her.'

Fru Berg tightened her grip and shook my arm like a piece of linen. 'You talk to her,' she said. 'If you know what's good for you – what's good for us all.'

When the rest of the family had retired to bed, I slipped into Tullik's room. It was late, but she was standing at the window, nibbling at her thumbs.

'Tullik, why are you not in bed?'

'I can't sleep,' she said. 'He's with her now, isn't he?'

'Who?'

'Milly. He's with Milly.'

'Milly is in Kristiania,' I said, confused.

'But in his head? In his head? Who is he with, Johanne? Is he with her or me? I cannot tell. *EM*. It says *EM*.'

'Where?' I said.

'There. In there. On all the paintings.'

Her eyes crossed to the wardrobe. Fear hung dark across her face.

'*EM*. *E* and *M*. Edvard and Milly. He even writes it in full view. For me to see. Is that his message to me?'

'They are his initials, Tullik,' I said. Edvard Munch. *EM*.'

She turned her thumb across her mouth and bit the skin at her knuckle, still staring at the wardrobe. Ignoring me.

'He did not speak to me this afternoon. He drank with Delius. Then he painted. Delius and I walked along the beach. When I left, Edvard didn't care. He didn't even say goodbye. Didn't look at me. What's happening, Johanne? I don't understand.'

'He's working,' I said, weakly.

'Working? Drinking. He's drinking. I must go to him again. I must know that it is me he loves. I can't bear it. I will go on Sunday, when Oda Krohg is there.'

'Do you think it's wise, Tullik,' I said, approaching her slowly, 'when he is working so intensely like this? And everyone's saying there will be talk – that your mother won't be able to bear the shame of it. Please, Tullik. Don't go. Not yet.'

'I must be with him,' she said, desperately. 'I must be with him or I will go mad.'

'But it is church on Sunday,' I said. And Thomas. I remembered Thomas wanted me to go with him on his father's boat.

'After. After that. I must go. You will come with me,' she said.

'I cannot come to Munch's again, Tullik,' I said, brushing her arm. 'There will be talk. And Mother's threatening to send me to Kristiania.'

'But you must come. We will tell them we are going berry-picking together. It's my heart, Johanne. I must follow it. I have to follow it. What else is there? If we do not follow our hearts, what else is there?' She reached out and held my face in her hands. Her thumbs were bleeding. Her eyes were so full of love and pain. 'You must follow your heart, Johanne, to the exclusion of everything else.'

Her words entered my body and lingered there for two days. At night I lay awake in Milly's bed, reading the book, trying to understand the colour of Tullik's heart. I read about the nature of colour, the force of colour, and how only the slightest

194

change has to take place in the component parts of bodies for the colour to change. Was I changed? Had I been mixed with Tullik's reds and Munch's blues? I conjured Thomas to my mind and stirred him into my palette, pouring the words over him to see if they would blend. *Follow your heart, to the exclusion of everything else.* Was Thomas my destiny, in the same way that Munch was Tullik's?

When Sunday arrived I was still asking the question. I was sitting in Borre church beside my mother. With its stone walls and aged flagstones, the church provided a refreshing coolness, but the ladies were still fanning themselves furiously with bibles and hymn books. The Ihlens sat at the front. The four of them were composed, fine and tailored. A clump of sadness lodged in my stomach. This pretty tableau would not last. Tullik's heart and soul were racing towards its very destruction. I clasped my hands together and prayed that she would not go. Not to Munch's. Not without me. Not today.

After the service we all poured out into the burning sun. The ladies rushed to seek the shade beneath the linden trees and the men made polite conversation in the stifling heat. I watched the familiar groups form, making boundaries with their backs. The Ihlens' circle was closed. Tullik was hidden within them.

We trailed home through the woods. The walk was laborious in the heat. Andreas and I walked together in silence with our parents. Thomas was behind me, further back; I sensed his presence, a budding thrill. When we reached the huts a group of youngsters broke away.

'We're going to the beach!' one of the boys called. 'Who's coming?'

Some girls brushed past me and I seized my chance.

'I'll come!' I said. 'Mother, I'm going with them. I'll be back later, for dinner.'

I was running before she had even had a chance to protest and I rushed away, aware of Thomas's eyes on my back.

By the time he caught up with me I had already reached the pier.

'So are you coming with me then?' he said, turning me round to face him. 'The boat's ready. It's all mine for the afternoon.'

'Yes,' I nodded. 'Yes, I'll come, but I have to be back for dinner.'

Thomas grinned and we rushed to the boat moored along the strip that stretched out before the Grand Hotel. It was only a small rowing boat, but it had a sail and room for five oarsmen and was enough to make Thomas feel like a captain. He stepped down into it and held his hands out to me.

'Madam,' he said, smiling so broadly his face must have ached.

I stepped down onto the slatted gangway and over the slime-covered edge of the pier. Thomas took my arm. The boat rocked as I landed and took a seat at the prow.

'Where would you like to go?' he said, settling down opposite me and taking up the oars. 'Kristiania? Denmark? France?'

'Take me out to Bastøy,' I said, 'to the lighthouse. We don't have very long.'

Thomas's powerful arms made light work of rowing. The boat cut through the calm waters and soon we were out in the fjord, bobbing like the sailboats in Herr Heyerdahl's paintings. The sun laid a white sheet over the water's surface and brought a sparkle to the crest of every wave. I leaned back on my hands and lifted my face to the sun, feeling a familiar tingle as the light washed over me. It made me think about Munch and how subjects in paintings grow and change; how they are life. I sat up straight and looked back towards the shore, hunting for the little mustard hut and the sloping garden, but we were too far out now. Thomas raised the sail. The wind filled it quickly and carried us closer towards the island of Bastøy.

'What are you thinking about?' Thomas said, when the sail was secured and our course was set.

'Paintings,' I said.

'What's there to think about?' Thomas said.

'What inspires the painter – the colours, the emotions in them.'

'There are no emotions in paintings, Johanne. They're just pictures of things.'

'Not if you look closely,' I said. 'They can make you *feel* things too.'

'Like what?'

'Sadness, fear, joy, longing, love.'

The last word caught his attention.

'How can you feel love by looking at a painting?'

'I don't know,' I said, thinking about the pictures Munch had painted of Tullik. 'You just feel it. You feel what the painter felt.'

'How do you know the painter feels anything?' he said, climbing to the bench opposite me.

'Because that's what art is. It's an expression.'

Thomas laughed.

'I think you've been spending too much time with those lah-di-dahs from Kristiania. You're starting to sound like them,' he said.

'Oh? And how do you want me to sound? Like a fisherman's wife? With talk of cod and mackerel and scales and fillets?'

'Don't be angry, Johanne,' he said.

It was only then that I realised I was.

'I just want you to sound like you,' he said, coming to my side, 'with your talk of fruit and the forest, and nature and seasons.'

'What makes you think I know so much?' I said, as he embraced me.

'You grew up with it. You're a child of that forest. You belong to nature.'

'Perhaps,' I said.

'Funny girl.'

He kissed my shoulder and I waited for my anger to melt. I closed my eyes and listened for the voice of my soul to speak up, to tell me this man was my destiny, that I was following my heart.

'I will look after you,' he said, putting his strong arms about me, 'when we are married. I will provide for you. You will never be lacking. You know that, don't you?'

Again I urged my soul to speak up.

'Yes,' I said. 'I know.'

I held his hand. Thomas was a good man. I did not doubt that he would care for me, or that we would have a good life together, but could he truly understand me? This urge to paint that I had, and the way it made me feel. Everything Munch had taught me. Would Thomas take it away from me? Would I have to give up my soul to become his wife?

I kissed him.

He cupped my face in his large hands and pressed his lips against mine. I allowed his hands to roam across my breasts. Deep-blue violet. Plum to pink. All my senses stirred and we moved closer together, gradually leaning back against the tip of the boat. I ran my fingers through his hair and he groaned heavily. Longing. He kissed my neck. Hot fire. Licked my earlobe. Sweet. A sweet gasp of pleasure. Burning. He held my hips. Pulled me closer. Tight together. Cerise. His hardness wanting me through his clothes. Hunger and lust. Blue. Red. Scarlet. Panting. Kissing. Unable to deny my own pleasure.

But my heart was silent. How could I follow it, to the exclusion of all else, if it wouldn't tell me where to go?

'Have we reached Bastøy yet?' I said, sitting up and straightening out my dress.

Thomas's chest was heaving. He sat up on his elbow.

'The lighthouse is around the next bay, where the rocks point out like a needle.'

'Take me there,' I said. 'It's so long since I've seen it.'

His chestnut eyes stung with frustration, but he pretended not to care and stepped across the boat to alter the sail. I watched him work the mast and the rigging as he steered us carefully around the rocks and brought the boat into the coastline where the lighthouse teetered on the very edge of the island.

'There!' he said. 'There it is!'

I clambered round in the boat and looked up at the cylindrical tower, staring at the light that guided the ships. I wondered then if my heart might speak up and guide me to it like a boat lost at sea. I held my breath and closed my eyes, but all I heard was the aching call of the distant gulls.

14

Dark

As yellow is always accompanied with light, so it may be said that blue still brings a principle of darkness with it

Theory of Colours, Johann Wolfgang von Goethe

By the time we reached Åsgårdstrand pier, the afternoon was fading and the sun had lost the stab of its heat. Thomas moored the boat in the harbour and I climbed out swiftly, with a ferocious guilt biting at my heels. I scanned the harbour but didn't see the face I feared the most: Mother's.

'Thank you for the trip,' I said.

'I'll walk you home if you like.'

'You don't need to. Mother will only remark.'

'So let her remark,' he said. 'What can words do?'

Something sparked at the base of my stomach and I smiled at him.

'There's a dance at the end of the week,' he said. 'I take it I'll be seeing you there, with Miss Ihlen? The two of you are becoming quite the talk of the town.'

'What do you mean?' I said, thinking of Fru Berg's warnings of 'talk'.

'I suppose people think it's strange, that's all, a maid and her mistress out together. Miss Ihlen doesn't act like the other ladies from the city.'

'Then let them remark,' I said. 'What can words do?'

I was about to walk away when I heard my name being called. I turned to see a tall man in a white suit striding towards us. Delius.

'Johanne!' he said, removing his hat.

I shrank away from him. Thomas stared.

'We thought we'd see you this afternoon. Are you coming?'

'No,' I said. 'I have to get back for dinner.'

'Oh, that's a pity,' he said, grinning at Thomas, awaiting an introduction.

'In fact, I'm really very late,' I said, 'my mother will be getting anxious. Goodbye, Thomas; goodbye, Herr Delius.'

I dashed away, leaving the two of them staring oddly at each other. Thomas called after me, but I didn't answer.

I plaited my hair hurriedly as I walked, conscious of how ruffled and undone I must have looked. It was dinnertime and the smoky smell of meat on the grill wafted from gardens and kitchen windows. Chimneys pumped out the aroma of stew and vegetable soup. People were setting tables outside, laying bowls brimming with fruit and baskets of bread. I watched Fru Nedberg carry a tray out to her husband who was smoking his pipe under the trees. She placed a bottle and two tumblers on the table, then lifted her hand to wave as I passed.

The brew of flavours in the air made me quicken my step. I was pleased when the fishermen's huts came into view. I would be home in time, and Mother's questions would be minimal. I had almost made it to the door when a shrill piercing sound stopped me. There was a dreadful shouting and someone crying out as if in pain. I turned to follow the sound. It was coming from Munch's garden.

I hurried over to the fence at the side that bordered the fishermen's huts. Too afraid to go in, I crouched behind a bush next to Munch's outhouse. When I peeked out to the side and saw a woman standing in the garden, I gasped hard and had to cover my mouth with both hands.

It was Ragna.

I was so shocked at the sight of her in Munch's garden that at first I didn't even notice Caroline standing further down the hill with her hands on her hips. The sound was coming from her mouth.

'You thought you could hide it from us, didn't you?' she was saying.

I dipped back and peeped around the lower side of the outhouse, where I saw Tullik facing her sister, her hands clenched and her chest pumping.

She'd gone. To Munch's. Without me.

'I knew you were here!' Caroline continued. 'You fancy yourself as quite the little bohemian, don't you? I've seen your books – all that filth you've been reading. All the filth that *he*'s filling your mind with!'

She pointed over her shoulder and when I swung to the other side again, I saw Munch standing on the steps at the back of the house. He was smoking a cigarette and leaning over the back railing. His eyes were cloudy and he was swaying unsteadily.

'Edvard and I love each other,' Tullik said. 'I don't care what you think about it. Neither of us do.'

'You're a fool, Tullik! That man loves Milly, isn't it obvious? You think you fit into this world, but you're out of your depth. All you're doing is making a damned fool of yourself. You're coming home right now,' Caroline said. 'Come and get in the carriage.'

Ragna's eyes flitted back and forth from Munch on the stairs to the warring sisters. She disapproved of all of it and seemed satisfied that Tullik had been exposed. I caught sight of other neighbours on the opposite side of the garden, peering out from behind trees and bending around the sides of houses. I wanted to go to Tullik, to defend her, but I was too afraid – afraid of being caught by my mother and losing my job with the Ihlens and being sent to Kristiania. I suddenly found myself worrying, like Mother would, about how all of this would look.

'I'm not going anywhere,' Tullik was saying, 'I will stay here with Edvard.'

Caroline lowered her voice to a menacing whisper.

'I can't believe you would stoop so low and act so selfishly as to do this to our mother,' she said. 'Ragna, take her.'

Ragna grabbed Tullik's arm and Caroline followed, clamping her sister's hands behind her back and jabbing her shoulder. 'Get in the carriage!'

Tullik looked as though she might spit in Caroline's face.

'This is not over,' she said, her words black with bitterness.

Lifting her chin, she was led away up the hill. She looked up at Munch, whose eyes dragged after her pitifully. Ragna and Caroline turned their backs on him as he lazily took the cigarette from his mouth and blew smoke out at them.

In that moment I hated him. Why had he not fought for Tullik? Defended her? Why had he let Caroline say that about Milly? Why didn't he tell them he loved Tullik? Why didn't he appeal to them at all?

After they'd gone, he stood there staring at the three easels as though watching the events unfold all over again in his mind. He flicked his ash into the hedge and slipped inside the hut to fetch another bottle.

I rose to my feet. Anger rushed in my blood. I was about to scale the fence to go after him when I heard my mother's voice behind me.

'Johanne Lien, get away from there!' she screeched.

I spun to face her and saw her calling me.

'Dinner's ready. Where've you been?'

'Out,' I said.

'Did you forget your head when you were out? Has your brain drifted off with the sea breeze? Get inside!' she said, poking my hips with her fingers. 'Fru Jørgensen has written to her sister in Kristiania to enquire about jobs. I think that would be best, don't you? We only want what's right for you, Johanne, and that means getting you away from . . . from all *this*.' She smacked the air and grimaced, shutting the door on the invisible evil that swam about her.

The evening was intolerable. I could think of nothing but Tullik. I'd tried to warn her, but my words held no sway over the danger that seduced her. Her very soul seemed to feed off it. And now she would be punished. She would not listen to me. Despite all the secrets we had shared, the countless times I had placed myself in danger for her. Had my loyalty and friendship meant nothing?

I could not bear to imagine her punishment, having brought such shame on her family, having been humiliated like that. Julie would be distraught, knowing that all the local folk of Åsgårdstrand and Borre were talking about her daughter and *that* man, again.

I did not sleep. Even without the creak of Andreas's bed above me, I could not have slept. Lying there in a fidgeting torment, with my chest a-flutter like a cage of insects, I felt as though a pitcher of ice-cold water was being poured into a hole in the top of my head, trickling down and freezing my blood. I didn't even try to close my eyes, afraid of the images my mind would summon. Instead I turned onto my side and stared at the uneven boards of the broken floor.

I rose before Mother and left without waking her. The morning was a grey monotone, with no convincing promise of sun behind the flat sheet of cloud draped across the sky. A haunting stillness had silenced the forest and I walked through its pathways like the only living being in a desolate world. I made my steps small and slow, never wanting to reach the house or face the Ihlens. I would have to be informed of what had happened, to hear the story of Tullik's shame. Ragna and Fru Berg would delight in its telling, relaying with relish the details I already knew.

There was no sun to brighten the house and it looked wan with sickness. Hiding in the shadows by the wall, I tiptoed to the back door, brushing past the lilac bush in full bloom. I took my apron from its peg, found my gloves and knelt by the stove, where I began to clear out the ashes from the day before. Above my head the floorboards creaked. The admiral and Fru Ihlen were always the first to stir. I shovelled the charcoal into my tin bucket and swept around the feet of the stove. There was no wood left in the alcove, so I set up my kindling and went out to the wood store to gather some fresh logs.

When I turned back to the house, I saw Ragna looking at me through the kitchen window. Our eyes met, but even though she knew I had seen her she continued to stare, sending a threat with her keen dark eyes.

'You're late,' she said, when I returned to the stove.

'Am I?' I said. 'I left early.'

'They're risen already. You'd better set the table. Only three places today, Miss Tullik can have a tray.' She said it triumphantly as though she was the one who had decided to banish Tullik from the dining room.

'Is Tullik unwell?' I said.

'*Miss* Tullik is confined to her room,' she said, taking her pestle and mortar from the shelf and a knife from the drawer. 'She's to stay there. All day.'

I lit the stove, then rushed to set the dining table, leaving Tullik's place noticeably bare. To fill the void I slid the jam jars and butter dish to Tullik's side of the table and laid the other places further apart than usual. But when the Ihlens arrived to eat, there was nothing that could compensate for Tullik's absence or the emptiness it brought. Fru Ihlen was downcast. She barely touched her food and left her coffee to stand, as though I had poured it for someone else. Caroline and the admiral talked about the weather. No one mentioned Tullik at all.

Fru Berg and Ragna were whispering in the pantry when I returned to the kitchen to make up Tullik's tray. I clattered about with cups and saucers and threw the teaspoon against the china, making it chime like a bell. It was the type of childish protest Andreas made at home. He was an expert at shouting without ever opening his mouth.

'Straight up and straight back down with that,' Fru Berg said, emerging from the pantry and tying her apron behind her back. 'Miss Tullik won't want to be pestered by you today.'

I went to the back door and cut a sprig of lilac from the bush, placing it in a silver vase on the tray.

'It's not her birthday,' Fru Berg said. 'There'll be no pleasantries for that one for a long time.'

I took the tray upstairs and let myself in without even knocking.

'Tullik,' I whispered, 'I've brought you some breakfast.'

She was lying in her bed. The sight of her was so shocking that I had to turn away at first, muttering about the food I'd brought her to divert my own eyes. Her face was a pallid, sickly white and her cheeks and eyes sunken and grey. It was the most extinguished I had ever seen her. There was no vibrancy or life in her at all. Even her hair, splayed out around her face, was dull and gaunt.

'Tullik,' I said, sitting down on the bed beside her. 'What happened?'

'They won't let me see him again,' she said. Her eyes were fixed on the wardrobe and she did not look at me when she spoke.

'Why didn't you listen to me, Tullik? I told you not to go.'

'I had to go,' she said. 'I had to be with him.'

I picked up her hand and held it in mine. Her fingers were limp and did not respond to my touch.

'What can I do?' I said. The ache in my chest had such a tight grip that I could barely speak.

Tears swelled in her eyes but she did not blink them away.

'I love him,' she said.

'You must try and eat something, Tullik,' I said, stroking her arm. I poured her a glass of apple juice and held it to her face, but she refused it and rolled over to face the wall.

'I'll come back later,' I said.

I bent down and kissed her cheek. She closed her eyes, locking herself back inside her own pain as the welling tears overflowed and rolled down her nose.

Tullik did not leave her room that day, or the next. Her separation from Munch was an illness so depleting that it affected us all. The house fell silent as the Ihlens' lives collapsed under the pain that emanated from Tullik's room. She suffered, just as she loved, in the extreme. For the first few days she could not have left her room even if she wanted to. Her body was drained, her spirit sucked out of her. All she could do was lie in bed, wasted like a flower deprived of water as the separation slowly eroded her.

At night, lying awake in Milly's room, I heard the sounds of Tullik's grief pass between the walls. Occasionally, if she had the strength, she would cry. I came to be thankful for her weeping as it was something I was able to identify with.

More frightening were the groaning noises, the long empty howls. The sounds were inhuman, like an animal tearing itself apart, chewing itself up and destroying itself from the inside. Tullik wailed and whimpered as though eating into reserves, destroying what was left when there was nothing more to expel.

She stopped talking and instead began to babble incoherently. I tried to make conversation with her, but she could not engage me. Her eyes were constantly dark and glazed: the glassy doorways to an anxious terror that lay deep within. When the Ihlens realised the devastating effect their punishment had on Tullik, they allowed her to take small walks with me in the forest, but she refused to go. By then the damage had been done. She was lost. Tongues whispered. Where was Miss Ihlen? *She is mad. She is a drunk. She is crazy like the artist Munch. She is engaged to him. She is with child.*

In an effort to quash the rumours, the Ihlens told everyone Tullik was suffering from influenza and could not leave her room. The lie was weak. Not like the strapping lies Tullik and I told. It didn't stop the tongues and couldn't quite clean the slate that had been so irrevocably tarnished.

Every day I tried to tempt Tullik out, to show the world she wasn't crazy, or drunk, or with child. But she would not be persuaded. Some days she talked, but not to me, not in proper conversation. She would ask me questions but wouldn't wait for the answers: *Is she coming? Is he with her? Is he there? Will you check? Is she coming?*

I bottled my emotions; the dark-brown hatred of Ragna, the grey resentment of Caroline and Fru Berg, the dirty rust frustration I felt towards the Ihlens. One day when I could no longer stand the torment of it, I ran to Munch's house without a care for who saw me.

It was a Sunday afternoon. He was standing in his garden amongst his paintings. His arms hung redundant by his side as he gazed out to sea. The sadness of his eyes had reached a new depth and they seemed clouded from strain.

'I need to paint,' I said, boldly.

He held his left hand up to my face. A piece of string had been tied around each of his fingers with a small knot.

'I'm trying to remember,' he said. 'Can you help me remember, Johanne?'

'Remember what?'

'Something. I tied these strings to help me remember what I was going to do. I can't for the life of me remember.'

'Paint,' I said. 'You were probably going to paint.'

'Is Tullik with you?' he said.

'No. They won't let her come here,' I said. 'She's in her room.'

'Won't you bring her to me, Johanne? I can't work.'

'Tullik is ill,' I said. 'She's not herself. She needs to rest.'

'Then take her this picture. I meant to give it to her.'

I followed him to the studio, where he rattled about among the canvases that were leaning against the walls. He pulled out a simple wash-painting on paper of a man crouching on a beach leaning towards the water where a woman swam to greet him. Their faces were abstract and each had only one dark eye. The washed-out sky was daubed on in layers of russet and lavender. Paint dribbled from the sky to the indigo sea. Brushstrokes visible. The woman was naked. Her hair

211

sank like rope in the brown depths of the water. The man was so drawn to her I could almost see him move. Munch had captured that charged moment of magic and longing, as noses and lips align, just before a kiss.

'This is beautiful,' I said.

'I never know if she's a mermaid or not,' he said. He rolled the paper up and handed it to me. 'Take it to her when you return. Now, you wanted to paint. I've been rearranging things in here,' he said, moving to the other side of the studio. 'I set up the easel at this end.'

The third of the despair paintings, the one on cardboard, was on an easel in the corner.

'Let me get this down and put yours up,' he said.

'I can paint without an easel, if you're using it.'

'I'll take this outside,' he said, lifting the painting down, 'it needs a bit of air. The horse-cure does wonders for them.'

I turned to look at the painting as he took it down.

As soon as I saw it, I heard a sound. A whine? A moaning, like Tullik in the night.

Munch had filled in the wavy sky. It was now a vibrant blood-red vermilion layered with bright gold. Worked into the sky was a stretched elliptical shape, like an eye watching me. The fjord was stark ultramarine edged with black curving lines, and the minute sail-less boats in the distance were sailing precariously close to the yellow whirlpool at the centre of the fjord. But the most shocking detail was the figure on the bridge. It was no longer a man in a hat, staring over the railings, but had become an abstract figure that had turned round to face us. It was still only an outline, but it curved like the flame of a candle in the wind. And the sound, the whining, seemed to be coming from this figure, this being, on the bridge.

'I don't know, Johanne. I can't give it a face. The longer she is away, the more it feels like it's not just me but nature itself that is screaming to be released from the hell of it. And what does the face of nature look like?'

'It makes a sound,' I said, looking closer, *listening* to the painting. 'It's the same sound she makes in the night.'

'I was told it was impossible to paint a sound, but you can hear it?'

I swallowed. The painting evoked such nervousness in my chest, a sense of panic and confusion. Had I really heard something? I looked again, then closed my eyes.

'Yes,' I said, as the whining returned. 'I hear it clearly.'

'I'll take it out so it doesn't disturb you,' he said, reaching for my own painting and setting it up on the canvas. 'We are both painting her,' he said, as he secured my picture in place. 'But you see her differently from me. In your painting she is turning away from the light. In my paintings she *is* the light.' His eyes drooped. His voice was soft.

'I didn't really think about it,' I said.

'No, and nor must you think about it. The moment we start thinking about our paintings is the moment we kill them,' he said. 'You could leave it at any minute, Johanne. It doesn't have to be finished in the sense that every single part of the canvas is covered.'

'I know,' I said, rubbing the outer edges of the painting with my fingertips. 'It's not the actual picture that isn't finished. It's the way I *feel*,' I said, suddenly feeling the prick of tears in my eyes.

'Mmm. Good,' he said. Without offering a word of comfort, he left me alone.

Face-to-face with my own creation, I tried not to think about it. I tried not to think of the woman being Tullik. Maybe she wasn't Tullik at all? Maybe she was someone else? Maybe she was me?

I took out the brushes and paints and hooked a palette over my thumb, the way Munch did.

A single deep breath.

Lines of taupe and brick and beige. The beach in the sun. I've turned away, turned my back. Turned my back on my family. Wading into the green water, the muddy marsh. I hear Thomas calling after me. His voice cream. Corn. Sand. I do not turn. Shades are darker. Tan and fawn. I move through colour. Feel through colour. The base of the ocean, green to red. Coral and auburn. Layers. Layers like sand and silt. Like Munch and Tullik, teal and ruby. Ragna: black. Julie: olive. Caroline: brown. Milly: blank to grey. And me: yellow. Return to the sun, the light. The love. I am pulled to the fire. The source of life. The source of the soul where all is connected, all is one. All is the colour of love.

15

Vermilion

Whoever is acquainted with the prismatic origin of red, will not think it paradoxical if we assert that this colour partly actu, *partly* potentia, *includes all the other colours*

Theory of Colours, Johann Wolfgang von Goethe

I met Thomas on the way home. Red. Heat. Flustered. He appeared on the beach, carrying netting under his arm.

'Johanne,' he said. His voice was uncertain, as though he wasn't sure it was actually me. 'Where've you been? I looked for you after church but couldn't—'

'Nowhere,' I said.

'What's that you've got?'

I hid Tullik's painting behind my back.

'Nothing.'

'And what's that on your hands? Is that paint?' he said. Fortunately he didn't wait for an answer. 'And who was that man you spoke to last week? He knew you. Who was he?'

'No one,' I said, 'just a friend of Tullik's.'

'Do you have any idea what people have been saying about Miss Ihlen?' he said, trying to turn me against her.

'She has influenza,' I said.

'You think people believe that? Haven't you heard the talk? Folk are saying that crazy-man Munch is possessed by the devil, that he's insane. They're saying Regine Ihlen has shamed her family and gone that way too,' and he hammered his temple with his finger. 'Crazy. They say she's engaged to the painter. Some are even saying she's with child. Is it true, Johanne?'

'What happened to "*What can words do?*"' I said.

'Johanne, they're talking about you too, you know. You've been seen in his garden, picking fruit, with her.'

'And?'

'Well, you're being pulled into something you don't understand.' He dropped his netting onto the beach and began unravelling it.

'Oh, and you *do* understand it then?' I said.

'You've changed,' he said. 'Spent too much time with your Miss Ihlen. I don't like what it's doing to you.'

I walked away.

Mother was no different. There was only one topic of conversation now every time I went home. She suffocated me with her endless questions from the moment I stepped through the door. Beside herself with concern for my own reputation, and hers, she worried that we would be forever tainted by my association with Tullik. I hid the painting by the fence behind Munch's outhouse and prepared myself for the barrage.

'There you are, Johanne,' she said. 'Where have you been?'

'Walking.'

'With her? Have you been with her this afternoon as well?'

'No, Mother. I was alone.'

'You must have known,' she kept saying. 'Didn't you know Miss Ihlen was mixing with those types? Didn't you see it? Didn't she tell you? Everyone's seen the two of you around town together. And Fru Jørgensen saw you in that garden.'

'I've told you, I was following orders,' I said, plunging my hands into the bowl beside her and scrubbing them hard. 'I have to do what Tullik says – she's my employer. I thought you'd be happy I was spending so much time with a Kristiania lady.'

'Not one who squanders her reputation,' she said. 'We must find you a new one. I'm expecting to hear from Fru Jørgensen any day now. I mean, what's to become of Miss Ihlen now? You will do your work, quietly, and you won't speak to her anymore. Only take your orders from Fru Ihlen and the admiral, no one else. Do you hear me?'

Later I lay on my bed, agitated, with my mind and heart at war with themselves. I had already strayed so deeply into the realm of my mother's fear that I knew my own reputation would probably sink with Tullik's. Thomas was afraid of it too, afraid of having a wife who conspired with the insane and indulged in reckless drinking and immorality for the sake of her art. Mother and Thomas were there together, taunting me, every time I closed my eyes.

But then there was love. The irrepressible pull that Munch conveyed so well in his painting. That heave of the soul in the mingle of kisses. The voice that speaks louder than any other, that controls us and drives us, in its pursuit, to peace, or to madness. It could not be for nothing. There had to be a reason, a purpose to the love that Tullik pursued so ferociously. How could I stand in its way?

In the morning I took the painting to Tullik. I had to bend the scroll to hide it under my shawl and when I got to the house I tucked it into my apron. By the time I reached Tullik's room I was afraid I had ruined it, but the beautiful painting glowed in the morning sunlight as I spread it out and admired it again. The suspense, the longing, the pull of two souls who could not be parted. He had done it so simply, so effortlessly.

'Look, Tullik,' I said. 'He painted it for you. It's you and him, together.'

I wanted her to look at it and be transformed. I wanted her to leap from the bed she had not left and escape the prison of this room. If she would only find her adventurous fire again, the passion that had led her to Munch in the first place. That fire would end this suffering, I was sure of it.

She cast her eyes over the painting with little enthusiasm.

'When is he coming?' she said. 'Is he still with her? Is he adrift? Is he in the air or beneath the sea? Where, Johanne? Where is he?'

'Tullik, he's at his house. He painted this for you. He said you were the light.'

I was glad he could not see her now. Her face was ghostly white, her hair a limp, dark mass. The eyes that used to sparkle with danger were sunken and defeated. She was a shell, an empty vessel that Tullik used to inhabit. All the light had faded and nothing but darkness prevailed.

218

'Strawberry Girl,' she whispered, 'bring me strawberries, in a bowl, freshly picked, juicy and sweet.'

'Of course, Tullik,' I said, rolling up the painting and hiding it in the wardrobe. 'I'll pick strawberries for you.'

She hunched up on her bed and lifted her hands to her ears, covering them as though the sound of my words was harming her. Her face was a sick pale green.

'Tullik? Are you all right?'

'After, after,' she said. 'Talk after.'

Her condition remained the same for another few weeks. She asked for strawberries every day and I found them for her, even though the season was coming to an end and the fruit was not as plentiful as it had been before. For a short while after she had eaten my strawberries, traces of the old Tullik would resurface.

'How do you know where to find them?' she said, one day. 'You must have picked all the strawberries in Borre and Åsgårdstrand.'

'Nature is generous,' I said.

'And cruel. Is it not a cruel nature that makes us love so hard? Or that ties us to souls who cannot be bound?'

She didn't mention Munch directly, but stared at the wardrobe with those glassy, fearful eyes.

I took the empty bowl from her and returned to the kitchen. As I passed the parlour, I accidentally overheard the admiral and Fru Ihlen talking by the door.

'But Gaustad?' Julie said, her voice shattering as she spoke.

'We will have to, if she does not improve,' the admiral said. 'If she gets any worse she will be beyond our help. And you, my dear – your nerves. We can't go through this again. I thought that business with Milly and that artist would be the end of us all.'

'Tullik is not Milly,' Julie said.

'No,' Admiral Ihlen said. 'She does not have her strength.'

On Sunday I ran to Munch's again, drawn to the paint and the peace of the studio. The studio door was locked and he was inside the house. I sat on the back step with my arms wrapped around my knees until he came out. When the door finally opened a woman appeared in the doorway.

'What's this?' she said. 'You have a visitor, Munch.'

I expected her to shoo me away, but instead she sat down beside me.

'Hello,' she said, 'who's this little angel? Would you like a cup of coffee?' Her voice was gravelly and sweet. She had a kind, open face and her eyes were soft and pretty.

A small dark man wearing a cap came after her.

'Who is the angel?' he said. 'Munch, Oda's found an angel on your doorstep.'

'What? A fallen angel?' Munch said, following the pair. 'Oh, Johanne, it's you. Won't you say hello to my friends, Oda and Jappe? Have you come to paint?'

'And to speak to you,' I said.

'Another woman who paints,' Oda said, reaching for my arm and lifting me to my feet. 'Thank God! There just aren't enough of us.'

I knew instinctively that she was Oda Krohg, wife of the famous painter Christian. I didn't know who the man, Jappe, was.

220

'Won't you join us at the table, Johanne?' Munch said.

'I'd rather go to the studio,' I said, as my eyes swept the neighbouring houses and gardens.

'I understand,' he said. 'Jappe, get the wine, I'll be with you in a minute.'

Jappe and Oda drifted to the table in the garden and I followed Munch to the studio.

'You are washed out,' he said, closing the door. 'What is it?' I could not look at him.

'It's Tullik, isn't it? What's happened?'

'She doesn't leave her room, doesn't eat much – only strawberries. She doesn't read. They won't allow her to leave the house alone, but she won't come out with me. She's withering,' I said, 'her fire is out. Sometimes I don't even understand what she's saying. Fru Ihlen and the admiral are talking about sending her to Gaustad.'

Munch said nothing. Then he pulled me round to his easel where the painting still sat. 'You must take this to her,' he said. 'She will know it. She will understand it.'

I looked at the painting and shivered. The abstract figure, neither a man nor a woman, was now skeletal in form, its head a skull with sunken, empty eyes. It was holding its hands to its face, covering its ears, and it appeared to be screaming from its gaping mouth. I felt as though I had been struck, hard, in the stomach. I wanted to run. Frightened, I saw Tullik in the image. The fiery red and orange sky was like waves of her hair, the anguish of the face was everything I had seen in her: the green streaks around its nose and mouth were like the sickness I saw in her face; the way she had held her hands to her ears was uncannily similar to the figure in the picture. Even the ominous whirlpool in the background gave me a feeling of impending, inescapable doom, like the hurricane Julie Ihlen seemed to have predicted.

'It's her,' I said, backing away from the painting and turning to him. 'It's her, as she is now.' The whining sound that came from the painting had become louder. 'It's screaming,' I said, 'like her.'

'It's nature,' he said. 'Have you ever felt that blood-red scream of nature? So vast, so overwhelming? That is what tears at our souls. The loss that comes from separation. But we are not separated, we are joined. Everything in nature is joined. You must give her this and tell her I understand. Tell her this is the *Scream*.'

He went to lift the painting down from the easel but I stopped him.

'I can't take it with me now,' I said. 'It's Sunday, I'm staying at home tonight. I will have to return for it in the morning.'

'Then I will leave this door unlocked,' he said. 'Now, paint if you wish.' He lifted a different canvas from the floor and took it outside with his newspaper bag and his paints.

Scream stared out at me with its round white eyes. Its tortured cry scared me, but I was also strangely attracted and found a part of myself connecting with it at some deeply unreachable level. I covered my ears with my hands to block the sound and slowly leaned in closer to inspect it.

He'd used egg tempera to help it dry quickly. I'd seen the tubes lying around the studio. On top of the paint, lines of colour were etched on in crayon and chalk: blue and green

222

on the sea, orange and red in the sky, and white and yellow highlighting the skeletal screamer's face. Parts of the cardboard remained untouched – unfinished, as he would say – as if to give some taste of where this painting came from. It had a sense of its own creation. Like nature, it carried a force, simple and undeniable. To be with it was to know the terror of being parted from the self, the things that make us who we are, the parting of souls, and the fear of a world without love or meaning. It was chaotic and terrifying and yet it was profoundly connective. Something in it unified us all. Perhaps it would heal Tullik? Perhaps it would comfort her to know that Munch had been there, at the edge of madness, too.

It was another sleepless night. Andreas kept hanging over the side of the bed and asking me a torrent of questions I did not want to answer.

'So it was true about Miss Ihlen then? Is she engaged to crazy-man Munch? Is she crazy too? Does she talk about him to you? What's going to happen to her?'

'I don't know,' I kept saying, wishing it were true. 'I don't know anything, now get to sleep.'

I closed my eyes, but all I could see was the horrifying face of the figure in Munch's *Scream*: the vacant eyes and the gaping mouth. I could not shake the image from my mind, nor could I ease the breathlessness from my chest.

As soon as I felt the sun on my face I rose and dressed quietly. I stubbed my toe on the uneven floor, which still rattled and wobbled even though Andreas and I had covered it with a thick mat.

Mother was awake, but in bed, when I came into the parlour. 'You're early,' she said.

'There's a lot to do today,' I said. 'The cleaning's more thorough now the season's winding down.'

'The Heyerdahls are leaving next week,' she said, 'but the cherry tree at the Central Hotel might still have some fruit. Be sure to take them a bowl. There's still time for him to finish a painting, you know.'

'Yes, Mother.'

I slipped out of the house and walked the wrong way to fool her.

As soon as I had passed the huts, I cut up a narrow lane between the houses and joined Nygårdsgaten, doubling back on myself to return to Munch's house.

I hesitated at the gate as the image returned to my mind. Picturing the blood-red sky and the hollow mouth, I realised I had not stopped thinking about it all night. Already, it haunted me.

The screams began as I crept to the studio door. The volume of the painting was enough to fill my entire body with noise. I suddenly thought of my father and his longing for silence. He could not have looked at this painting – it was too unsettled, too deafening. At the thought of Father, everything around me came into sharp focus: the droplets of dew shimmering on the morning grass, the shapes and sizes of all the other paintings scattered throughout the garden, the burgundy walls of the studio and the faded white door with its flaky, peeling paint.

I reached for the handle, jerked the door open and edged my way in, feeling the wall behind me for support. The painting was sitting where Munch had left it on the easel. I approached cautiously, the way the farmers did with wild horses. No sudden movements, no signs of fear, no direct eye contact. I let my eyes stare vacantly until they became blurred, then concentrated on the bottom edge of the painting, latching onto the wavy figure's black body so that I wouldn't have to look at its face. But it forced me into submission and drew my eyes upwards, pulling me into its anguish. I met its unearthly stare. There was something raw about it, a deep sense of anxiety, something I wanted to run from, but I knew there was no escape because part of it was part of me. Looking at the figure again and its long wavy hands, I began to wonder if it was actually shielding its own ears from the sound. Perhaps it was not the figure that was making the scream but the landscape around it? Is that what Munch meant when he said *It's nature*? I sank into the wavy lines of the fjord, the shoreline, the sky: red, blue, green, yellow. The primary colours that wove and curved together to produce a primal scream.

I lifted the painting down from the easel and clamped it under my arm, pulling it in close to muffle its cries. It was not a large painting, only a foot or so by two, and because it was painted on cardboard it was lighter and easier to carry than the canvas had been. But *Scream* was the hardest painting I had smuggled because the circumstances were now so altered. Tullik was confined to her room. Caroline had charged Ragna with keeping a close eye on me, and Ragna was as inquisitive as ever, lingering in rooms longer than necessary and using the vantage point of the kitchen window to observe any outdoor activity. It was impossible to avoid her. I would have to hide the painting until nightfall and bring it into the house after

225

Ragna had gone to bed. Getting caught with it was unthinkable. The repercussions would be devastating.

Munch was not yet awake. I closed the studio door behind me and headed out to Nygårdsgaten, half running, half walking to the mouth of Fjugstad forest. Although I was carrying out Munch's instructions, it felt like a theft. All the other paintings had been given to us; this one had been swiped from the painter's studio itself. But it wasn't just that; it was the depth and intensity of emotion in *Scream*. It was as though I was stealing a feeling, stealing Munch's own soul.

I could not take it to the house immediately, so I veered off the footpath and trod through the plants and undergrowth, chopping at leaves and branches with my free hand, pressing the painting to my body. Eventually I found the cluster of rocks where Thomas and I had kissed on the night of the dance. I knelt down in the moss and managed to slide the painting into a crevice between them.

'You will have to stay here until it is dark,' I said. 'Then I will come and find you.'

The painting seemed only to scream louder as I walked away. It was like abandoning a child.

I returned to *Scream* in the middle of the night. A high full moon had come out to assist me, illuminating parts of the path between the whispering trees. I inched my way out of the house painstakingly slowly, barefoot and in my nightgown. First I stole into the dining room and took a tablecloth from the dresser, then I waited at the back door. I did not turn the handle until the clock in the hall struck two, hoping its chime might conceal any noise. As soon as I was across the road I began to run. I would have to work quickly and get back to the house with the painting before anyone awoke.

The forest was cold. Gone were the balmy nights of the summer. The air had not yet grown the teeth that would bite us in the winter, but there was a sharp nip to it that heralded the approach of autumn. Everything was bland in the moonlight. The leaves colourless, merging into one. Rocks protruded like gravestones in the shadows, grey-white slabs against the dark undergrowth. Then I saw it, the blazing red and orange – Tullik's fire – alive in *Scream*'s troubled sky.

'You waited,' I said, talking to the painting to calm my own nerves. 'That's good. I've got you. There we are.' I lifted it up from between the rocks and covered it with the tablecloth. 'I need to wrap you in this, so they don't see you.' A rumble crossed my chest and my breathing grew fast and shallow. *Scream* was angry. It did not want to be hidden. 'Tullik will see you,' I said. 'In the morning, Tullik will see you.' I hugged the painting to my chest as I folded and secured the cloth, then slid it under my arm and ran back to the house.

I was relieved to find everything just as I had left it. No one had stirred and the rooms were still dark. In the kitchen Henriette greeted me with a loud meow, then she circled me suspiciously as though sensing the waves of sound that streamed from the painting. The noise reverberated through my body. I was a fool to think I could sneak a scream into the house unnoticed.

I had learned how to move through Solbakken quickly and quietly in hurried steps from one point to another. My first

227

point was the post at the bottom of the stairs. I glanced at the clock. It was almost a quarter to three. The pendulum swung as though timing my movements. I held my breath and dashed out to the stairs. The next point was the back window in the curve of the staircase. When I reached it, I turned back on myself to check that no one was behind me. The last point was my bedroom. I was about to spring forward again when I heard the conspicuous whine of a door.

My heart thumped hard in my ears and, coupled with the noise of the painting, it was impossible for me to locate the sound. I didn't know if it was above me or below me, in front of me or behind me. I leaned *Scream* up against the wall, detaching myself from it and stepping away. Then I realised there were two sounds. One was the tread of footsteps in the hall downstairs; the other was a bedroom door. The only person who could possibly have been below me was Ragna. I peered over the banister and saw the top of her head approaching the staircase. Gathering *Scream* up into my arms, I ran to my room without knowing whose bedroom door had opened or who had seen me.

I threw the painting under Milly's bed and leapt under the covers. My feet were filthy from the forest and I tried not to let them touch the sheets, hovering my legs uncomfortably above the surface. I sucked at the air to force my breath to slow, but I could hear Ragna's footsteps on the stairs. She was getting closer. From my bed, I saw my door handle twist. I clung to the sheets. Peering over the side of the bed, I noticed that a corner of the tablecloth was showing: *Scream* was peeping out. The door opened. I shuffled the coverlet with my knees and hoped it would drop to the floor before Ragna saw anything.

Before she came in, I heard her voice, whispering, loudly.

'I heard a noise,' she said.

'It was me,' I heard Tullik say. 'You can go back down now.'

'Shouldn't I see you back into bed, Miss Tullik?' she said. I could almost hear her black eyes scanning Tullik's body. I could tell from her tone that she knew it was me she had heard on the stairs.

'No,' Tullik said. 'Go.'

Tullik waited for Ragna's footsteps to recede before she came into the room.

'Johanne?' she said. 'Are you awake?'

'Tullik!' I swung my dirty feet off the bed and sat up. 'Thank goodness it was you. Are you all right?'

Her eyes seemed clearer, brighter, in the moonlit room.

'I heard a moaning sound, a wailing,' she said. 'Were you crying?'

'No.'

'Johanne, you're freezing,' she said, touching my arm as she sat down beside me. 'Where have you been?'

'I went to the forest. I have a painting for you.'

'Is he here? Is he here?' she said.

'Sort of. He said you would know it and understand it.'

'Show me,' she whispered. 'Where is it?'

I got down on my knees and pulled *Scream* out from under the bed. Standing opposite her, I peeled away the tablecloth and let it fall to the floor, holding the painting up with the screaming figure facing me. Slowly, I turned it around.

229

Tullik's mouth dropped open when she saw it and her hands flew up to her ears. She was its mirror image.

'Look at the strokes.' She ran her fingers across the lumps in the cheerless blue fjord. 'The sky is on fire. We are afraid . . . of everything around us – of this world. For if we are parted there is nothing but pain. Our souls scream. It is a vast, endless scream.'

She collapsed back down on the bed.

'I must go to him,' she said, her face bright, yet sober.

'Tullik, are you sure?'

'I see it clearly now, yes. I must go to him.'

'But your parents will—'

'They don't have to know,' she said.

'They'll find out. It's too dangerous. Ragna is watching our every move.'

'I'll think of something,' she said.

She took the painting and ran her finger round the gaping O of its mouth. She could hear it too.

'Make sure you hide it well,' I said, as she left.

She didn't answer.

Morning found me in nightmares of blood-red skies and the dizzy swirl of whirlpools, and boats with no sails being pulled by the current into the dark-blue depths of the fjord.

Fru Berg was knocking at my door.

'Johanne, you're late,' she said. 'What the devil's got into you? Up! Up!'

I felt her chunky hands on my shoulders as she shook me awake.

'Johanne! Come on! The breakfast!'

'Sorry,' I murmured, sitting up in bed, confused. 'I was having such a terrible dream.'

'Well, if you don't hurry up it will come true. Come on, girl!'

As she walked away she slipped on the tablecloth that was still lying on the floor.

'What in the Lord's name is that doing here?'

'It's for the laundry,' I said. 'You can take it. I brought it up with me last night by mistake.'

She bent over and gathered the cloth to her bosom.

'Hurry, girl!' she said, as she waddled out.

Ragna was visibly outraged when I arrived in the kitchen. Her bony shoulders twitched with tension and her eyes flashed from side to side, watching me hungrily. She knew she had been close to catching me in the night and was furious I had escaped her. Throughout the morning she deliberately over-heated every soup and every sauce, blackening the bases of the pots and pans so that they would not come clean without a vicious scouring.

She eagerly stacked them up, knowing I would have the task of cleaning them. Around mid-morning, when I had finished the dusting and the floors, I went outside to wash the pots in a steel tub by the hen coop. To fill it, I had to use a heavy double-handled pot from the stove and it was labor-ious work. Kneeling over the tub's deep edge to lift and scrub the pots was back-breaking and, exhausted from my lack of sleep, I was close to tears. But it had been worth it, just to see a glimmer of fire return to Tullik's eyes again.

I was just lifting a potato pan from the water when a cry shot out from Tullik's room. Crimson. White. The window was open and the ear-splitting howl was so sudden that I dropped the pan. Then the cry changed shape and it became the sound of my own name.

'Johanne! Johanne!'

At first I did not recognise the voice because I had never heard it raised before. It was Fru Ihlen. She was shrieking helplessly.

I fled from the wash tub and, with my hands still dripping with water, ran up the stairs to Tullik's room.

'Johanne!' Fru Ihlen was shouting. 'Oh, Johanne, there you are. Thank goodness. You must help us.'

She was flanked by Ragna and Fru Berg, who were staring at the floor as though someone had just died. Tullik was sitting on her bed with her arms folded across her chest. An oppressive droning sound weighed the room down.

My trip to the forest and all my efforts to conceal *Scream* had been for nothing.

Tullik had hung it, blatantly, in the middle of her wall.

'You must get this dreadful thing out of here,' Fru Ihlen said to me, pointing at the shocking picture. 'I can't even bear to touch it. Where did you get this filth from, Tullik?' Julie said.

'Edvard,' Tullik said, defiantly.

'Johanne.' Fru Ihlen set her clear eyes on me. 'You must take this dreadful thing away from here and burn it.'

'No!' Tullik yelled.

'Take it,' Julie said, indicating to Fru Berg and Ragna to restrain Tullik.

Tullik tried to reach for the painting but the two women wrestled her back down onto her bed.

'Johanne! No!' she pleaded. 'Don't take it! Don't take it from me.'

'Pay no attention to her,' Fru Ihlen said. 'It's for her own good.'

I knelt on Tullik's bed and, following Julie's orders, reached out for the painting.

'No, Johanne!' Tullik cried. 'You're my friend. You understand it, don't you? It's him. He's in this. It's him and me. It's our pain. Our pain together. Don't take it!'

'Don't listen to her,' Julie said. 'Take it away.'

Ragna and Fru Berg tightened their grip and, with her arms pinned down, Tullik started kicking. Her foot thumped against my stomach as I leaned towards the wall.

'Johanne!' she shouted. 'Don't do it!'

My arms dropped.

Julie touched my shoulder, then bent down to hold Tullik's legs.

'Please, Johanne,' she said, calmly. 'It must go. Quickly.'

I lifted my arms, but then lowered them again. I couldn't take *Scream* from Tullik. I would be stealing part of her soul too.

'For heaven's sake, girl!' Ragna shouted over Tullik's cries. 'Take the damned thing away.'

'Hurry, Johanne,' Julie said. 'Get it out of here.'

I moved in and lifted *Scream* down from the wall without looking at Tullik. I could not bring myself to witness any more of her pain and I was ashamed of my betrayal. I fled the room in silence and Fru Ihlen hurried after me.

'There is no place for something so inhuman, something so monstrous, in this world. Burn it,' she said, solemnly. 'Do not come back until it is done.'

16

Natural

Let the eye be closed, let the sense of hearing be excited, and from the lightest breath to the wildest din, from the simplest sound to the highest harmony, from the most vehement and impassioned cry to the gentlest word of reason, still it is Nature that speaks and manifests her presence, her power, her pervading life

Theory of Colours, Johann Wolfgang von Goethe

Scream and I were alone in the woods again. This time there was no tablecloth and the picture was exposed, as it wanted to be. Fru Ihlen had given me a bottle of turpentine and a box of matches, but I had no need for them. When I reached the shelter of the forest I cast them into the bushes. Looking at the face of *Scream* again, I began to cry. Pale-blue tears. I didn't know why I was crying.

'I won't burn you,' I said, looking at the forlorn face and the hollow eyes. 'I will protect you.'

But how?

'I can't take you back to Munch,' I said, wiping my eyes. 'He'll think it's a rejection. He wants you to be with Tullik.

I just need to keep you safe for a while, until she can get you back again.'

I ran to the rocks and slid the picture into the crevice that had protected it the night before. I had to find a safe place for it, but needed help. Who could I trust with this secret?

Lifting my face to the sky, I closed my eyes. With my hands held out and my palms turned upwards, I wandered round in circles, silently begging the forest for help. It was only when I tripped over a fallen branch that the answer came to me and I sped from the woods, leaving *Scream* alone.

I raced through Åsgårdstrand and went straight to our hut. Hunting inside and out, I had to know it was empty. Then I rushed to the pier to look for my brother.

'Andreas! Andreas!'

My cries caught the attention of the fishermen by the walkway.

'You're in a hurry, Johanne,' one of them called. It was Thomas's father. His hands were full of worms that he was threading onto hooks.

'Have you seen Andreas, Herr Askeland?' I said.

'He was on the other side of the boathouse this morning,' he said, pointing across the pier. 'He and the lads were fishing.'

I tore away and ran to the boathouse at the end of the beach. Rounding the corner, I found Andreas with his friends Markus and Petter. He was sitting with his feet hanging over the ledge at the back.

'Andreas!' I said, gasping for breath. 'I need you to come and help me.'

'I'm fishing,' he said, waving his pole at me.

'It's important.'

'This is important,' he said, unmoving.

'Just hurry, will you!'

He handed his rod to Petter.

'Hope you have more luck than me,' he said, stepping over his friend's legs and pulling his cap tight on his head.

'Where's Mother?' I said.

'How am I supposed to know? I've been here all morning.'

'I need you to go to Father's workshop. Ask him for some spare sailcloth or an old sail he doesn't need.'

'What for?'

'Just do it. And get a hammer and some nails.'

'Why can't you ask him?'

'I'm supposed to be at work, aren't I? I don't want any questions. Leave the hammer and nails in our bedroom and then meet me in the woods with the sail. Don't tell a soul. We need to hurry, while Mother's out.'

I threw a stern look at him, then turned and ran back to the forest.

By the time Andreas caught up with me I had lifted *Scream* from the split in the rocks and found a place for it behind the birches by the Nielsens' farm. I crouched behind the trunks, snatching glimpses out to the path. When Andreas appeared, I came rushing out, ambushing him unawares.

'What are you doing?' he said, jumping away from me and dropping the sail he was carrying.

'Sorry,' I whispered. 'No one can see us and we must work quickly.'

'Lord, Johanne,' he said, turning pale. 'Have you killed someone?'

'Don't be a halfwit,' I said. 'I'll kill *you* if you breathe a word about this.'

'All right, all right,' he said. 'So what are we doing?'

'Come with me.'

I led him off the path and through the thick of the trees.

'Lay the sail down,' I said, helping him spread it out.

'It's not a proper sail,' Andreas said, 'just what he had left over. I told him I was making a raft.'

'Very good,' I said. 'Now, we need to wrap this painting in it.'

I lifted *Scream* from behind the bushes and laid it down on top of the sail.

'Almighty God!' Andreas said, covering his mouth. 'It's the crazy man, isn't it?'

'It's Munch's painting, yes,' I said, underplaying the shock of the screaming skeletal figure and the unsettling landscape, 'but I need to hide it.'

'Why? Where did you get it?'

'Don't ask any questions. Just help me wrap it up.'

We eased *Scream* into the tightly woven hemp sailcloth, folding the cloth neatly along the edges.

'We'll take it back to the hut,' I said, stretching my arms around it and holding it to my hip. 'If anyone asks, we tell them it's a sail, for Father. You'd believe that, wouldn't you?'

'I suppose so,' he said.

Andreas walked beside me and shielded as much of the folded sailcloth as he could, as I carried the painting back to our hut.

'Good, she's still out,' I said, when we got back. 'Let's get it into our room.'

We laid the painting down on the bottom bunk.

'Now what?' Andreas said. 'It's not exactly hidden *there*, is it?'

'We're going to fix this floor,' I said. 'Did you get the hammer and nails?'

Andreas reached up onto the top bunk, pulled the tools down and laid them out on the floor.

'Right,' I said, lifting the mat and tossing it aside. 'Help me lift these loose boards.'

It was heavy, dirty work. The floorboards were old and thick and we had to lift one at a time and stack them on a small oblong of floor by our beds. Below them was a shallow pit, dusty and soiled by rats and vermin.

'That's five,' Andreas said, when we approached the opposite wall. 'There's only one more. Do we have enough room yet?'

I ran my hand between the joists.

'Maybe if we turn it round this way,' I said, waving my arm up and down the wall end.

We lifted the painting from the bed and gently lowered it into the floor. The sailcloth gathered and ruffled as we squeezed it under the crossing joist. I bent over and pulled it tight as Andreas carefully slid the corners of *Scream* into place.

'There! It's in!' he said. Then he looked at me with a puzzled expression. 'What's the matter?' he said.

I was crying again. Streaks of blue rushed down my face.

'I don't know,' I said. 'It's just so sad. It doesn't want to be covered up like this. I can tell. It's like I'm burying something that's not dead.'

'Johanne, it's a *painting*,' Andreas said. 'A crazy, stupid painting. Come on now, we need to put all this back.'

One by one we lifted the boards and lowered them into place, this time hammering them with new nails to hold them securely in position. We were just about to pick up the last one when our mother returned. She came flying into the house and started screeching when she saw it was occupied.

'What's going on here?' she said, staring at the two of us kneeling on the floor.

'We're fixing the floorboards,' I said. 'They were loose and we kept tripping on them.'

'Why aren't you at the Ihlens'?' she said.

'I'm out on an errand for Fru Ihlen.'

'Well, you'd better get on with it then,' she glowered, 'instead of wasting the woman's precious time on your bedroom floor. Honestly, Johanne.'

'It's my fault, I asked her to help me,' Andreas said, rescuing me. 'I can manage the last one on my own. You should be getting back to work.'

'But while you're here,' Mother said, her mouth tightening as though her lips were being sewn together, 'you might want to pick some fruit for the Heyerdahls. Didn't I tell you they were leaving this week?'

'Yes, Mother,' I said, walking past her. 'Hammer that board hard into the joist, Andreas, nice and tight. It won't be bothering us any more.'

'Did you hear me, Johanne? The cherries for Herr Heyerdahl?'

'I'll be back tomorrow. I'll do it then.'

If I had not been required by the Ihlens, Mother would have beaten me for my insolence. Instead she snarled and gave me a dig between my shoulders as I left.

'Clean up all this mess, Andreas,' she said. 'Look at the dust.'

I left Andreas to finish the job under the suspicious eye of my mother. My brother and I rarely chose to spend time together and I knew she would question our cooperation, but I imagined she would only be interested in the floorboards with a view to cleaning them, not to finding out what lay below them.

On Saturday, Fru Ihlen allowed me to go home early. I returned to Åsgårdstrand and, true to my word, I picked cherries for the Heyerdahls. A dance was to be held at the Grand Hotel in the evening. It was the last one of the season but I would not be going, not without Tullik. Herr Heyerdahl was talking about it as he invited me into my own home.

'How delightful! Cherries! Christine, come and see what Johanne's brought. Come in, Johanne,' he said. 'Christine's just looking for a dress in the trunk. There's a dance tonight, at the Grand. Are you going?'

'No, I don't think so,' I said, stepping through the deluge that had been created by the Heyerdahls: an avalanche of canvases, easels, palettes, spots of paint, rags and dust sheets. Mother would relish cleaning up the debris after they had gone.

'Oh, but it's the last of the season,' Herr Heyerdahl said.

'I'll put the cherries on the bench here,' I said, ignoring him. 'They'll be good for a day or two, but no longer.'

'Then we'll eat them tonight, before the dance,' he said. 'Are you quite sure you won't come?'

'Not without Tullik.' The words were out with my breath and I couldn't pull them back in again.

'Miss Ihlen? Yes, Edvard said she'd disappeared. Is she all right?'

'They won't let her see him,' I said, no longer caring who knew what, or where my talk might lead.

'You must tell her to forget him,' he said.

'That's impossible. She cannot *be* Tullik without him.'

'Edvard's not a man for love, Johanne. Not with a woman. He loves his art. He is married to his art.'

'She knows that.'

'He's so intensely wrapped up in it. It engulfs him, takes up his whole soul.'

'I think she knows that too,' I said, with a heavy sadness.

'Then she will know that the only way to truly love him is to let him go. You know he's planning a trip to Germany? He'll be leaving soon, with all the rest of us. We'll leave you in peace to get on with your lives again.'

I wondered how there could ever be any peace for Tullik, or how she would be able to get on with her life, now that it seemed to be over.

'When will he go?' I said.

'I don't know. Soon. He received an invitation from an admirer of his who wants him to exhibit in Berlin. He's lucky to get the opportunity – can't sell a sketch in Kristiania.'

'He doesn't like to sell them. Tullik said he calls them his children.'

Herr Heyerdahl laughed raucously, clutching the side of his substantial paunch.

'I suppose they are,' he said, looking through the window at his own children playing outside. 'Poor Edvard.'

'I must be going,' I said, feeling somehow offended. 'Mother needs my help.'

'I expect you'll all be glad to get back into your own house next week,' he said.

I masked my disagreement with a smile and left him, relieved that the cherries had not sparked the inspiration that my mother so desperately craved. Relieved there would be no more paintings of me, no picture portraits to freeze me in time.

In the evening, after dinner, when the plates were cleared and the leftovers stored, I felt my father's hand come to rest on my shoulder.

'I hear there's a dance tonight, Johanne,' he whispered. 'Last one of the season. Why don't you go? Enjoy yourself.'

I was empty, not in the mood for dancing.

'I don't need to go, Father,' I said.

'Who in the world ever *needs* to go to a dance?' he said. 'You go because you *want* to. Don't you *want* to get out of here?' He gave me a wink and tipped his head towards Mother, who was dozing in a chair by the stove.

'I suppose I could do with some air,' I said.

'Then off you go, dear.' He stood back and raised his arm towards the door as if I didn't know where to find it.

I untied my pinafore and draped it over the chair.

'Thank you, Father,' I said, kissing him on the cheek before I left.

Across the road Thomas was sitting on an upturned fishing boat, waiting for me. I didn't know how long he had been there. He held a striped terracotta stone in his hands and rubbed at its surface with his thumbs. He knew I liked those stones, the ones that were hard to find.

'There's a dance tonight,' he said, smiling, 'remember? I was hoping you'd come.'

He stood up and walked towards me, reaching out his arms.

'I don't feel like dancing tonight,' I said, brushing him away. 'Not without Tullik.'

'It would do you good to be without her,' he said. 'Isn't it enough to be with me?'

His question brought a lump to my throat that words could not shift.

'Isn't it?' he said, his eyes dimming.

And then there was Tullik in my head, and her arms around me and her hair like fire and her voice as seductive as roses. Red and ruby, reeling and flowing and breathing with life. The exhilaration of scarlet, the indulgence of deep burgundy. The freedom that colour brought. And then Thomas again, before me. *Was* it enough? Was he enough? Would he take my colours away?

'You don't have to answer,' he said. 'I can't give you what Munch gives you, or Miss Ihlen, or any of those Kristiania guests. I'm just a fisherman.'

He turned away from me and cast the rock out to the beach, throwing it so hard and so far that I didn't hear it land. Then he sniffed and shook his head and began to walk away.

'Thomas, please,' I said, 'I . . .' The sentence stopped, losing conviction on its way out. I wanted him to come back, but on what terms? I couldn't say. A burst of magenta chased after him. Swirls of scarlet spun about his chest and surrounded him in a halo of reddish light. But he held his hand up, without looking back, and at once it all faded to grey. His big strong hand that used to hold me. Now it was a wall, a stop sign. It told me not to follow, but to turn around.

To leave.

The summer days were dwindling and the moon had grown impatient. It paraded out early, claiming ownership of the sky the second the sun had faded. In its yellow glare, I crossed the grassy mounds and found myself drawn, as always, to the sea.

I followed the stones, picking my way over them without looking down. The tide rushed in and out with a rhythmic whoosh, making the mix of seaweed and salt bloom and then fade in the cool night air. I matched my breathing to the flow of the waves, inhaling and exhaling with the water. Some nights I thought I could walk forever along the Åsgårdstrand shoreline. I could follow the coast through Borre and Horten and keep walking up to Holmestrand. If I stayed by the shore I would curve round to Svelvik and even get to Drammen. Eventually I would reach Kristiania. With the waves lapping gently by my side, I was sure I could walk all the way to Sweden and never tire.

From time to time I had to remind myself to stop before I went too far. The first of these self-notifications came at the edge of the forest where the coast rounded inwards and made a horseshoe shape, which was lined in trees. My boots sank gently into the sand and pebbles and, although it was dark, I still knew my way.

I looked back and saw the lights of Åsgårdstrand twinkling behind me: the lanterns strung along the back of the Grand Hotel and the light from the windows where the guests would be dancing and where Christian and his friends would be charging their fiddles. I remembered how Thomas had spun me until I was dizzy when we danced on the night I first saw Tullik. It seemed like years ago now.

A small stone jetty stretched out into the fjord at the far end of the horseshoe. An invisible hand moved around my shoulders and directed me to it. Without question, I followed the force. It was only when I was halfway out that I saw Munch. He was sitting at the end of the jetty, facing towards Borre with his knees up. I did not need to see his face to know it was him.

When I was close enough, I sat down beside him without saying a word. He knew I was there. He knew it was me. It was just as it had been before, when I was younger, sitting with him, although being apart. The moonlight caught the wave of his hair tossing about his face in the breeze. He looked longingly towards Borre with a yearning so palpable it pierced my chest.

We sat there consumed by nature: the water that sloshed around us, the wind that picked at our hair and clothes, the great pine trees whose branches reached out to us but could not bridge the divide. Time passed unchecked. He was less of a mystery in the silence and I began to understand him, the way a bud understands how to ripen. In the arms of the atmosphere we were not separate individuals but two elements of nature, conversing through feelings that required no words. His sadness and restlessness coursed between us like colours squeezed from a tube. *I can't help you, Munch*, I thought, beginning to sense that no one, not even Tullik, ever could.

It was cold and the stone pier was starting to numb my legs.

'I'm leaving,' he said, breaking our silence. 'I'm going back to Germany to exhibit.'

'When will you go?'

'Soon. Maybe next week.'

'Will you tell her?'

He dipped his chin and ran a hand through his hair.

'I will say goodbye.'

A sharp breeze froze my neck and I pulled my shawl tight.

'What do you think is best, Johanne? The dream of happiness or the dream of imagined happiness? I have my art and capacity for nothing else. And then there's my disposition, this sickness I've inherited from my parents – the physical weakness of my mother and the nervousness and anxiety of my father. Would Tullik really be able to cope with that? Because I cannot get rid of it. If I were to be rid of my sickness, then what would happen to my art? And my sister Inger says that work is the best thing for us. It gives us strength. I've always put my work before everything – a woman would only stand in the way, wouldn't she? And could I live amongst them? They read their silly romance novels and gossip and go to birthday parties. Don't they ever dare to be alone? The women go parading arm-in-arm down Karl Johan, the men have their clubs. They are always so busy. But busy with what? What will they have to show for it all when their time comes? For we all know that when we go on through the valley of death, we must wander alone. We must wander alone in the dark, if we don't have the light with us. So we should follow those who are the light, those who bring the light. But what do we do? We persecute them. People don't see the light that is there, they see only darkness.'

I could not respond to his cascading thoughts but I could see that, for him, loving another would always be secondary to his work. His life would be his art.

'I came close to death several times as a child,' he continued, 'so close I felt his cold fingers about my shoulders and the shudder that prickled down in my bones. There were times I thought I would not recover, and times I did not even want to. But then, when I was well, I understood that death would call again, and that I would have to face him one day and have something to show for the life he allowed me to lead.'

'And that is your art,' I said.

'Precisely.'

The wind picked up again and whipped at his body as though he and the breeze were shaking hands. My legs were bitterly cold and I stood to bring them back to life.

'I should be getting back,' I said, 'it's late.'

'I will go with you,' he said, turning.

'No. There's no need. I know the way.'

'I know it too,' he said. 'We all know the way back.' His eyes were dark and his voice as weak as the chirp of a thrush. 'It's the way forward that is less certain.'

I left him sitting on the jetty and returned home chilled, my nose and cheeks red with cold. Mother was sleeping and Father murmured something incoherent from his bed when he heard the door. I whispered a lie: I'd been to the dance, yes. I'd enjoyed myself, yes. I sneaked into the bedroom where Andreas was sound asleep. The floorboards no longer creaked. I walked over them as I undressed, feeling the smooth old planks under my feet. When I lay down in my bed, I closed my eyes and prayed that sleep would come quickly. But all I could hear were the haunting cries of the *Scream* howling at me from beneath the bedroom floor.

17

Black

In darkness we can, by an effort of imagination,
call up the brightest images

Theory of Colours, Johann Wolfgang von Goethe

The storm began on Monday evening after dinner. At first we didn't think it would ever break. The air was alive with tension, flickering with lightning and rumbling periodically like chronic indigestion. Fru Berg was rushing about the house carrying baskets of linen, unable to decide what to do with them.

'There's a badness brewing,' she said, passing me on the stairs as I went up to check on Tullik. 'You can feel it scheming. It's conspiring against us. God is angry.' I leaned back against the railings where Henriette was circling and sucked my breath in to make way for Fru Berg. She shoved Henriette with her foot. 'Out of my way, cat,' she said, tramping off to the kitchen in her own puffed-up bubble of fear.

Tullik had been sleeping all afternoon. After her brief moment of lucidity at the sight of *Scream*, she had sunk again into her darkness, her tangled world of panic and confusion. She had withdrawn so fiercely from the ritual of the Ihlens' daily lives that I feared it would not be long before her parents yielded to the call of Gaustad.

No one was more concerned than me. Watching Tullik sink into this dreary existence, this half-life, with her torturous wailing by night and her lethargic drowsing by day, was like watching her wade through clay. For one who had been so vital, she had become her own shadow, dark and indistinct like the spectre that loomed over Laura Munch in the painting. Like Laura, Tullik could not escape it.

The air was stuffy when I entered the room. I opened the window to the growling skies. Small snakes' tongues of lightning flashed from the slate-grey clouds, chased by the menacing snarl of thunder.

'What's that?' Tullik said, from her semi-conscious daze.

'A storm's coming,' I said. 'Fru Berg's terrified. She thinks God is angry. But I think it'll be good to clear the air. Won't you come down and eat some supper?' I said, spying the bread I had brought up earlier curling and drying on the tray.

'I'm not hungry,' she said.

'Then what can I get you?' I gathered up her hand in mine.

'Open the wardrobe,' she whispered. 'Bring him to me, Johanne.'

'What about—'

'Bring him,' she said, climbing out of bed.

I checked the upper landing to make sure we were alone, then silently closed the bedroom door. At the wardrobe I carefully unpinned the false back: the dark sheet that covered the

251

paintings. I dug my fingers into the drawing pins and wrenched them out until the fabric gave and a rush of paintings flopped towards me through Tullik's clothes. I lifted them out one by one and held them up to her like dresses.

'He's here,' I said, 'Edvard's here, in every one.'

Her eyes popped open like two bright moons in the dusky room as I held up first *Mermaid*, then the heartbreakingly poignant painting of the encounter of the man and woman on the beach. Tullik made me put them on the floor. She began to dance around them, as though bewitched by the storm's dark energy. As the mermaid she was enchanting, emerging from the indigo water by the light of the moon that shone from a towering column and rippled across the water. She was moving like a mermaid, kicking up her legs like a tail fanning the waves.

I looked at her glorious hair in the painting, hanging forward over one shoulder, pouring into the water, becoming the pools around her. It was pushed back over the other shoulder, exposing her breasts, her hips and her thighs, exactly as it had been on that day when she felt so daring, when she was so full of fire and reckless abandon.

I showed her *The Voice*, the moment when she stood before him that night in Fjugstad forest with her hands clasped behind her back and her face lifted towards him. I remembered how fascinated I had been by the passion of their kisses, how they had consumed each other like starving animals.

'He loves me,' she said suddenly, still dancing around the pictures and waving her arms.

'Of course he does.'

'And I must go to him.' Her eyes were alive again. I sensed their danger but could not say I was sorry for it.

The Ihlens had long retired to bed before the first of the rains came. Perhaps they were even sleeping. I was standing in my nightgown at the window, curiously attracted to the storm, to the strength of nature and all its mightiness, which reminded us we were forever at its mercy. The heavens opened in a thunderous downpour and the rain battered at the windows like an invasion. Hard droplets pelted the glass like stones while water accumulated in the gutters, sending small water-falls spewing to the ground.

The sky was ripped apart by thunder and the house shuddered helplessly with every blast. I imagined Fru Berg quivering in her home, convinced that God must be furious with us all. A flash of lightning lit the church and for a second I could see the beams of the gable end and the thick door bracing itself against the onslaught. I wondered how many times the church had weathered such storms in all its hundreds of years. It seemed unflinchingly resilient, as though it knew God would not attack the very place where He was worshipped.

The blasts continued, rocking the foundations of Solbakken with violent determination. An unclosed window somewhere rattled in fear. A door downstairs slammed shut. Open and shut. Open and shut. Tullik's hens were unsettled and clucked feverishly in their coop. To them the thunder must have seemed like a thousand Fru Bergs threatening to roast them for the admiral's dinner. Each boom was more ferocious than the last as the storm built to a never-ending crescendo. I felt the sea levels rising. My inexplicable connection to the water sent uneasy ripples through my chest and I retreated to my bed for some stability.

Between the cracks and flashes I listened for Tullik but could not hear her. There wasn't a whimper from her room, but for some reason that did not console me. The silence was sinister, as though some other threat was lingering in the troubled air. I tried to put it out of my mind while the storm raged on, breathing deep and slow to subdue my agitation. An hour passed, maybe two, as I napped fitfully to the changing moods of the storm.

An explosion of thunder awoke me and I sat up in bed, my heart beating fast, my neck and head pulsating with urgency. The rain was still lashing against the windows. Its impatience dragged me from my bed and I stood there in the middle of the room, confused, wondering why I was on my feet, cold and afraid. Then the frenzied pattering on the glass seemed to divide itself into two syllables, two repetitive syllables that said, *Tull-ik*, *Tull-ik*, *Tull-ik*.

I ran to her room.

'Tullik,' I whispered. 'Are you awake?'

The room was in shadow. The window was still open and rain was pooling on the windowsill and spilling down the wall.

'Tullik!'

I went over to her bed but couldn't see her. Feeling blindly for her body in the dark, I stretched my hands out and patted them down on the bed, but the sheets sank below my fingers. I tore at the bedclothes, pulling them aside, ripping them off and throwing them on the floor. I spun round, checking the floor, the chair by the window and the bed again, but Tullik had vanished.

I came back out into the hall and listened at the top of the stairs, hanging my head over the banister. Perhaps, unable to sleep, she had ventured down to the kitchen? My ears strained for a moment, filtering out the sound of the driving rain and the crashing thunder, but downstairs nothing stirred.

'No!' I whispered. 'No, Tullik. What have you done?'

I rushed back to my room and dressed in a hurry, racing through my hooks and laces, missing the loops and button-holes that held me in place. Grabbing my shawl and tying a scarf around my head, I slipped out and prepared myself to face the storm.

The night was blacker than tar. I found the lantern in the shed, but it was of little use in the rain and only created more shadows ahead of me. The fallen rain made tides across the submerged ground. The road was a sea, the fields a swamp. By the time I reached the forest my boots were already wet right through. Water was running down through the trees, and the leaves and branches provided no shelter. The lantern swung back and forth as I hurried along the path, a boggy sump of mud and mush.

Another barrage of thunder broke above my head. It was so loud and angry that I cried out, jolting back and cowering behind a tree. The branches were arching under the weight of the rain, pointing at me with slippery black fingers. They brushed my face eerily as I passed, and moaned as though they might snap in the howl of the wind. I remembered Tullik talking of trolls and huldrefolk, how she'd walked these woods at dusk and seen shapes and shadows, moving like ghosts among the trees. I had dismissed her fantasies then, but now I believed them. A troll or a tribe of huldrefolk would not have been out of place in this storm and, as the thunder and lightning tore at the trees, my head began to picture frightening images of ghosts and monsters lurking behind every branch.

Even the soothing rush of the sea had disappeared, subsumed by the omnipresent flow of water. I lifted my ear towards the shore, but the waves had abandoned their rhythmic surge and were now churning angrily in all directions, crashing against rocks, clapping together with a loud smack, then rumbling in a threatening gurgle.

I slipped and stumbled along the soggy pathway, pummelled by the vicious rain that showed no sign of abating. Water was running down my nose and cheeks, trickling into my open mouth and dripping from my chin. It was as though I was swimming in the sea. I shook my head and tried to blink away the rain, but every time I cleared my eyes a fresh onslaught would fill them.

When I finally reached the Nielsens' farm I was exhausted. Flopping against the wall, I removed my headscarf and wiped the mud speckles from my face. My hair was soaking. I wrung it out tight like a rag and repinned it in the darkness, scraping the straggly wet strands into a knot at the back of my neck.

In the middle of the stormy night Åsgårdstrand was deserted. The streets were abandoned and left to the ghosts. Windows were dark and empty. I heard the sounds of gates swinging and clanging at the latch. Trees bent powerlessly over fences, hanging, as if in shame. Nygårdsgaten was a waterlogged cesspool flowing with twigs and stones and pulpy horse-dung. I hopped through the filthy pools, sticking to the middle of the road to avoid the brimming cart tracks. I heard the Andersens' baby crying as I passed our hut and thought about all the children who would be unable to sleep tonight, shaking and frightened, seeking refuge in their parents' beds, consumed, as I was, by tales of trolls and huldrefolk who come in the night. And then I thought of Andreas and wondered if he could hear the cries of the *Scream* above the raucous bellow of thunder.

At Munch's house the gate was already open, leaning pathetically against the house as though it had been wrenched from its hinges. The shutters were closed at the side window and I couldn't see in. I noticed that all his paintings were still outside, even in the beating rain. Perhaps he was glad of it? Perhaps he thought they needed rain just as much as the fruit and vegetables did? In the darkness all I could see was the effervescent glow of Inger's dress in the painting where she was sitting on the rocks at the beach.

I hurried up the stairs at the back as the thunder crashed on in angry condemnation. I banged at the door with my fist and waited, but no one came. A candle in the neck of a wine bottle was flickering at the window behind a stream of raindrops that gave a liquid veneer to each pane.

I returned to the bottom of the steps and patted my hand against the glass.

'Tullik!' I shouted. 'It's Johanne! Let me in!'

From the ground, the base of the window was at my shoulder. Standing on tiptoes I could just see into the house, but everything was obscured by the rain and apart from the flickering candle most of the hut was in darkness.

'Tullik!' I continued. 'Are you in there?'

With no response, I started to panic. If Tullik was not here, then where could she be? I had to get in, or at least be able to look inside. I searched the garden for something to stand on and found a few large rocks, but my hands kept slipping on their wet surfaces and none of them were sturdy enough to hold my weight. Then I saw the garden bench that Tullik and Munch had been sitting on the night I found her here, drinking with him. At the first heave the bench hardly moved and I had to push it with my back and rock it with my knees until there was enough purchase to drag it to the window. The sodden grass churned beneath the legs of the bench and left two muddy lines in the earth. I managed to pull it up to the house and positioned it with its back towards the wall.

'Tullik!' I shouted again. 'It's Johanne! Are you there?'

For a few seconds I looked up and waited, but no answer came.

Holding up my lantern, I stepped onto the bench and leaned in towards the window.

At first there was nothing but shadows moving behind the wavering candlelight. But then I wiped away the rain and cupped my hand to the glass until I could make sense of the shapes that swirled within.

I almost cried out when I caught sight of Tullik and thought for one horrible second that she might be dead.

She was sprawled out on the bed, her right arm hanging out as if it had been abandoned by the rest of her body. Her hair was strewn in auburn waves about her head. Draped across the top corner of the mattress, it hung over the side of the bed and the tips of it brushed the floor. Her blouse was open and her breasts were exposed. Beneath her petticoat one leg was straight and the other bent up at the knee. Her eyes were closed, but when I studied her face I could see that she was not in pain, or lifeless, but serene, like a goddess or an angel. Her cheeks were flushed pink and her full lips slightly parted; her eyes were closed gently beneath lightly arched eyebrows. Never before had she seemed so tranquil, so free from longing or question or pain.

'Tullik.' My voice was barely a whisper.

Munch was sitting on a chair by the bed. He was naked from the waist up. His sketchbook was propped on his knee and his arm was moving in squiggles and circles across the page as he watched Tullik, sketching the outline of her body with a stick of charcoal. His moustache moved softly as he talked to her in a low, inaudible voice. An empty bottle of wine and two glasses stood on the table by the bed. Tullik and Munch were oblivious to the rain, to the thunder, to me – to anything other than each other. Here, in the midst of this monstrous and violent storm, the lovers had found their peace.

Seeing Tullik so untroubled made me reluctant to disturb her, but the rain was beating down so relentlessly and I was so cold and wet that I knew I would develop a chill if I stayed outside all night waiting for her. And then there were the questions we would have to answer in the morning: *Where had she been? What was she doing out in the storm all night?* This time I would not be able to defend her. Caroline would know exactly where she had been, and Tullik would be banished. She would never see Edvard again. I had to get her home before sunrise.

I picked up a stone and tapped it hard against the window until they noticed me. Munch was the first to respond.

259

He looked over his shoulder to locate the noise and I drove the stone faster, tapping like a woodpecker to draw his attention.

He laid his sketchbook down on the bed and Tullik stirred, sitting up and buttoning her blouse.

'It's me!' I shouted through the window. 'It's Johanne.'

Munch came to the back door.

'Johanne, what are you doing out in this storm?' he said, pulling on his shirt as I entered the house. 'Look at you! You're soaked to the core. Come in, for heaven's sake.'

'I need to get Tullik back before they find out she's gone,' I said, trying not to look at him.

'Johanne, darling!' Tullik drawled, as though I were a guest at a Kristiania party.

'Tullik, I was worried about you. If they find out you're gone, they'll—'

'Oh, who cares about what *they*'ll do,' she said. 'They can't stop me.'

Munch handed me a towel and I wiped my face.

'But what if they send you away, to—'

'There's nothing they can do,' she said, flatly.

'You know how Caroline feels about this,' I said, 'and your mother and father.'

Tullik sauntered over to Munch who had returned to the chair. She climbed into his lap and slipped her arms around his neck, tipping his head forward and bringing it to rest at her breast. Her hair fell over them both in long fiery tendrils as they embraced. Tullik pressed him closer and he nestled against her heart with his arms around her waist like a child with its mother. She leaned down over him and kissed his

260

neck, softly, tenderly, whispering intimacies I could not hear. I tried to avert my eyes, but felt them pulled again to the lovers and could not look away.

'You can take me home if you like, Johanne,' she said, when she finally drew away from him. 'Things will be different now anyway.' She lifted Munch's face and cupped it in her hands, bringing his strong jaw up and brushing his lips with her thumbs. 'Won't they, dear?'

He hadn't told her. About Germany. About leaving. He hadn't told her.

'Tullik, we need to go,' I said sharply, infuriated that he could be so detached. Like the day in the garden, with Ragna and Caroline. He didn't fight for Tullik, didn't want to protect her fragility. He was planning to leave and her poor soul would be crushed. But Munch had his art. His one singular love, and that was all he needed.

'Take this sketch with you, Tullik,' he said, tearing a memory from his sketchbook. And I have another canvas for you, over here: *Moonlight*, a landscape.' He crossed to the side of the room and picked up a rectangular painting of the coast-line, pale turquoise with the column of the moon lying phallic across the sea. The sketch and the painting were pieces of him, the only pieces he could give, the only pieces she could keep.

'Look, Johanne,' she said, taking *Moonlight* from him. 'It's Åsgårdstrand. Beautiful and still, in the night.'

She sank into the tranquil picture and I guided her out into the street. As we headed back to the storm-battered forest, she seemed unfazed by the flooding and the rain as if they were doing her good; her own horse-cure. We carried the art back to the house and she skipped through the pools as if her skin was made of oil and she couldn't get wet.

'I think he's going to ask me to marry him,' she said. 'In fact, I'm sure of it.'

I wished I could have contradicted her. I wanted to tell her the truth: that he was leaving here and going back to Germany. But how could I blight her happiness? It was the first time she had been at peace in weeks. I allowed her to believe it.

'We should marry in Borre,' she said. 'He won't want to get married in Kristiania.'

'We must hurry back,' I said. 'I don't want you to get ill out here.'

The thunder had finally subsided and given way to a constant drizzle that showed no sign of diminishing. The lantern dangled at my side with no real purpose other than providing a false sense of comfort in the dark.

At the church the road was coming up for air after the storm's attack. Small islands had appeared on higher areas where the fallen rain had receded, running into ditches and sinking deep down into the earth. The ground would be sodden for days.

We walked along the side of the house as water overflowed from the gutters above us. My clothes were drenched and sticking to my skin. I was shivering. Icy blue. My head was fuzzy. At the back door, I dropped the painting. *Moonlight* clattered to the ground and I reached for Tullik's arm.

'Get me inside, Tullik,' I said. Then blackness enveloped me. My knees keeled and I sank to the ground.

18

Burgundy

*Colour becomes fixed in bodies more or less permanently;
superficially, or thoroughly*

Theory of Colours, Johann Wolfgang von Goethe

I awoke on the kitchen floor. A blanket was laid over me. My
head was heavy. Deep purple. A painful burn passed across
my brow. I rose to my knees. Ears throbbing. My hair was still
damp and my clothes were cold. Something was tapping. At
first I thought it was my own head, but then it became clearer.
There was knocking at the back door. I picked myself up and
tried to tidy my hair. I pulled a clean apron from the peg. The
knocking ended.

Curious, I went out into the misty grey morning. It had
stopped raining, but the constant dripping and the sound of
running water pouring from every orifice of the house gave the
appearance of rain. It was as though the whole house was leaking
from the inside. In the back garden the plants were battered.
The lilac bush had changed shape; it had been pounded in the
middle, turning it into a sort of a heart with a rounded bottom.

The rain had wrought unmitigated disaster to the hen coop. Ingrid and Dorothea, whom I was now able to identify by appearance alone, were over in the far corner of the cage, unable to scale a large puddle that covered the ground. Water was pouring from the hutch where the roof had bowed under the weight of the rain. The hay was flat and wet and the other birds were pecking about miserably, unsure of where to lay their eggs.

'Come on now, ladies,' I said, reaching for the brush, 'we can fix this.'

I swept the water to the side where the ground was uneven and there was enough of an incline for it to drain away. Then I lifted the roof and poured the water off. I was about to fetch some fresh straw from the shed when I heard the gritty clop of hooves at the side of the house.

I turned and squinted against the mist. My head boomed. It was too early for Fru Berg and she never arrived by horse and cart. I leaned the brush against the hen coop and peered round the side of the house. A man was approaching, walking alongside a large black horse, holding the reins in his hand. As he drew closer, I could see that he was wearing a naval uniform: a peaked cap and a blue jacket with silver buttons and silver brocades that shone through the mist. It was as if I was seeing just an outline of a man.

'Hello?' I called, clinging to the cage.

'Is there someone there?' the man said. He had a heavy Swedish accent.

'Yes, I am here. I'm Johanne, the maid.'

'Forgive me for the hour,' he said. 'Our ship got tossed to Horten in the storm and we arrived early.'

I guessed the man was a friend of the admiral's.

'Can I help you, sir?'

'I am a naval officer in the service of Prince Carl of Sweden. His Royal Highness and four of his officers would like to dine here with Admiral Ihlen this evening. It would also please His Royal Highness if he could sleep here until tomorrow morning, if it's not too much of an imposition. Perhaps you could tell your mistress?'

My chest was fluttering. I felt as though I was being arrested, guilty of some unknown crime. Did he say *His Royal Highness*?

'Won't you come inside? I was about to light the stove.'

'Much obliged,' he said, looking for a place to tie his horse.

I waited, stupefied, unable to find words to help him. He hooked the reins around the fence post and pulled them tight, slapping the mare on the neck before turning to face me.

'Let me show you to the parlour,' I said.

As he followed me through the house I listened to the alternate clip and thud of his boots as he walked across the rugs and the bare floorboards. All I could think about was Tullik and the painting. Had she been caught in the night? Did she manage to hide the pictures?

'I will put on some coffee and let my mistress know you are here,' I said, bowing clumsily as I left him alone. I ran upstairs and pummelled on the Ihlens' bedroom door.

'Goodness, Johanne,' Fru Ihlen said, appearing in a sleepy haze, her hair still tied in rags. 'Whatever is the matter?'

'I'm sorry, Fru Ihlen, a man is here – a naval officer. He says he has come from the ship of Prince Carl of Sweden and that the prince and four of his men would like to dine here tonight. If it's not too much trouble, the prince would like to sleep here too.'

Julie's eyes widened. She stood there staring at me in horror, as though I had thrown a bucket of cold water in her face.

'Prince Carl?' she said. 'Here? At Solbakken?'

'His man is waiting in the parlour.'

She inhaled, filling her chest with ideas.

'Run down and tell him he must join us for breakfast,' she said. 'Put on the coffee and awaken Ragna. I will inform the admiral and the girls.'

'Yes, Fru Ihlen.'

I scampered back down the stairs and hurried to the kitchen, where I lit the stove and put the water on to boil. Ragna was already awake. She sneaked in behind me, tying her apron.

'What's the fuss?' she said.

I turned to face her, wringing a dishcloth in my hands.

'Why is your hair wet?' she said, eyes darting. 'And your clothes, they're damp.'

'The Prince of Sweden and four of his men are coming for dinner. The prince will stay here tonight. His officer is having breakfast with the family. He's waiting for coffee in the parlour.'

Ragna chewed at the insides of her lips, gnawing with her incisors like a mouse through rope. Her eyes fixed on a stain on the floor as hundreds of meals rushed through her mind. I had seen her do this before, when forced to make a banquet out of very little, and I had to admire her resourcefulness. She knew cooking the way I knew fruit.

'I will go up to Gannestad to get chickens,' she said, still staring at her spot as though plotting a crime. 'I'll leave after breakfast. You will go over to the rectory and ask for salmon, milk and cream. Find as much fruit as you can in the garden; there's still rhubarb and apples – I will make a tart. Bring it as quickly as you can.'

A whooping sound at the back door told me that Fru Berg had arrived.

'Whose is the mare?' she said, flabbergasted.

'We are to have a royal guest,' Ragna said, 'Prince Carl of Sweden.'

'What? Here? At Solbakken?' Fru Berg searched Ragna's face for a shred of humour. 'Are you trying to put me in an early grave?' She grabbed her bosom.

'It's true,' I said. 'One of his men is here now, he's staying for breakfast. There will be five of them for dinner, including the prince. The prince will sleep here too.'

'Lord have mercy!' Fru Berg said, as though the prince's visit was a test sent directly from the Lord Himself. She began babbling about cleaning agents and furniture polish and started charging about the room.

'That's enough, Benedikte,' Fru Ihlen said, gliding gracefully into the kitchen with immaculate composure. 'Johanne, dear, we will have to ask you to sleep at home tonight; the prince will have Milly's room. We need the best china and silver, polished until it's gleaming. The rugs will need to be beaten and I need fresh flowers in the parlour and dining room. I will have Caroline fetch the family's finest bed linen and tablecloths from my sister in Horten. What we keep here at Solbakken won't do. Oh, and the glasses . . . use the crystal on the top shelf of the dresser. Johanne, make sure you can see your face in it. After breakfast I want you all to set to work. The prince and his men are due to arrive at five o'clock.'

The three of us nodded in silence and I returned to the coffee.

'Bring a tray with three cups, Johanne,' Fru Ihlen said. 'We will take it in the parlour.'

The day was a blur of excitement and tension. We gathered the best of everything we could find and spent every minute sweeping, polishing, brushing, washing and shining. Fru Ihlen sailed amongst us like an ocean liner in a stormy sea, swaying with the tides, overseeing the preparations with a steady but gentle hand. Even when she herself spilled a bottle of carbolic acid in the admiral's office, creating an overpowering odour in the house, she simply closed the door to the office and opened all the windows, asking me to bring fragrant flowers. I cut sprigs of lavender and left them to stand in vases about the house.

Due to the commotion, it was late morning before I got to Tullik. She had not left her room and wasn't present at the breakfast table. When Caroline took the carriage to Horten, I raced up the stairs and burst into Tullik's bedroom.

'Johanne, are you all right?' she said.

'Just tell me what happened.'

'You collapsed. You were not well. I heard noises downstairs and couldn't carry you, so I had to leave you there. I wrapped you in a blanket and took the painting and came to my room.'

'Good. That's good, Tullik,' I said.

'Are you ill?'

'I have no time to be ill. The Prince of Sweden is coming here tonight. You must get ready.'

'Who cares about a prince?'

'Your family does.'

'A prince is nothing to me. I have Edvard. And soon I will be his wife. I'm sure he will propose any day. Did I tell you that? Did I tell you he is going to propose to me?'

'Yes, Tullik. But I must go now. You should get dressed.'

Caroline returned from Horten laden with treasures and heirlooms that spanned generations of Julie's family, the Nicolaysens.

'Aunt Bolette let us have the embroidered tablecloth,' she said to her mother as they prepared the dining room, 'and when Grandmother Aars heard the prince was coming, she gave me a set of wine goblets that were one of *her* mother's wedding gifts! I was almost afraid to bring them back. They're packed in the chest, but the slightest bump could have cracked them all.'

Throughout the day Ragna kept trying to interrupt Caroline, indicating she had something to tell her. Each time, the pit of my stomach fluttered with fear. If Tullik was exposed – if the Ihlens found out she had seen Munch again – I knew she would be sent from here, sent to live with Grandmother Aars or Aunt Bolette. Anywhere away from Munch. They could not know that he was leaving and the threat he posed to their daughter would soon be gone.

Thankfully, Caroline was too busy trying to turn Solbakken into a palace to be pestered by Ragna and fobbed her off at every attempt. Having a royal prince as a guest would no doubt elevate her position in Kristiania to new and dazzling heights. It was the stuff of Caroline's dreams and she wanted everything to be perfect.

'What shall we talk about?' she asked Julie as they unpacked Grandmother Aars's goblets.

'I was thinking perhaps I could tell him about the animal-protection group and our lobbying. Maybe he could offer some support?'

'Do you think he'll want to talk about animals?' Caroline said, horrified.

'Perhaps? And naval issues, and politics: Norwegian independence, maybe. The Sweden issue is rather delicate, but I'm sure your father will handle the conversation beautifully. He has met Prince Carl before, you know.'

'You mean he won't want to discuss life at the palace?' Caroline said.

'Prince Carl is a naval commander, dear. I'm quite sure he will have no desire to discuss anything but the navy with your father.'

'But what about me?'

'You and Tullik will be quiet and not utter a word unless you are spoken to. Otherwise, you will be courteous and polite.'

'Well, you know Tullik won't be. She'll be downright offensive.'

'Tullik knows how to behave properly when she needs to, and anyway she seems much more like her old self again today: brighter, happier.' Julie smiled with relief. 'I'm sure she will be charming.'

* * *

270

The man we all anticipated was a rather stuffy gentleman, stiffly packed into a starched uniform, full of salutes and perfunctory airs and graces. But the man who came to Solbakken was quite the opposite.

The group arrived punctually, shortly after the clock in the hall had sounded. Fru Berg, Ragna and I were lined up on the front porch in our bleached white aprons and caps. Fru Berg had steamed and pressed every crease into submission until the cotton fabric had lost the will to defy her. I felt as lifeless as my pinafore, standing with my back erect and my chest pushed out, my feet apart and my hands clasped behind my back.

The flag was flapping proudly on the flagpole as the first two men arrived on horseback, one of whom I recognised as the messenger who had found me in the garden earlier. The other two were seated with the prince in a carriage that rolled up by the front gate where the Ihlens were waiting to greet them. Julie and the admiral stood on one side of the path, and Tullik and Caroline on the other. Naturally, word of the royal visit had spread and across the road a small crowd had gathered. I could see Isabel and her mother amongst a group of neighbours, and the vicar, all grinning with pride to see a member of the royal family in their quiet little town. There could not have been royalty in Borre since the Viking kings who were buried by the shore.

Prince Carl was wearing the same light-blue uniform and cap as his men. His jacket was trimmed with gold brocade, golden buttons and thickly roped epaulettes. A ledge of medals gleamed at his chest. He had a flushed complexion, a long straight nose and a black moustache that was twisted into

271

points at the edges. He seemed embarrassed, or even unworthy of the attention he was receiving, and waved to the onlookers, as much to dismiss them as to greet them. He jumped down from the carriage and smiled at the four awaiting Ihlens as he swept through the open gate. Graciously he kissed Julie's hand, then Caroline's and Tullik's, before greeting the admiral with an informal handshake and a pat on the shoulder.

'Nils, how good of you to put me up like this, at such short notice,' he said. 'I hope it's not too much of an imposition.'

'It's a pleasure and an honour,' Admiral Ihlen said.

Inside my stiff uniform, my heart lurched with pride for the family whose housemaid I had become.

They went inside and I set to work, ignoring the scarlet burn of my forehead and the cold shivers that had become progressively worse throughout the day.

Tullik was dressed finely, in a bright burgundy gown. Her hair was drawn back from her face, rolled up and secured with gold pins that sparkled in the candlelight. The table had been extended with two extra inserts to accommodate the Ihlens and their guests. The prince sat at the head of the table and the admiral at the foot, in Fru Ihlen's place. Fru Berg, Ragna and I served them quietly. I concentrated hard to clear the plates at the right moment and fill glasses that were less than half full.

One glass I never had to fill was Tullik's.

With all eyes on Prince Carl, I was the only one who noticed how much she was drinking, helping herself to the carafe and constantly guzzling wine. Between courses, I removed her glass altogether and took it to the kitchen, but when I returned she had somehow procured another, which sat brimming beside her.

The conversation moved as easily as a waltz. Caroline was determined to make herself shine. She talked about politics and the matter of the constitution as tactfully as was possible. Did we want independence from Sweden? Of course we did, but it was to be conducted in a peaceful manner. Yes, she said, Norway would be the first country in the world to gain independence through peaceful negotiations rather than war. There had been too many wars. On that matter, I agreed.

It was only when the evening was drawing to a close that Tullik finally drew attention to herself.

'But tell me, Prince Carl, who are the prominent painters in Sweden?' she said.

The prince turned to Tullik and smiled at her.

'Well, Anders Zorn is a marvellous painter. I have met him on several occasions.'

'Oh yes, Zorn,' she said. 'Isn't his wife's name Emma?'

'That's correct. Her portrait is one of his many stunning pieces.'

'Wasn't Emma from a wealthy family?' Tullik said, as the other conversations around the table began to pitter and die.

'I believe so,' the prince said.

'And yet she married a poor painter?'

'Yes. He's a genius.'

'How did her family ever allow her to marry him?'

'I'm not entirely sure,' the prince said patiently, 'but by the time they married I believe Zorn was becoming very successful. He must have been able to support Emma, financially.'

He gave a small nod and took a sip from his glass. It was clear to everyone else that the sip signalled the end of the conversation, but Tullik pressed on.

'And he likes to paint nudes, doesn't he? Fuller-figured ladies, bathing, and sitting in boats, bending and arching in compromising positions. Doesn't he?'

'Really, Tullik,' the admiral said, 'is this entirely necessary?'

'And ordinary working folk,' she said, ignoring her father. 'Doesn't he paint life as it is?'

'You're quite the art critic, Miss Ihlen,' the prince said.

'Forgive her,' Caroline said, pleadingly. 'She gets carried away with these things. Never seems to know when her interest and enthusiasm become tiresome.'

'Not at all,' Prince Carl said, 'culture is important for a country. Miss Tullik is quite right.'

After dinner, the men retired to the green room and Julie and her daughters drifted upstairs to bed. I could hear Caroline scolding Tullik when they reached the top of the stairs.

'Do you only know how to be rude and shameful?' she said. 'You can't even behave before royalty. Your vulgarity will be the end of this family, Tullik.'

Tullik laughed.

'I won't be part of this family much longer,' she said. 'I will be a painter's wife, just like Emma Zorn.'

19

Fade

The art of painting is so circumstanced that the most beautiful results of mind and labour are altered and destroyed in various ways by time

Theory of Colours, Johann Wolfgang von Goethe

The chill night air brought a cool relief to my lungs, which had been unable to inhale fully for most of the day, labouring as they were with the same tiny pocket of nervous air. Despite Tullik's outburst, the dinner with Prince Carl had gone well and, once the table was cleared, I had been dismissed.

The forest was fresh and fertile after the storm. The crisp smell of pine needles filled the air and the trunks of the birches shone with new life now that the rain had scrubbed their silver skins clean. The familiar sound of waves could be heard through the trees as I walked along the forest path. Everything had settled back into place, having been so thoroughly distorted in the storm. I emerged from the woods feeling cleansed, despite my sneezes and the chill that I could not shake.

In the clarity I thought I heard my heart whisper.

Thomas, it said.

Thomas.

I longed for the comfort and familiarity of him. Not a prince, or a painter, but a simple fisherman. Like the sea that soothed me and the forest that sheltered me, Thomas was a part of my unwavering sense of belonging, to this place, to Åsgårdstrand, and to him. There was nothing left to fear. If he loved me, he wouldn't take my colours away. Like cadmium pigments, he would only make my colours brighter, more brilliant.

But as my heart finally began to speak, it also began to break. For in one simultaneous realisation, I knew that I loved him and had lost him all at once.

Mother was sewing at the table in the dim candlelight when I came in. A pair of round eyeglasses pinched the tip of her nose and she was leaning towards the flame, concentrating on the elbow of one of Father's shirts. I could hear a sound like someone was crying, the Andersens' baby perhaps.

'What are you doing here?' Mother said when she saw me.

'The Ihlens have an important guest, so they needed extra space,' I said. I still hadn't told her I slept in Milly's room. 'I'll go back in the morning to do the breakfast.'

'I see,' she said, straightening the shirt. 'An *important* guest indeed?'

'Yes, Mother. It's Prince Carl of Sweden.'

At this she dropped my father's shirt altogether and swiped the glasses from the end of her nose.

'Really? The *Prince* of Sweden? Halvor!' She sprang to her feet and crossed to the bed where my father was sleeping. 'Halvor! Wake up! Johanne's met the Prince of Sweden!'

Father grunted and moaned in his sleep. Mother pulled the nightcap from his head and shook his shoulders. 'The Prince of Sweden!' she shouted. 'Well, what was he like?' she said. 'What did they eat? What did they talk about?'

For the first time in my life I held my mother captivated. It was what *she* wanted. It was *her* fairytale: a chance to meet a prince. My story allowed her to dream and she melted in its telling. She even draped her arm about my shoulders as I spoke. I couldn't be angry with her. I felt a sense of satisfaction in her pleasure, just to see her face relaxed, without tension, and with the smallest hint of pride. She would not settle until I had told her every little detail from start to finish; from the moment the messenger arrived with his horse in the mist to the moment I had been dismissed. She relished every word, as though eating every forkful of their meal herself.

'I knew it would do you good,' she said, 'to work for that family. Even though that business with Miss Tullik was most unpleasant. Look what it's brought you. You've met an admiral and a prince! That's where you want to be, Johanne, not with that vulgar painter and those despicable people he entertains. I don't know why Miss Ihlen would choose those types over *princes*. She must be out of her mind. Mustn't she, Halvor?'

Father had pulled the sheets over his ears and turned to face the wall. The wailing continued to drone in the background.

'Do you hear that?' I said.

'Hmm?'

'The baby?'

'No,' Mother said. 'Solbjørg got him down early tonight – haven't heard a peep.'

'I should get to bed,' I said. 'I feel a chill coming on.'

'Let me fill the bed-warmer for you,' she said, rushing to rekindle the stove. 'We can't have you getting ill and missing the prince in the morning now, can we? Heavens, no.' She unhooked the copper bed-warmer from the wall, lifting it by its long wooden handle and putting a pot of water on to boil. 'Go and get ready,' she said. 'I'll bring it in for you.'

When I opened the door to the bedroom where Andreas was already sleeping, the forlorn crying sound intensified and I realised it was the cries of the *Scream* from beneath the floorboards. It suddenly became vivid in my mind: the long thin hands thrust against the skeletal head, the empty eyes, the blood-red sky, the nauseating waviness of it all, the movement of that frightening sound. The colours filled my head: blue, green, black, bright crimson and yellow. I could feel the mysterious eye shape in the sky looking up at me through the sailcloth, penetrating the floorboards and piercing my heart.

I climbed into bed. Mother came in with the warmer and slid it under the sheets.

'Roll over,' she said.

I turned towards the wall and she moved the copper pan up and down the bed in long strokes.

'Now, don't touch it with your bare feet,' she whispered, leaving it at the end of the bed. 'You'll burn yourself, and we can't have any injuries or illness, no, no. You must be bright in the morning and up early for the prince!'

278

'Yes, Mother.'

I drew my knees up by my chest and eventually dozed off to the sounds of the *Scream*.

As it happened, the bed-warmer did nothing to relieve my symptoms and the next morning my head was thick with cold and my nose was streaming. I forced myself out of bed and dressed lethargically. Mother brewed a pot of nettle tea. I couldn't remember the last time she had paid me such attention.

'Drink your tea and I'll fix your hair,' she said. 'We can't have you looking sick, can we?'

She dragged a comb through my hair and rolled it into a tight knot on the top of my head. The combs and pins felt like razor blades across my pounding scalp and I winced at her attentions as I supped my tea.

'The fog has drawn in across the water,' she said, glancing out the window. 'It just needs the sun to burn it away. Off you go now. Take my shawl – it's thicker than yours – and your straw hat. Wait and I'll pin it on for you.'

'I'm only going to work, Mother, not to church.'

'You want to look your best for the prince, though, don't you?' she said, fitting the hat over my hair. 'Should I get a ribbon? Or a feather, perhaps?'

'I'm only going to take it off again in the scullery, Mother. The prince won't even see it.'

'Well, make sure your hair is tidy and your hands are clean when you get there,' she said, chasing me out of the house. 'And we want a full report. Don't we, Halvor? Halvor? Are you awake?'

I left her prattling and walked down to the beach, where a group of noisy oystercatchers were prowling the shore. Their red bills pecked at the rocks and sand in the hunt for mussels and sea worms. I felt their staring bright-red eyes on me as they piped. They seemed to be mocking my fancy hat, as though they knew it wasn't Sunday and it was all a charade for nothing.

The mist hung low over the forest and the trees were swathed in ghostly wisps. Along the path I felt fallen cupules from the oak trees crunch underfoot. Soon the leaves would be turning golden. The blackbirds in the branches were already lamenting, as though singing summer's final song. Behind me there were footsteps. I turned sharply and saw Munch, plodding along in his grey jacket and straw hat.

'Hello,' he said.

'Munch?'

'I'm leaving. I must say goodbye to her. They're entertaining a prince. A prince! All the more reason for me to leave.'

'She will be sorry to see you go, Munch.'

I couldn't tell him that Tullik was expecting a proposal.

We walked to the other side of the forest in silence, the weight of Munch's thoughts leaving no room for conversation. His sketchbook was tucked under his arm and he was fiddling with a stick of charcoal, turning it in his fingers, then throwing it into his pocket, only to retrieve it immediately and start twisting it through his fingers again. When we reached the church he abandoned the charcoal and took out a clump of tobacco.

'When is Prince Carl leaving?' he said, rolling a cigarette.

'After breakfast.'

'Then I'll wait until he has gone,' he said. 'Here, under the linden tree.'

On my way into the house I picked a small cluster of raspberries from a bush beside the church. The last of the season, they had a bluish tinge, but the colour was consistent and they came off effortlessly in my hand. Another day or two and they would have been overripe and wasted, and I could not pass ripe fruit without picking it.

I found a plate for the raspberries in the kitchen, where Ragna was already up and preparing breakfast.

'Don't dawdle,' she said. 'Light the candles and set the table. They'll be down at eight.'

I left the fruit on the kitchen table and took a new apron from the scullery. When I reached the dining room I sneezed until my head pounded and my eyes watered. I took a handkerchief from my pocket and wiped my nose. My brow was clammy and I pressed my head against the window to cool it. Across the road in the churchyard I saw a circle of smoke spiralling from Munch's cigarette. A nervous shiver crossed my chest. No one else knew he was there.

I decided not to tell Tullik. The family had enough to concern themselves with and they needed her present and charming at the breakfast table, not distracted by Munch. I set the table and lit the candles in the silver candelabra. Another item on loan from Horten, it was ornately carved and formed of two dragons. The dragons' tails held the two outer candles and their heads met at the centre column, nose-to-nose.

I couldn't help but think about Tullik and Caroline when I saw them, head-to-head in constant battle.

When the clock in the hall chimed to announce the last fifteen minutes of our preparation, there was a buzz of activity as Fru Ihlen and the admiral came down, followed by Tullik and Caroline. They gathered in the parlour to wait for the prince, who did not appear until quarter past eight.

'I beg your pardon,' he said, when he arrived at the foot of the stairs. 'Your bedroom beats a ship's bunk by far. That's the most comfortable bed I have slept in for many months. I slept like a baby.'

This was such an impressive compliment that when Fru Berg and I overheard him say it from the kitchen door, she prodded me in the back.

'Listen to that!' she whispered. 'I wonder if it's more comfortable than the palace! That's my sheets, that is. It's *my* sheets that did it,' she said, 'my perfectly laundered bed linen.'

The breakfast ran like clockwork. Even I was impressed with my own serving and waiting skills. I could never have imagined when I first arrived at the Ihlens' at the beginning of the summer that by the time the season was over I would be serving a royal prince. But I swallowed back my sneezes and managed to conceal my fever as I moved around the table delivering pots of coffee and baskets of eggs in the right place and at the right time.

Fru Ihlen was kind. She graciously whispered, *Thank you, Johanne* every time I put down a bowl or replenished a cup. I sensed that her fear for Tullik had subsided as she watched her beautiful daughter chatter politely to the Prince of Sweden

282

with such effortless ease that it could have been the very activity she had been born to do.

Still no one knew that Munch was waiting.

When the breakfast was over and I was clearing the table, I noticed a crowd had gathered again outside the house to give the prince a farewell fanfare. Word must have spread because there were at least double, perhaps even triple, the number of people that there had been the day before. The morning sun had burned away the fog and cast a copper tone over the garden, where the grass was twinkling with dew and the rosehip hedge was glowing a luscious green. When the carriage arrived, a wave of excitement passed through the crowd. I could hear them exclaiming with 'oohs' and 'aahs', just like Fru Berg, and chattering to each other in eager anticipation.

The Ihlens bade the prince farewell. He handed the admiral a small box containing a gold tiepin as a gift of thanks, over which they all fawned, Caroline more than any of the others. They followed Prince Carl out to the gate. Fru Berg, Ragna and I took up our positions on the front porch by the table and chairs and the hoisted flag. The prince waved and the townsfolk cheered. I saw Isabel and her mother waving white handkerchiefs. A little girl in a yellow dress ran out to the carriage and handed the prince a small bunch of roses. He accepted them obligingly and patted her softly on the head. She leapt back to her mother, who pressed her against her skirts with a gleam of pride.

The carriage pulled away and, as the prince disappeared down Kirkebakken, the crowd rushed in. A group of children ran to the fence. A black dog skittered after them barking and wagging its tail, thinking everyone was there to play with him. When the royal carriage was finally out of sight, a voice in the crowd piped up and shouted, 'Do you have any souvenirs for us, Fru Ihlen? Something to remember the prince by?'

Julie looked at the admiral and raised her hands questioningly.

'I know!' Caroline said, to the crowd. 'Wait here!'

She disappeared inside the house and was gone for a few minutes. She returned with her hand outstretched, her index finger and thumb squeezed together. She appeared to be holding nothing at all.

'What is it?' a woman shouted.

'I can't see anything!' said another.

Caroline was grinning mischievously.

'Here are three hairs from the prince's pillow,' she said. 'Who wants three hairs from the prince's pillow?'

Hands shot up: five, ten, fifteen – too many to count.

'Very well,' Caroline said, 'I shall have to auction them to the highest bidder. Who will give me two kroner? Good. Yes. Two-and-a-half? Three?'

The prince's hairs were sold in minutes. Tullik walked away, shaking her head.

'It's gone completely to her head,' she said to me.

'Come, girls,' Fru Ihlen said, 'Johanne brought raspberries this morning. Let's go to the back and eat them.'

Caroline and Tullik followed their mother to the back of the house, while the admiral went to his office to fetch his robe and cigar box.

284

As the crowds dispersed I caught a glimpse of a figure by the linden tree. Too shy to come near while people still skirted the house, he busily sketched everything he saw.

'I'll take a coffee out here on the veranda, Johanne,' the admiral said, when he returned.

'Yes, sir,' I said, and hurried to the kitchen.

I waited for a fresh pot of coffee to brew and laid a tray exactly as the admiral liked it, with a cup and saucer, a silver teaspoon, a small bowl of sugar and a folded napkin.

By the time I took it out to him, the townsfolk had disappeared and a calm had descended over Solbakken. Nils Ihlen was admiring his new tiepin and smiling to himself at the success of the prince's visit. He took a fat cigar from his tin and clipped the end of it with his silver cigar-cutter, then popped it in his mouth and lit it, sucking hard before he exhaled.

'What a fine morning,' he said, settling into his chair as I put the tray down on the table beside him. 'Thank you, Johanne. That will be all.'

As I turned to go back into the house I heard the latch click on the gate and behind me Admiral Ihlen jumped to his feet. When I looked across the garden I saw Munch, clutching his sketchbook under his arm. He removed his hat and walked up the path, offering his hand to the admiral, as vulnerable as a mouse. Admiral Ihlen struggled to shout and lower his voice at the same time.

'You?' he said, grabbing Munch's arm and leading him back to the gate. 'You have the audacity to come here?'

'I understand you are angry, sir,' Munch said.

285

'What do you want?' the admiral said. 'What is it about this family? About my daughters in particular? Why are you so fixed on destroying their reputation? They are not like you. They are innocent, honourable young women.'

'You are right, sir. I came only to say goodbye.'

The front door was open and I heard footsteps in the hall.

'Johanne, could you bring us some coffee?'

It was Tullik.

I raced up the front steps and ran into the house, closing the door firmly behind me.

'What? What is it?' Tullik said, seeing through the yellow sickness in my face and finding the blushing deceit beneath it.

'Nothing,' I lied. 'Your father wishes to be alone, that's all.'

I stepped back and pressed my hand against the door.

'Johanne,' she said. 'What are you hiding?'

'Nothing.'

I was trying so hard to block her passage that I didn't think to guard the dining room. She hurried to the window, then gasped and let out a little yelp.

'He's here!' she said. 'He has come to propose! Oh, Johanne, this is it! Look at him. Is he not honourable to come? To do the right thing by my family and ask my father's permission like this? Wait . . . what is my father doing? He has him by the arm. Johanne? Move. Move!' she cried, fleeing from the dining room and peeling my hand from the door. 'I must go to him.'

'No, Tullik,' I said, 'it's not wise to interrupt them.'

With a demented strength, she shoved me aside. Her hands sank to the door handle and she flung the front door open with such force that it smashed against the wall, denting the wood.

286

'Edvard!' she shouted.

Munch was already in the road.

'Where are you going? Edvard!'

She flew out after him, but the admiral was too quick for her. He stepped into her path and took her arm.

'No, Tullik,' he said, throwing the butt of his cigar to the ground.

'Edvard!' Tullik pleaded.

Munch turned at the gate and looked at her. He raised his hand to his head and politely dipped his hat.

'Edvard!'

'Inside, Tullik,' the admiral said, wrestling with her. 'Johanne, help me get her inside, would you?'

I took her other arm but she jerked away from me, writhing and twisting her neck back to look for Munch.

'You sent him away!' she said. 'How could you?'

'Get inside, Tullik,' the admiral said. 'There doesn't need to be a fuss.'

'But Edvard – you sent him away! He asked for my hand, didn't he? But you refused him. You would deny my happiness, just like that!'

'That's not what happened, Tullik. Come on, dear, inside.'

We jostled the wriggling Tullik to the door, where the admiral held her firmly and pushed her inside.

Before he closed the door, I saw Munch across the road. He lifted a cigarette to his mouth and lit it, before he finally turned his head and walked away.

20

Shadow

Colour itself is shade ... and just as it has an affinity with shadow, so too will it merge with it as soon as the right conditions are given

Theory of Colours, Johann Wolfgang von Goethe

The door slammed shut. A blackness spread. My brow burned. Lungs clogged. Thick chewy air.

'Let him go,' Admiral Ihlen said. 'Won't you just let the idea of it go, Tullik.'

'But we were to be married!' Tullik said.

'He did not mention that, I swear,' the admiral said. 'He told me he was leaving, for Germany.'

'You're lying!'

'It's the truth. He is leaving the country.'

Tullik wrestled against her father's grasp and tried to pull away.

'Let me go!' she shrieked. 'I must go to him. It's not too late.'

'No, you mustn't,' Admiral Ihlen said. 'You must forget all about that painter.'

'I *love* him!'

'Tullik, don't be silly now,' the admiral said, locking the front door. 'Why do you have these silly notions of marriage? You can't marry *him*, dear. What kind of life would that be?'

Tullik did not reply in words, but let out a sickening cry and collapsed to the floor grasping her stomach, then her chest, as though she was trying to escape from her clothes, her skin, her flesh, herself. She turned pale, then pure white as the blood drained from her face. With a gurgling eruption there was a piercing scream.

It eroded her. Ate her up from the inside. Mouth stretched. Lips taut. Lamenting. Soul ripped clean from her being. Tearing. Snagging on memories on its way out. Gasping and brutal. Her heart was dissected before me. Fragmenting. Splintering. The sound: primal. A force of nature. Unstoppable. Unyielding. Face contorted. Chest concave. Pain searing across her eyes.

It came from the back of her heart. The power of the blast was as shocking to Tullik as it was to everyone else. I rushed to her side and grabbed her arm, but she tossed me away. The admiral was on his knees trying to placate her. Julie and Caroline came running, Fru Berg and Ragna at their heels.

Tullik's grief was stunning. Petrifying. The innate knowing that this life would have to be played out without him. All the woven strings that had bound them together split and frayed as her soul was stolen from her. Her power source, life source, dimmed, and the shine blotted out, leaving her blank, bereft. The pain in her eyes, the agony that clamped tears. The dry, arid, empty cry of loss.

Julie and Caroline gripped her arms and waist as her body sank beneath her. Frightened, they looked at each other, not knowing what to say or do while Tullik screamed on. Throat rasping. Convulsing. Tiny, whimpering pleas repeating his name: *Edvard, Edvard, Edvard.* The brutality of it repulsed me. Like an animal at the slaughter. She raged forward, charging at some imaginary evil, the beast that had stolen her soul. Then howling. Clawing at the air. Vicious revenge.

The admiral picked her up, but she thrust her arms out against him. Scraping and slashing. Scratching his face as the blood-curdling scream raged on. He used all his strength to press her arms into submission, but she fought back. Demonic and demented. Lashing out at him, tearing at her own hair. Seeking escape from herself.

I thought it would never end. She shook and writhed with wretched desperation. All the fire of her soul blazed livid as the scream that possessed her, tortured her, erupted into being. Waves of sound. Piercing and sick. Jagged blades and serrated edges. Savage. Ferocious. Barbarous and insane.

When it finally began to recede, Tullik slumped to her knees devoid of energy. Wasted, she crouched on the floor. Hands and knees. High-pitched cries continued to rip through her like the aftershock of an earthquake. Then his name again in a panicked race: *Edvard, Edvard, Edvard.* Crazed and slurring. Saliva building in the corners of her mouth. Mucus dripping from her nose. Cheeks flushed red. Sweat beading at her brow.

Julie was shouting at me. Terror in her eyes. I could see her face and her mouth changing shape, but could not hear what she was saying. Then the admiral was holding my arms.

290

He ordered me to fetch the doctor. Horten. Horten. Doctor in Horten. Caroline was crying. Fru Berg blubbering. And Ragna staring. Staring. Black eyes staring.

Horten. Horten. Doctor in Horten. Go, Johanne. Go now!

I staggered to my feet and threw myself at the door. In horror, I fled.

I ran so fast I couldn't feel my legs. Running without purpose. Just running. My chest tight. My sight blurred. And still there was the terrible deafening screech of Tullik's cries in my ears, in my head. The taste of blood in my mouth. The taste of screaming, of Tullik's *Scream*.

I stopped before the rectory and bent over, stooped, shaking. Threw my hands to my knees. Nausea pulsating in my stomach, in my blood. My skin perspiring, but shivering with a feverish chill. I had to find Isabel. Horten. Horten. Doctor in Horten. I lifted my head and wiped my brow with my sleeve. Sweat trickled down the backs of my knees. The sound still swirled in my head, on and on like the drone of bees.

The sun lit the front of the rectory. It glinted white, too harsh and blinding to look at. I turned my head and searched the distance. With the sun behind me, I caught sight of Munch walking down the path to the forest. He followed the curve of the track, then cut across the field and headed towards the shore. He wasn't smoking now. Just walking. Hands in pockets. Sketchbook under his arm. Forcing one foot out in front of the other. One at a time. Purposeful. He stopped at the edge of the field where the land dipped down to greet the water. Staring out to sea, he stood. Solitary. Haunted. Alone.

I cleared my throat and sprang forward, racing to the back of the rectory and into the dairy without a thought for the customers milling at the counter or the little girl beside them holding a basket of eggs.

From behind the cash register, Isabel was staring at me fearfully, as though a wild animal had come crashing in.

'Johanne?' she said.

'Horten!' I shouted. 'Horten! Doctor in Horten!'

'You want Doctor Karlsen, dear?' Isabel's mother said, coming round to steady me. 'Get her into the wagon, Isabel,' she said, as the customers covered their mouths and pinned themselves to the walls.

They propped me in the back of the milk wagon, where Isabel sat beside me holding my arm. I tried to explain what had happened, but found myself unable to say anything but *Scream, Scream, Tullik's Scream.*

'I don't understand, dear,' Isabel's mother said. 'Has Miss Tullik's influenza worsened? Are we fetching Doctor Karlsen for Tullik Ihlen?'

I nodded my head as the cart pulled away, then slumped back against the side. Isabel backed away from me and leaned across to her mother, who cracked the whip hard, as if we were being chased by an army.

'Mother, I think Johanne is sick,' she said. 'We should get the doctor to see her too.'

I did not hear Fru Ellefsen answer. I was slipping in and out of a delirium. Tullik's sickening cries circled my head. The movement of the wagon shook my bones and I shivered with cold. By the time we reached Horten, my fever had pulled

292

me under, into a world of terrifying hallucination. Screams, blood-red skies, whirlpools and hollow, empty eyes.

I woke up in the bottom bunk at the fishermen's hut. Two days had passed. Father was sitting at the end of the bed reading a newspaper, leaning forward to catch the weak light from the window. I guessed it was late afternoon. The gulls squawked in the distance.

I looked at Father for a moment, waiting for a skeletal figure to pounce at me from over his shoulder, mouth gaping, throat rasping, pulling on a sickness deep inside that refused to come out. I listened for the wailing that would rise to hysterical screeching and then recede back to a long, mournful moan. I studied his face, afraid it would turn crimson and his eyes would flare scarlet until his entire head started boiling and bubbling like molten lava, until his features had melted away and he was nothing but a volcanic fire. Such were the horrors of my dreams.

When he turned to find me awake, he threw the newspaper to the floor and moved up the bed, gently gathering my hands into his.

'There you are, my dear girl,' he said. 'You gave us all a terrible fright. I'll fetch your mother. Get you some tea.'

'No, Father,' I said. 'Stay here with me a while.'

I drifted away from the nightmares slowly, checking Father's pockets for bony fingers as he came nearer and searching my bedclothes for streaks of blood, stains left over from the violent flow of red and orange fire. I sniffed the air for the suffocating mix of thick oil paint and turpentine, the fumes that had laced my delusions. But the air was clear and my father was perfectly normal. The only screams were the calls of the seagulls.

I glanced down at the floor.

'Do you hear anything, Father?' I said, lifting my head from the pillow.

'No, dear,' he said, craning his neck, 'just the gulls at the pier.'

I sank back down onto the bed.

Scream had finally been silenced.

Mother and Father delayed the return to our own house because I was too sick and weak to be moved. Herr Heyerdahl stopped by to deliver the key before he left for Kristiania. The sight of his portly frame at the door delighted Mother almost as much as his arrival had.

'She's definitely on the mend,' she said, grasping at the hope that he might want to paint me in my sickbed. Perhaps the sight of me, frail and emaciated, would provoke a revival of the trend for painting girls dying in their beds.

'Johanne.' My name sounded like the peal of a church bell when it exited Herr Heyerdahl's booming mouth. 'I heard you'd been ill,' he said, entering the room and pulling up a chair by the bed. 'I brought you these.'

He handed me a bunch of flowers: purple clover, blue asters and white bindweed.

'Oh! Aren't they just divine!' Mother said. 'Let me put them in water for you.'

She clattered about the kitchen, desperate to find something more elegant than the cracked ceramic jug we used at the table.

'How are you feeling?' Herr Heyerdahl said.

'Strange,' I said. 'Empty. Cold.'

'We all feel like that at the end of the season,' he said.

I leaned forward to the edge of the bed and dropped my voice to a whisper.

'Munch?' I said. 'Where is he?'

'Oh, he's gone. Germany,' he said, 'to the exhibition in Berlin.'

'He's left?'

'We all have to leave at some time,' he nodded.

'And Tullik? Did she see him before he left?'

'No, Johanne.' His face darkened, his eyes sloped with sadness. 'I'm afraid not. Listen, he gave me this. Take it, please.' He handed me a rusting key. 'It's for the studio. He wanted you to have it. You might want to hide it.'

I took the key and slid it under my pillow as my mother swept back in with the flowers that had been forced into a tall beer glass. 'Aren't they splendid?'

She put them on the windowsill and we all looked at them with pity and regret, as though they were not just the last flowers of the summer, but the last flowers ever to grace the earth. I studied the blue stars of the aster, the open white petals of the bindweed and the sweet purple clumps of the clover with a feeling of things coming to an end. It struck me then that all three of these flowers were food plants for larvae, and as such were part of its transformation. They helped the larva become a butterfly. Perhaps it wasn't the end of the summer after all? Perhaps it was just the beginning of autumn?

'Will you stay for some tea, Herr Heyerdahl?' Mother said, in her sugar-coated voice.

'Thank you, but I must go,' he said. 'Christine and the children are waiting at the pier.' He reached out and placed his hand on my brow. 'You're not burning any more. I think she's out of danger now, Sara.'

'Thank the Lord,' Mother said. 'She gave us a dreadful fright.'

'I'm sure she'll make a full recovery once she gets back home again. Here's the key. Thank you again for your kind hospitality. I'm afraid the place probably won't meet your high standards, after I've been there with my paints and easels and rowdy children.'

'Not at all,' Mother said. 'It's a pleasure to have you. We hope to see you again next year.'

Herr Heyerdahl tipped his hat like the perfect gentleman and swooped out of the hut.

I looked again to the flowers. All the stems were squashed together in the glass: lines of green and yellow that varied in shade and texture. The morning sun streamed through the window and lit the petals, firing them with a bronze glaze. As people passed by outside and cast their temporary shadow, the petals darkened: purple to indigo, blue to black, white to grey. And then they were all plunged into darkness as a man stopped and looked in at the window, hands cupped around his face.

How dare he? I thought at first, but on closer inspection I saw it was Thomas.

'Come in!' I said, beckoning with my arm.

'She's still very fragile,' I heard Mother say at the door.

'Let him in!' I shouted, my weak voice wavering.

'Just for a few minutes then,' Mother said.

He strode in, carrying all the rays of the morning sunshine with him. His face was bright, his cheeks flushed, his brown eyes gleaming like polished chestnut.

'Johanne!' He stood by the bed, holding his cap in his hands.

'Sit down,' I said, pointing at the chair Herr Heyerdahl had just vacated.

'I was so worried,' he said. 'We all were.'

'There's no need to worry anymore,' I said. 'I'll be well again soon. Mother won't let me be idle for too long.'

I watched his long lashes sweeping up and down as he blinked. There was something calming about him. He stretched out his arm and slipped my hand into his big square palm, where something warm and tingling was rekindled. I heard a quiet voice begin to whisper again. It was not a wild, screeching demand but a subtle innuendo, a hint that something, in time, would grow. The flowers may have been shedding their petals and the trees humbly unleafing, but it was the only way they could return again, resplendent, more glorious than before, the next time summer came around.

'Now, about that adventure,' Thomas said, 'to Denmark and France, and Egypt. Do you still want to come?'

'Yes, Thomas. I want to come with you,' I smiled.

'And we will return decked in jewels, and they will call us the King and Queen of Åsgårdstrand.'

'Yes,' I laughed, 'the King and Queen of Åsgårdstrand.'

As soon as my mother heard my laughter she rushed back into the room to scold us.

'Johanne needs rest now, Thomas. If you don't mind.'

'Of course, Fru Lien. You're right, she must rest.'

He stood up and returned his cap to his head.

'We've a haul of coalfish over at the pier. I'll bring you some if you like?'

Thomas was so amiable that my mother struggled to hold her stern expression in place. It cracked at the corners of her mouth, where a smile was begging for release.

'Thank you,' she said, 'that would be very kind.'

He was not an admiral, nor was he a prince, but Mother could not disguise her pleasure at the benefits Thomas's courtship brought. There was much to be said for having an ordinary fisherman as a son-in-law.

'You're too young for marriage,' she said, when he had gone. 'Charming as he may be, you're too young.'

'Yes, Mother. I know. I don't want to get married, not yet.'

'Good. You must make sure you find the right man,' she said. 'Look where it got Miss Ihlen, falling for that painter.'

'Tullik,' I said, revived by the name on my lips. 'Is she well again, Mother? Have you heard any news from Solbakken? Has Fru Berg been to call?'

'They brought you here the night Miss Ihlen became ill,' she said, 'Fru Ellefsen and her daughter, Isabel. They said that Doctor Karlsen had instructed them to bring you home as quickly as they could. He said he would have brought you himself, had he not been going back to Horten immediately with Miss Ihlen.'

'Tullik's in Horten?' I said.

'No, Johanne.'

'Well, where is she?' I said, suddenly remembering how Herr Heyerdahl had looked so sad when I asked about her.

Mother was shaking her head.

'Where is she?' I pleaded, sitting up in bed.

'We didn't want to upset you,' Mother said. 'Look how excitable you're getting. You need to rest. Fru Ihlen said you could be released from their service, now that the season is over. You don't need to go back there again. You don't need to think about the Ihlens now. Not any more.'

'Tell me. Tell me, Mother! She's my *friend*,' I screeched, grabbing her arms. 'Where is Tullik?'

Mother sat down on the bed.

'Very well. But do lie down, Johanne,' she said, 'you're still very weak.'

I settled back reluctantly onto my elbows.

Mother was quick and sharp.

'She's been committed to the asylum. Gaustad. Doctor Karlsen thought it would be the best place for her. The family agreed.'

All my nightmares had come true.

'Gaustad?' I said. 'At Ekeberg?'

'Yes. It's a facility for women. She will be cared for by professional people. Fru Berg said she was beyond the reaches of the Ihlens. There was nothing more they could do for her.'

'Will she be locked up? In a cell?' I said.

'I don't know what goes on in these places,' Mother said, 'but she will stay there until she's feeling better.'

299

Gaustad. It was the place where Munch's sister Laura was confined, wrestling with madness, unable to talk, lost in the darkest depths of her own mind. I thought of Laura and the painting, and how Tullik had said she could be that way too. Munch had sketched Tullik into the painting, merged her with his sister, entwined them with strokes of charcoal. It was Munch who had brought them together, and now they were both languishing in Gaustad trying to escape their own shadows.

21

Harmony

Thus, if two opposite phenomena springing from the same source
do not destroy each other when combined, but in their union
present a third appreciable and pleasing appearance,
this result at once indicates their harmonious relation

Theory of Colours, Johann Wolfgang von Goethe

Returning to our own home was both liberating and confining at once. Free from expectation or demand due to my convalescence, and without the constraints of employment, I was able to fill my time as I pleased. However, being stuck in the house with only my parents and Andreas for company was not conducive to recovery. I moped from room to room, much to the irritation of my mother, and was only really happy in the garden. I sat outside for hours at a time, wrapped in blankets. Eventually I managed to convince my mother it would be good for me to paint. Although she was alarmed by the idea, Father brought me a tin of oils and two horsehair brushes, and after that no one could stop me.

The garden was changing but, although it was almost October, some orange asters were still flowering and the rose bush by the potting shed was a breathtaking sight, full of fist-sized cerise flowers with petals like silky pink handkerchiefs. It was this bush that I painted, over and over again. Just as Munch had said, the subject of my paintings grew and changed, depending on my mood or the time of day. The internal reflected the external. When Thomas came to visit, or on sunny afternoons, the roses came out large and bright, the petals formed from generous globules of paint that I dabbed on loosely with my biggest brush. On days when I could not remove Tullik from my mind, the rosebush seemed to shrink in size. It became a muddy burgundy and the leaves dark like coffee beans. On those days, all I could see were the shadows.

Some days my heart was so heavy that I could not paint at all. I sat there on my chair in the garden with my eyes closed, listening to the sounds of nature. In my head I chanted Goethe: *Nature speaks to other senses, to known, misunderstood and unknown senses: so speaks she with herself and to us in a thousand modes*. He was right. It was there in the hectic cries of the birds fanning the skies in their wide V shapes, preparing to migrate; the rustle of the breeze through the trees, building its strength, gently plucking the leaves, one by one from the branches; the occasional tapping of the woodpecker and the furtive patter of a squirrel. Even in a quiet garden, nature spoke if you listened hard enough.

It was on one of these mornings, sitting alone, with my eyes shut, that I heard something unusual, something unnerving. It was a Sunday and the others had gone to church. *Everyone* was

302

at church. But approaching the garden there were footsteps. Smacking against the road. Hard and fast. Gasping breath, interspersed with a low lamenting whine. And then my name, unsteady and fluctuating: *Jo-han-ne. Johan-ne. Jo-hanne.*

When I opened my eyes, I jumped from my chair and threw off the blankets, leaving them in a heap on the grass. There was a woman at the gate. She was dressed in dark red and had a head of wild flaming hair.

'Tullik?' I shouted. 'Tullik! Is it you?'

'Johanne! You must come quickly!'

'Tullik! You're back!' I ran towards her, tears springing in my eyes.

She grabbed me fiercely and we clung to each other, both of us crying.

'You must come,' she said. 'You must come back to Solbakken with me at once. I don't have time to explain – just come. Now.'

Her words were slurred and her eyes manic and intense. I wondered if she had escaped from Gaustad, if she was still crazed? Regardless of her state of mind, I had no choice but to obey her. She spoke in a way that told me to run, to run as fast as I could, even though I had barely used my legs for weeks. She dragged me from the garden and we tumbled down the hill, crying, shaking and gasping for breath. My legs were as flimsy as flower stems and the pathetic weight of my body felt too cumbersome for me to carry. Blood surged in my mouth, the metallic taste that told me I was going too fast, too soon, with nothing to fuel my efforts. When we reached Fjugstad forest I leaned against a tree and vomited.

Tullik was ahead of me. She was running so hard it took her a few minutes to realise I was no longer at her side.

'Hurry, Johanne!' she screamed, when she turned back and saw me retching. She could see that I was unwell, but did not come to help me. She seemed locked in her own space, unable to move forward or back. 'Johanne, hurry. Hurry!'

'Tullik, *please*!' I said. 'I have not been well. I must rest.'

'There's no time to rest,' she said.

'What in God's name is so important, Tullik?' I said, spitting strings of saliva from my mouth.

'Ah!' she cried, running back towards me again in brisk, reluctant strides. 'You must hurry. It's Ragna.'

'What? What about Ragna?'

'Oh, Johanne, she's found the paintings, every single one of them. They emptied my wardrobe. Mother has ordered her to burn them after church. They've stacked them up in the garden.'

'No!' I said, wiping my mouth. 'They can't do that!'

'They can! They are! You must help me stop them. I ran from the church. Said I needed water. They didn't stop me, but they will be home soon. Johanne, please hurry.'

She yanked my arm again and somehow I started running. My head was a fire of anger and fear. *Burning the paintings? All of them? Munch's work. Destroyed.*

We tore through the forest and emerged on the other side, a pair of heaving wreckages. Crowds of people were gathering in the graveyard. The service was over. I couldn't feel my legs and my chest was a whirlpool of nausea and fear. Then the house appeared before me, its windows watching me, judging me as they had before. I was a stranger once again.

The smell of smoke and turpentine clogged the back of my throat.

We were too late.

Tullik was weeping.

We ran to the back garden, past Tullik's hens, which were agitated, clucking and flapping erratically.

Behind the house, it had already begun. Where the white table and chairs had been, a heap of canvases were stacked on top of each other. Several sketches lay around on the ground. Images of Tullik were everywhere. Ragna and Fru Berg held more in their hands: sketches and scrolls of paper. There were more even than I knew of: small drawings and paintings that Munch must have given Tullik every time they met. Ragna saw us coming and casually tossed one into the flames that had begun to lick the base of the pyre.

'Stop!' Tullik screamed. She cast herself forward and thrust her hands into the fire, despite the growing flames. Fru Berg grabbed her arms and pulled her away.

Ragna threw on another painting and another. I rushed out. Circled the fire. Pictures burning. Columned moon. Tullik's hair. Tullik in the woods. Tullik on the beach. Canvases peeling back to the frame. Black lines. Paintings shrivelling. Flapping. Charred edges. Thick smoke. Fire belching. Spreading. Flames licking. Tullik on her knees. Howling.

Helpless, I watched *Moonlight* burn. The black charring spread in seconds, crossing the painting from right to left, wiping out the tranquil sea, the column of the moon, the beach, the trees. Gone. Then I saw the couple on the beach. I reached out my hand but in seconds that charged moment – that pull of desire so effortlessly captured – was erased from the world.

Before I even knew what I was doing, my hands were grasping at Ragna. First her shoulders and then her neck.

'Why?' I shouted, plunging my fingers into her scrawny neck. 'Why? When she's been so fragile, so tormented? What are you trying to do to her?'

Ragna's mouth was round, her black eyes so wide I could see red feathered lines straining outwards from her inner eye.

I shook her hard, shocked by my sudden strength. Her bones were as vulnerable as a bird's beneath my angry hands. I could have twisted them until they snapped. I wanted to.

'Just following Fru Ihlen's orders,' she coughed. Her face was full of spite and hatred. Even with me at her throat, she was still trying to throw another painting on the fire.

'You!' I snarled. 'Just because you've never known love. Just because you were rejected, cast aside for another, someone better than you!'

'Johanne!' Fru Berg shouted, prising me from Ragna's neck. 'That's enough!'

My grip was so tight that my nails left red scratch-marks on Ragna's skin. She slipped out of my grasp and hurried about the garden, picking up the remaining pictures and tossing them on the fire that was now roaring out of control in a blazing conflagration.

The last painting to burn was the beautiful mermaid. A searing pain tore across my chest when I saw black circles begin to scorch the yellow moonlight, then her golden skin and her mesmerising eyes. The picture burst into flames and the fire ate through it with a ravenous hunger. Seconds later, it was gone.

Tullik crawled around the fire on her hands and knees, unable to get up. Unable to look. Motes from the charred paintings floated up into the air. My eyes followed them, dry and stinging from the intensity of the fire. Up and up they floated, leading me to the back window on the far side of the house. There I saw Caroline, arms folded across her chest. A smug line of satisfaction danced at her mouth.

When the paintings had gone, Ragna smacked her hands together, a macabre applause. Then she sneakily pulled something from her apron pocket.

'No!' I screamed. 'Not that. That's *mine*!'

She didn't even look at me. Calmly, she slung the book into the flames. I watched its cover char and the name *Goethe* blacken on the spine before the hungry fire bit into it, darkening all the colours in its pages and devouring the secret drawings I had cherished for so long.

'No!' I cried. 'How could you?'

'It's just silly nonsense,' Fru Berg said. 'Come on, Johanne, come away.'

I ran to Tullik, who was whimpering on the ground, clasping the singed grass in her hands and moving, wounded, around the fire.

'Get up, Tullik,' I said, throwing my arms around her waist and pulling her to her knees. 'Hold onto me.' I placed my hands under her arms. 'Come on. I'm taking you away from here.' She looked at me with misty eyes. I lifted her to her feet. 'There's nothing we can do.'

We were both coughing from the sickening fumes, the choking blend of turpentine and smoke, our hearts wrenched from us, raw and burning. Part of us had burned with the paintings. I glanced back to see Ragna and Fru Berg poking at the blaze with fire irons, as though they were watching leaves burn. To them it was nothing more than a cleansing, part of the disinfecting and laundering process, the end-of-season sanitisation. They had to get rid of the dirty paintings and remove every last trace of that vulgar man.

Tullik and I staggered away, mere fragments of ourselves. I didn't know where to go or what to do, but found myself heading to the sea. We walked along the shoreline, halting and shaking until we came to the jetty where I had sat in silence with Munch. Now I sat with Tullik in the same spot, voiceless, spiritless and bewildered. Rounded over, with our legs dangling above the waves, I held her hand in mine, but hardly felt it as my body was so numb.

Ages passed before I found a sense of reality. A wave crashed against a rock and, as the spray tossed up, it spattered my face and told me that I was here, at the jetty, with Tullik, and that we were the survivors of some terrible catastrophe.

'Are you all right?' I said, turning to her.

She continued to stare at the water. Her eyes were cold and lifeless. A few strands of her hair blowing about her face in the wind were the only part of her that moved.

I wrapped my arm around her shoulder.

'Tullik, I need to know. Are you all right?'

'I am *sane*, if that's what you're wondering,' she said, staring blankly at her feet.

'I didn't mean that.'

I took her shoulders and turned her round to face me, searching her eyes for a spark, for the tiniest glimpse of the Tullik I once knew.

'Did they really send you to Gaustad?' I said.

'They did,' she nodded, 'but it wasn't for long. They knew I wasn't mad, just broken, and the doctors didn't want me there. Strangely, it was good to be alone. You can think so clearly when you're locked away.'

'Even if you're forced to be there? Against your own will?'

'As long as you don't hammer at the door and beg for release. That's the root of true pain, Johanne; far worse than idleness or imprisonment is the constant screaming, the pleading to be freed from an unavoidable, inescapable situation.' She straightened her dress as though preparing to stand up, but then she threw her arms around me and we embraced. 'My dearest Johanne,' she said, 'you have been a true friend. We will stay friends, you and I. Forever.'

'Forever.'

'And now Edvard has gone to Germany,' she said, releasing me, 'free to wander his path, to follow his art, as he must. What my father told me is true. He did not ask for my hand. I can accept that now. I know he must be free to paint. It is the only way for him. And now all his paintings are gone and I shall have to accept that too.'

'They're not *all* gone,' I said. 'There is one left.'

She lifted her chin and looked at me with beautiful, hurt, sloping eyes.

'What do you mean?'

'*Scream*,' I said. 'The one you hung on your wall.'

'Mother ordered you to take it away, to burn it.'

'And I did take it away. But I didn't burn it. I hid it.'

'Where is it?'

'I hid it in my bedroom, under the floorboards of the old fishermen's hut. It's still there.'

'Does anyone else know it's there?'

'Only my brother. But he's sworn to secrecy – he won't tell anyone.'

'You hid the painting?' she said, as a tiny smile lifted the corners of her lips.

'I think the huts are still empty,' I said. 'I can get it back for you!'

'No,' she said. 'Let's leave it there. You keep it. It will never be safe with me. If they find it, they'll burn it and I won't be able to hide it for ever.'

'But Tullik, he painted it for—'

'It's too painful, Johanne. Looking at it will only take me back to that place, that loneliness, that terrible anxiety, and I don't want to think of us as being apart. Edvard and I will always be together. We are together somewhere else, somewhere above this ocean and above this sky, but at the same time we are inside every part of it. There is no separation. He always said that, and I understand it now.'

I looked up at the clouds and watched the yellow, blue and grey puffs rush across the sky. I tried to see the light, as *he* would have done, to find the sun and see where it fell.

'We are leaving Solbakken in the morning,' Tullik said, 'so I will have to say goodbye to you now, Johanne. I should go back.'

'Tullik,' I said, as we stood. 'My dear Tullik.'

We embraced.

I wanted to restore her fire, to have the joy returned to her soul, to see her as she was before the summer, with all her vibrance and vitality overflowing in bright waves around her. But the leaves were falling from the trees now. It was the season for endings and Tullik's fire had gone out. She held me limply and stroked my cheek.

'I will write,' she said, 'when I get back to Kristiania.'

'And I will be here,' I said, 'waiting for you, until next summer.'

'Send me your pictures,' she said, as we wandered back to the forest.

We stood with the stream flowing under the bridge beside us. Rusty maple leaves swirled in the water, gathering pace and spinning in russet and ochre circles towards the sea.

I kissed her on the cheek.

'Goodbye, my friend,' I said.

She walked back to Borre, where Julie and Nils would be waiting. They would sail from Horten and soon she would be slotted back into her place as a young Kristiania lady: beautiful and privileged, yet wonderfully untamed.

I wandered to the edge of the forest beneath the vast arching trees high above my head. The pathway was soft and cushioned with leaves. A dazzle of late-afternoon sun found its way through the branches and lit everything ahead of me in a stunning golden light. It cut amber lines through the shadows of the path and made the leaves around me gleam with a wondrous auburn sparkle.

311

I did not go home directly, but first walked along to the pier, passing the fishermen's huts where the *Scream* still lay. *Rest now*, I whispered to it as I crossed in front of the window, *she is with you. There is no separation.*

The gulls crossed the sky, soaring, diving and gliding in freefall. They cawed from their perches on boat masts and fence posts and I imagined they were hailing a queen returning from adventures in far-off lands: the Queen of Åsgårdstrand.

As the Queen of Åsgårdstrand, I cut through Munch's garden without shame or apology. It seemed barren without the paintings and I found myself looking for them, seeing them in my head still standing in their positions: Jacob, the bathhouse attendant, in his chair; the pregnant lady with her basket of cherries; Inger on the beach; Laura with her shadow. They too had come to the end of a cycle and had moved on to new surroundings.

The house was empty now and the doors locked. I placed my hand on the mustard wood. It was warm in the sunlight and I rested there for a moment, listening to the sounds of the birds. *Until next time, Munch*, I whispered, *I will look for the light.*

And so I brought myself home to the house on the hill where the last of Mother's late-flowering sweet peas greeted me at the fence. I brushed my fingertips through the light-pink froth and inhaled the unfathomable depths of their gentle, seductive fragrance. With my hand on the gate, I was about to return to the Painting. One more step and I would be the Strawberry Girl again: the child with the blue eyes and the messy cornfield hair. Uncomplicated and simple, I welcomed her back and took on the mantle like a comfortable old coat. I would return to her, for another year perhaps, or until the season changed.

ÅSGÅRDSTRAND
1947

EPILOGUE

Dreams

I walk calmly in my dreams which are my life –
only like that can I live

Private Journals, Edvard Munch

I sit alone. The seats are hard and uncomfortable, designed not for comfort but for practicality. Inger is on the front row, squashed onto the fold-out chair, and the excesses of her plump body hang over the sides. She doesn't complain. Her spotted scarf is tight at her throat. Too tight for a day like this. She alters the angle of her dark hat and reveals a bounce of pure-white hair. Twisting in her seat, she notices me and smiles.

A male choir is gathered beside the studio, two lines of heads at different heights. On the back steps is the mayor, August Christensen, holding the key. He gleams like a bright new button, hopeful and optimistic, as many of us are. The house will be a museum, preserved in time, the way it was when he lived here. Our country's greatest artist. My friend, Edvard Munch.

He wouldn't have liked all this pomp and ceremony. Recluse that he was. But he would have liked the park they have created out of his garden and the surrounding land, and he would be happy that Åsgårdstrand has the house now, not some private owner who could do with it what they would. He left everything else to Oslo. It's been years, but I still can't get used to calling it Oslo. It will always be Kristiania to me. Kristiania got his paintings, thousands of them. He kept them all with him at his house at Ekely. His children. Seems fitting that we should get this little cabin, the only house he ever called home. He hadn't been here for years, though. It was more a home to the ants and the rats than to anyone else. They cleared out anthills from the rafters that were a ton in weight. Munch always let the vermin roam. Left the cupboards open for the rats. Didn't like to think they'd go hungry while he was away.

The band plays.

Behind me sit the Gjermundsen sisters and one of Fru Book's girls. She used to cook for him in the early days, after he bought the house. For now, I can't remember her name. It'll come back to me. There are others: models, cleaners, people who cared. We all knew him in our own way and at our own time. He wrote to us, sent us money when his paintings started selling. Even bought me a new pair of shoes one summer. He didn't forget us. The little people of Åsgårdstrand.

The choir is singing. The notes drift up and up and dance on the air. Lilac, purple, blue, blue, blue. Rising to pink. Swelling to red. Scar-let. Red. Crim-son. Red. Scar-let. Red. Crim-son. Red.

In red I think of her.

It is five years since she died, but she lives within me, in a dream that never ends. Dear Tullik.

Even without the proposal, she married him. Even though they never spoke again, she married him. That summer in 1893. She was married to him all her life.

When the admiral died, Julie and Tullik came to live at Solbakken permanently. Tullik suffered poor health, but cared for Julie and her hens and seemed more content with her life in Borre than she ever could be in Kristiania. Fru Ihlen lived to be eighty-two. She was devoted to Tullik, and to animal rights, writing articles for *Aftenposten* and editing the organisation's magazine right up until her death. With Julie gone and Milly and Caroline married and away, I was the only one left to care for Tullik.

She often became ill with fever. Eventually someone would come calling, a maid or a girl from the dairy. Thomas was always at sea and I'd have to leave my boys with a neighbour to go off and nurse her. She always wanted me. Never a doctor. I'd sit by her side through the night, holding her hand, mopping her brow, calming her. I would be her maid again. When it was bad, I'd stay for several days at a time. I couldn't leave her.

Some mornings I would see *him*. Standing in the churchyard. Odd times when the streets were deserted, he would come. Even after many years, when he was over sixty years old, there was never any mistaking it was him: the strong jaw, the sad eyes. Untethered he came. Untethered he went. Like a boat without a sailor.

I asked Tullik if she saw him too.

'Occasionally, when I open the window at sunrise.'

'Do you never want to call to him?'

'Why would I do that?' she said. 'He must be free, to walk his path. It's better if I don't call. It can't come from me, can it? You say it yourself, Johanne, you don't say hello to him. You wait. It must come from him. You see him everywhere: in the forest, at the beach, on the lanes. He closes up for long periods at a time, but when he meets you he lets it all out. You say yourself that it comes flooding from him. That's because you've never tried to capture him. Only he can decide when to stop and when to walk on.'

I have often wondered if it gave him strength to know that Tullik had given him her faith, with no thought for anything in return. She seemed to emerge and reappear in his paintings over the years like a recurring dream. I always recognised her. It was Tullik, no matter what anyone else said. There was no denying his devotion. But Tullik could not have bound herself to a man like Munch. It would have destroyed them both. Instead they fought on through space and time, somewhere *else*, as she always said. They were not together here. They did not live together or see each other, but they were tied with stronger strings than if they had been under the same roof for a lifetime, drinking coffee from the same cup.

August Christensen clears his throat. He talks about freedom. Yes. The Germans are gone now. Norway is free. My boys risked life and limb in the Resistance, even though they were both in their forties by then, middle-aged men emboldened by patriotism. The freedom we did attain, peacefully, from

Sweden in 1905 was proudly won and proudly defended. Strange when I think about it now. Munch's patrons who had made his works so popular were German, but so too were the Nazis who stole our freedom. Hitler labelled Munch's work *degenerate art* and made a mockery of it. Then the Nazis who took control of Norway tried to make a hero of him for their own gain and popularity. They wanted to make their own Honorary Board of Norwegian Artists. Munch wasn't interested and, without his support, nothing ever came of it. He didn't live to see our liberation. Inger was incensed that the Nazis turned his funeral into an event to promote their own propaganda. They took control of the proceedings and she was pushed out, helpless. Despite her fearless protests, his coffin went up Karl Johan draped in swastikas in a procession of guns.

We join the choir. We sing. We listen to the mayor.

After, there is a lunch at the Victoria Hotel.

I look at my hands, pockmarked, paint-flecked. I should have brought my gloves, but it's too hot for them today. There is applause, then we all move on. The heat intensifies as we climb the hill. Thomas is waiting for me at the Victoria. Up ahead I see Inger shaking his hand. He removes his cap and makes polite conversation. The King of Åsgårdstrand he is not, but a good man he is. He never got to Egypt, but he inherited his father's boat and had adventures aplenty just by working hard to provide for us. Now the boys have a trawler of their own.

Thomas never really understood my painting, but he got used to it and eventually realised it was not something I had to

319

do, but rather something I *was*. It helped when I started selling. He only really saw the good of my art when he could equate it to food on the table or clothes on the boys. Simple things.

Jens Thiis, the man I met in Munch's garden all those years ago, was an art dealer. He went on to become the director of the National Gallery in Oslo. Shortly after Thomas and I were married, Jens sold one of my first paintings to a collector in Lillehammer, a simple landscape of the boats in the harbour with Bastøy and the fjord beyond. After that I sold more and, when the little fishermen's huts came up for sale, it was my painting money that provided our deposit.

Thomas couldn't understand why it had to be that hut, precisely *that* one. But I was stubborn and wouldn't back down. Upstairs, where the Andersens lived, is our kitchen and living room. Every day I sit in my chair and gaze out into the great blue forever that fills the window. The view may be the same, but nature is always changing. It presents the fjord to me in every imaginable colour and texture. Light I cannot describe in words. Sunrises. Sunsets. Stunning. Intense. Through the seasons, within the seasons, no two days are ever really the same here in Åsgårdstrand. The water gives me such joy, such inspiration – still, after all these years.

Downstairs are our bedrooms.

At first I worried the boys would hear it, that they might cry in the night or have bad dreams. But *Scream* is content. It has remained silent and neither my children nor my grandchildren have ever mentioned it. I still talk to it, of course, when no one else is home.

Andreas and I are the only ones who know it's there. Tullik never saw the point in taking it back, and Munch painted four more versions of it over the years. Once, when he was very hard up, I offered to dig it out for him so that he could sell it. He joked that no one would want it. Another version had already been ridiculed in Germany. This one was mine, he said, and he always called it *The Strawberry Girl's Scream*.

Now his sister is sidling up beside me. She is holding a painting. She unravels it carefully because it is torn at the edges and the paper is aged and fragile. A crumpled parchment.

'They found it in the wall of the studio when they were renovating it,' she says.

I look down and I see Tullik. Tullik, with her hair windswept and alive about her head. She is standing opposite him and they are close. Noses touching. In the background are the branches of the pines of Fjugstad forest. The central point of the painting is the bright column of the moon reflected on the water. It splits the trees. His head is in darkness, almost a silhouette, with black, hollow eyes, dark hair and shoulders. Tullik is light. Her face is bathed in the yellow shine of the moon. The strands of her golden hair stretch out to him, reaching like arms, tying their two souls together. Uniting them for all eternity.

'To think that it must have been hidden for years,' Inger says. 'How can that even be possible? A painting hiding like that? I'm so glad we found it.'

'Yes,' I say, 'paintings are meant to be seen. One way or another, they will find their way out.'

But I am speaking only half-truth. Not all paintings must be seen. Not mine. Mine is safe beneath the floorboards of my little fisherman's hut. There, it has found its home. There, it rests. There, it is content. And when Andreas and I die we will take this secret with us to our graves, for it cannot belong anywhere else. The other *Screams* will be seen and maybe even heard by some, but not *The Strawberry Girl's Scream*. It will never be found.

AFTERWORD

Living in Norway, it's impossible to ignore Edvard Munch. He is one of our most significant tourist attractions and a fundamental part of the fabric of Norwegian culture. Incredibly though, I *did* manage to ignore him for quite a long time. I lived alongside Munch for over a decade before I really started paying attention to him. I suppose he was such an integral part of Norwegian life that I didn't find him a mystery. I thought I knew him. My ears pricked up when *The Scream* and *The Madonna* were stolen in 2004, but it wasn't until the record-breaking sale of *The Scream* at auction in 2012 that I was finally roused from my Munch slumber. By then, I had been in Norway long enough to feel a sense of pride, and perhaps even a little ownership, of this great Norwegian artist. Now I was intrigued. I started asking questions: *What makes a painting sell for $120 million? Who was Munch? And why is this disturbing painting so universally appealing?* Ironically, it was only then that I began to discover just what an enigma Edvard Munch really was.

I had an idea to write an epic story about *The Scream*, spanning time periods, with multiple narratives and ending with the Sotheby's auction in 2012. But my research took me in a different direction and kept me much closer to home. It took

323

me to a beautiful little coastal town, under an hour's drive from where I live: Åsgårdstrand. It was love at first sight, and as soon as I set foot on the beach, I knew my story had to happen there. I would write about Åsgårdstrand, in the summer.

I read everything I could find about Munch's life in Åsgårdstrand. I spoke to local people, read the periodicals of local history associations, and went to every Munch event and exhibition in the area. It wasn't long before I came across an old memoir by a local woman, Inger Alver Gløersen, whose stepfather was a friend of Munch's.

In her book, *Lykkehuset: Edvard Munch og Åsgårdstrand*, Gløersen devotes a few pages to a story about a young girl, Regine, the daughter of an admiral, who lived in Borre and had a summer romance with Edvard Munch. According to Gløersen, the artist gave Regine paintings throughout the summer, which she hid from her disapproving parents, and at the end of the season when the maids cleaned the house, the paintings were discovered and burned.

The story inspired me, and the seeds of *The Strawberry Girl* were planted. I was determined to find out who this 'Regine' was and if there was any truth to the story.

It is common knowledge that Edvard Munch had a romantic relationship with Milly Ihlen, the daughter of an admiral, who spent her summers in Borre. So for a while, I presumed Milly Ihlen must have been the girl named 'Regine' in Gløersen's memoir. But I wasn't satisfied. Eventually, I came across an old photograph of a child called Tullik Ihlen. Coupled with census records and a local account of Prince Carl's visit to Borre, it finally dawned on me that 'Tullik' was a nickname. Tullik's real name was Regine Ihlen. The records confirmed it; Regine was Milly's younger sister. Suddenly the plot became juicier: two sisters, having an affair with the same artist.

Whether there is any truth to Gløersen's story remains unclear, but it is unlikely. Munch makes no reference to anyone named Tullik in his journals (although he often used codenames for the people in his personal life) and none of the experts I have spoken to, or whose work I have read, can corroborate the story. In fact, Tullik Ihlen seems to have vanished into history. Her name appears only in her father's obituary in 1905, and a couple of obscure letters and articles, nothing of any substance. However, it was enough to spark my imagination and I fabricated my own tale out of these wisps.

I decided to set the novel in 1893, as this was the year Munch painted the first version of *The Scream*. For this reason, I have altered the dates of his paintings to suit the story. Some of them would not yet have been painted in 1893, for example *Mermaid* (1896), and *Fertility* (1898) while some would have been painted earlier. Also, Munch did not rent the cabin in Åsgårdstrand before he bought it. His family rented a house ('Thorine's house'), further along the same road, but he didn't buy the cabin until 1897.

The members of the Ihlen family were all real. Admiral Ihlen, his wife, Julie, and their three daughters occupied 'Solbakken', the house in Borre, during the summer. The house had been gifted to the Ihlens as a wedding present by Julie's parents. Later, when the admiral died and the two older girls were married, Julie and Tullik came to live at the house permanently. The census records state that Tullik (a housebound 'sick' daughter), Julie, and a housemaid called Ragna, were living there in 1910.

Although they were real, I have completely invented their personalities. Some fragments do provide an insight into the kind of people they were – old newspaper archives report Julie Ihlen's work with the animal protection lobby, and the obituary in *Aftenposten* of Admiral Nils Ihlen (admiral, director and founder of the Norwegian marine insurance company *Det Norske Veritas*), portrays a highly esteemed and extremely well-respected man. Milly was a part-time actress in Oslo (Kristiania) and it is clear from Munch's journals and paintings that, for a while at least, he was rather obsessed with her and eventually, she broke his heart.

The artist Hans Heyerdahl was from the city of Drammen. He was an incredibly talented artist, popular for his portrait paintings. Although older than Munch, the two artists knew each other and both spent summers in Åsgårdstrand. Over the years, Heyerdahl has been somewhat eclipsed by the likes of Munch and Krohg, and although his paintings may not have been as innovative as Munch's, they were nevertheless beautiful, and give a rich insight into nineteenth-century Norwegian life.

There is some speculation as to who Heyerdahl's *Strawberry Girl (Jordbærpiken)* actually was. One theory claims she was Karen Gjermundsen, one of the local Åsgårdstrand children, whose sisters, Henriette and Marthe, also feature in Munch and Heyerdahl paintings. However, records from the Lillehammer Art Museum suggest that *The Strawberry Girl* was Albertine

Sofie Olsson – known as 'Albertine with the eyes'. She was the daughter of an Oslo mechanic, who tragically died at the age of seventeen, having predicted her own demise.

Regardless of who the girl in the painting really was, the character of Johanne is entirely fictitious. I needed a voice to narrate the story and was fascinated by what this girl might be able to tell us – a very ordinary, poor girl, finding herself living amongst these extraordinary painters and befriending a rich young woman. I enjoyed exploring that contrast, and the possibility that the Strawberry Girl might have been artistic herself.

As for Edvard Munch, I have attempted to portray him as sympathetically as possible, whilst at the same time showing his flaws and eccentricities. He was a deeply complex and intense man, but on the whole, a person I have come to genuinely like and admire. He was something of a paradox; representing different things to different people, and accounts of him vary widely. Even if he were alive today and we were able to ask him about his life and his art, I don't think we would ever truly know him. I have discovered that an investigation into Munch is an unravelling, a peeling away of layers that go deep into the human psyche. Unafraid to explore his so-called 'madness', Edvard Munch made painting an emotional experience. This fearlessness pioneered the Expressionist movement and left a legacy that continues to engage and inspire us today. Indeed, it inspired me to write a book whereby I would take my reader by the hand and together we would walk through the gallery of emotions that is Munch's art.

LIST OF ARTWORKS

List of artworks by Munch that feature in the novel, either as pictures, or as scenes, in order of appearance:

The Insane (Lithograph, 1908/09)
Fertility (1898)
Evening on Karl Johan Street (1892)
Primitive Man (Woodcut, 1905)
Clothes on a Line in Åsgårdstrand (1902)
Arrival of the Mail Boat (1890)
Despair (1892)
Towards the Forest (Woodcut, 1897)
Summer Night. The Voice (Copperplate, 1894; painting, 1896)
Red and White (1899)
Inger on the Beach (1889)
Mermaid (1896)
The Dance of Life (1899)
Encounter on the Beach: Mermaid (1896)
The Scream (1893)
The Storm (1893)
The Day After (1894–95)
Vampire (1893)
Moonlight (1895)
Attraction II (Lithograph, 1896)

ACKNOWLEDGEMENTS

My heartfelt thanks go to my wonderful agent Bill Hamilton, for believing in this book and providing such expert guidance and support along the way. I'd also like to thank Becky Brown and the rest of the team at A.M. Heath.

To my brilliant editor Clara Farmer, and everyone at Chatto & Windus, for giving *The Strawberry Girl* the perfect home and for offering such a constant stream of warmth, enthusiasm and professionalism.

Thanks also to Shana Drehs and the team at Sourcebooks, USA.

I would like to acknowledge some of the particular sources from which I drew inspiration for this book, namely: *Lykkehuset: Edvard Munch og Åsgårdstrand*, Inger Alver Gløersen; *Den Munch Jeg Møtte*, Inger Alver Gløersen; *The Private Journals of Edvard Munch*, edited and translated by J. Gill Holland; and also, what must be the definitive Munch biography in English, *Edvard Munch, Behind the Scream*, by Sue Prideaux, which was an excellent resource.

For their immense generosity, I would like to thank: Tone Brunner at the Munch Museum in Oslo; Gry Pettersbakken at the Lillehammer Art Museum; and Line Berg Harstrom at Munch's house in Åsgårdstrand.

I am deeply grateful to Niall Williams, for being a mile-stone on my writing journey. Thank you for inspiring and teaching me, but also, simply for writing. I am so grateful to you and Christine Breen for the influence you have had, and the encouragement and generosity you continue to give.

To my fantastic coach and good friend Janet Whitehead, for providing inexhaustible reserves of what can only be described as pure magic! You helped me see so many new perspectives, reminded me to have fun with the process, and you never stopped believing.

Special thanks to Heather Hepburn, for over thirty years of unwavering hand-holding, for reading them all, and never giving up the absolute conviction that I could do it.

I am also grateful to the following people for listening and offering continuous support and encouragement: Heidi Andersen, Hege Nedberg, Kjersti Dovland, Robert Bjørka, Lene Mørch Kerrison, my parents, and all my UK friends and family.

Finally, to Dagfinn, Sofie and Kristoffer. Light. Nothing is possible without you.